D0672475

CHICAGO HEAT

AND OTHER STORIES

✱

OTHER BOOKS BY CLARENCE MAJOR

No

The Cotton Club

Reflex and Bone Structure

Emergency Exit

Dirty Bird Blues

One Flesh

Inside Diameter: The France Poems

Fun & Games: Short Fictions

Swallow the Lake

Symptoms & Madness

Private Line

Such Was the Season

Some Observations of a Stranger at Zuni in the Latter Part of the Century

Dictionary of Afro-American Slang

The Garden Thrives: Twentieth-Century African-American Poetry

Necessary Distance: Essays and Criticism

Configurations: New & Selected Poems, 1958-1998

Surfaces and Masks

Calling the Wind: Twentieth-Century African-American Short Stories

Juba to Jive: A Dictionary of African-American Slang

Come by Here: My Mother's Life

Waiting for Sweet Betty

All-Night Visitors

Myself Painting: Poems

Down and Up: Poems

My Amputations

Painted Turtle: Woman with Guitar

From Now On: New and Selected Poems, 1970-2015

Clarence Major

CHICAGO HEAT

and

Other Stories

GREEN WRITERS PRESS
Brattleboro, Vermont

Printed in the United States.

10 9 8 7 6 5 4 3 2 1

Green Writers Press is a Vermont-based publisher whose mission is to spread a message of hope and renewal through the words and images we publish. Throughout we will adhere to our commitment to preserving and protecting the natural resources of the earth. To that end, a percentage of our proceeds will be donated to environmental activist groups. We will also give a percentage of our profits from this project directly to Vermont-based environmental organizations and The Southern Poverty Law Center. Green Writers Press gratefully acknowledges support from individual donors, friends, and readers to help support the environment and our publishing initiative.

Green Writers Press

Giving Voice to Writers and Artists Who Will Make the World a Better Place
Green Writers Press | Brattleboro, Vermont
www.greenwriterspress.com

Library of Congress Control Number: 2016950127

ISBN: 978-0-9968973-2-7

COVER ART: The cover painting is by Clarence Major, entitled *Lady,* 2009, 60 x 36 inches; acrylic on canvas.

TITLE PAGE ART: Clarence Major, *Icon,* 1998, 30 x 25 inches; acrylic on canvas.

PRINTED ON PAPER WITH PULP THAT COMES FROM FSC-CERTIFIED FORESTS, MANAGED FORESTS THAT GUARANTEE RESPONSIBLE ENVIRONMENTAL, SOCIAL, AND ECONOMIC PRACTICES BY LIGHTNING SOURCE. ALL WOOD PRODUCT COMPONENTS USED IN BLACK & WHITE, STANDARD COLOR, OR SELECT COLOR PAPERBACK BOOKS, UTILIZING EITHER CREAM OR WHITE BOOKBLOCK PAPER, THAT ARE MANUFACTURED IN THE LAVERGNE, TENNESSEE, PRODUCTION CENTER, ARE SUSTAINABLE FORESTRY INITIATIVE® (SFI®) CERTIFIED SOURCING.

CONTENTS

ACKNOWLEDGMENTS

"Summer Love" originally appeared in *Boulevard*; "Innocence" originally appeared in *Witness*; "Chicago Heat" and "Sketch" originally appeared in *African American Review*; "Five Years Ago" originally appeared in *Ploughshares*; "Weaver" originally appeared in *Michigan Quarterly Review*; "Girl in a Boat" originally appeared in *Hearse*; "A Story of Venice" and "Bourbon for Breakfast" originally appeared in *Callaloo*; "My Mother and Mitch" originally appeared in *Fun & Games: Short Fictions* by Clarence Major; and "The Driver" is slightly based on an earlier story called "Scat," originally published in *Calling the Wind: Twentieth Century African-American Short Stories* edited by Clarence Major.

CHICAGO HEAT AND OTHER STORIES

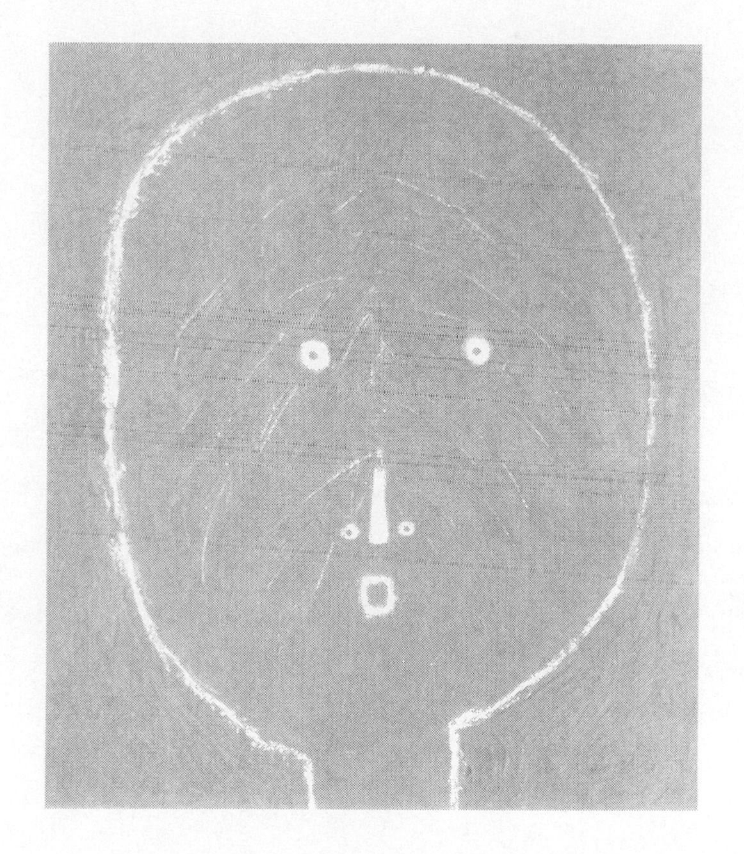

TEMPORARY BUSINESSS

I'M AT THE PIANO when the phone rings. A hesitant voice says hello with a question mark. Then another question, "Edward? It's Isa," she says.

It's Mercy's kid, *Ina*. She calls herself Isa. "I'm coming to New York. I can't get anywhere here in Iowa. Will you be around? Can I, uh, see you?"

I hesitate then quickly say, "Sure." Though I'm not sure what she means. Does she expect me to put her up? Why not? More affirmatively, I say, "It'll be good to see you, Ina."

"Isa." No anger but quiet insistence.

"Sorry. Isa. When are you coming?"

"Tomorrow."

"Come on in," I say to Isa as she stands in my doorway holding her stuffed suitcase. She's a stunning young woman in a leather car coat and jeans.

But what am I going to do with her? I tremble from nervousness as I reach out and embrace her. In that instant she lets out a gasp and drops her suitcase and throws her arms around me, kissing my cheek. She pulls back and kisses me on the mouth. Salty sweetness.

I have a bunch of questions. Has she quit her job? What about her husband? Did she have a fight with him? What about my friend, her mother? Why is she here suddenly like this?

It's the beginning of fall and the first few days are careful days. We seem to keep watching each other for signals—of what I don't know.

At one point she picks up my old flute from a corner and struts around the apartment actually playing it. And she's not bad.

Isa, with her great splash of red hair, her musical voice, her intelligence, has brought brightness into my opaquely varnished life here on East Fifty-Third and Lexington.

But her responses to my questions are cryptic: "Did you and Bentley have a fight?" "No." "Did you agree to separate?" "Yes, sort of." "Did he approve of your coming here?" "Yes." "Why?" "He had no choice. Can we talk about something else?" "No. How long are you going to be here?" "How should I know? As long as you want me." "Does your mother know you're here?" "Yes. She thought it was a good idea." "Why?" "Because you're mature."

Isa and I are at my small kitchen table eating dinner. I pick up the saltshaker and vigorously sprinkle salt on my spaghetti. She's watching and blinking. She wrinkles her nose. I know *that* expression. She disapproves. I snatch up the olive oil bottle and shake olive oil all over the steaming hot pasta. She wrinkles her nose even more.

"It's none of my business, but you use too much salt and oil. My father had a heart attack. I guess I'm just *conscious*. But—" she shrugs, "if you want to kill yourself, it's your business."

I concentrate on my spaghetti, determined not to argue.

We do the museums, see movies, and walk in the park holding hands. When I'm at the piano composing. she reads *The New Yorker* or some other magazine or collection of stories. Isa's ambition is to write stories for popular magazines. She saturates herself with stories in such magazines as part of her training.

I'm a composer. I spend a lot of time at the piano and the computer, writing short scores for TV commercials, sitcom theme songs, and the like. But my serious stuff is never far from my mind. Sometimes I give concerts.

The week before Isa came, I was out in Waterloo, giving a concert at their civic center, staying at Mercy's boarding house, when I met Isa.

In fact, Isa has been at my place just twenty-four hours before Mercy calls. I know it is she before I pick up the phone. Mercy and I are of the same generation. She and I hit it off right away three years ago when I first gave a concert in Waterloo. "Edward? I guess Isa is there by now. I couldn't stop her. Nobody could. So we said, go. You know she's so young. But I felt pretty good about her coming to you. I knew you wouldn't misuse or mistreat her. She wants so desperately to be a writer and she's got it in her head that New York is the only place where it can happen. Is she looking for a job yet?"

Isa finds a temporary job through an agency. She's typing a manuscript for a famous novelist whose eyes are bad. He's very old and there's talk that he may die soon. Last year they gave him the National Book Award. If he makes it till next year, word has it—according to Isa—they will give him the Nobel Prize.

I'm a bit surprised that Isa's husband, an assistant professor at the University of Iowa, hasn't called. "I'm not," she says.

Word comes by way of a letter from Mercy that Bentley has quit his job and moved to San Francisco where he has openly joined the gay community. Mercy says Bentley will never return to Iowa. "He had a hard time here," she says. He's become politically active in the Gay Movement.

Isa says she's happy for him. She believes in freedom of choice. Sexual preference is a human right.

I'm not good at this temporary business. When there's no commitment, no promise of endurance, I feel insecure. But many of Isa's generation seem to thrive on insecurity. Many of them seem to fear intimacy. I'm preaching again. Isa has said more than once that "The future's job is to take care of itself." Maybe I should listen.

This is our bed ritual. At bedtime I want to watch TV for a while. The TV is at the foot of the bed. She watches for maybe a half hour then becomes angry. At first I don't know why. Then it comes out: "You watch too much television." She says it rots my brains.

"Okay. There. I turned it off."

"Thank you. Reading is better for you."

I pick up a novel. Reading, I grow sleepy. I reach over and turn off my bedside light. She's still reading by her own light.

In sleep I turn and snuggle up to her backside. She jumps and pushes me away. She murmurs, "I don't like to be touched while I'm sleeping."

We're now at the kitchen table having coffee. I'm now hesitant about touching her, even by accident. Often we make love in the afternoon, lying across the bed, half dressed. "I don't like to do it naked in bed," Isa says.

I look at her. "I'm depressed," I say.

"Take an aspirin."

One day we're walking in Washington Square Park and see a couple walking in the opposite direction. The man is obviously twenty or more years older than the woman. (I'm fifteen years older than Isa.) They're holding hands. Judging from appearance, it's not likely they're father and daughter. "Look at them, will you," Isa whispers.

"What about them?"

"He's old enough to be her father or even *grandfather.*"

"Maybe. So what? I'm old enough to be your father too."

"No, you're not." She is still looking at them. "They couldn't *possibly* love each other. It must be his money she's after."

"Maybe not. Maybe he doesn't even have any money."

She says nothing in response but gives me a hard look.

This is a month after Isa's arrival in New York:

"My mother called. Says my Uncle Geoffrey is in New York on business. He wants to see me." The uncle is a lawyer with a practice in Cedar Rapids.

When Isa returns from dinner, in a fancy midtown restaurant, with her uncle, it's 10 PM. I'm at the piano picking out a kink in a new composition. "How was dinner with your uncle?"

She's taking off her clothes. "Fine. He's going to give me his three-year-old car because he's buying a new one. He drove it here. He's buying a new one and driving it back to Cedar Rapids." She pauses. "He gave me the key."

"That's great news, Ina."

"Isa."

"Isa, I mean."

She's in her robe now and she comes and stands at my side, resting a hand on my shoulder. "The condition is that I must leave New York. He and Mom think I should go somewhere less crowded. Get my life together. You know?"

"I know." Do I ever!

She suddenly throws her arms around me. I play a fast run on the keys to put an accent on the moment then look up at her. But the music creates more irony than accent.

"Oh, don't be sad. I'll probably come back. But I've agreed to drive to San Francisco. See Bentley for a while. Talk with him; see how things are going with him. After all, Bentley and I *are* still friends, still married, you know."

"Give the marriage another try, huh?"

"I wouldn't put it like that."

I'm still looking up at her remarkably young-looking face. She's a baby. I see tiny dancers, well choreographed by my imagination, in her yellow-blue eyes. There's an edge of happiness there I haven't seen before. "When are you leaving?"

"Don't act like this, Edward. Don't be sad. Please."

"I'm fine. When are you leaving?"

"Tomorrow."

Tonight I'm helping Isa pack. I throw in a few of my fiction paperbacks, the ones she was planning to read. I take the flute she liked and stick it in too. She protests and I say forget it. I want her to have it.

Tonight we make love a long time. Eventually we stop because she's sore.

My sleep is unusually restless. I sense she's hardly sleeping either. She keeps turning, kicking at the covers, talking in her sleep.

This morning I'm up before Isa. Here's the plan: Uncle Geoffrey will leave the car parked somewhere in the block, hopefully in front of the apartment building, sometime during the night.

It's now 6 AM. Pulling on my robe, I walk up to the front and look out and there is the dull blue Ford parked at the curb.

While I'm making coffee, Isa comes naked into the kitchen, yawning. "Did you look to see if the car is out there?"

"It's there." I hand her a cup of coffee.

She goes up front with her cup and comes back. "Sure hope it holds up on the road. Has nearly a hundred thousand miles on it already."

"Should be all right."

She puts her cup down and comes into my arms. I hold her and she holds me for a while. I feel her tremble. "I'm going to miss you."

"I'll miss you, too." I can't believe I'm feeling so goddamned sorry for myself I'm about to cry. But I knew all along it would end this way.

We awkwardly kiss.

Then she says, "I'd better get dressed. I want to get an early start."

I walk down with her, taking the suitcase, open the trunk, put it in, close the trunk, and turn to her standing there on the curb in her sweater and jeans. We embrace again. Then she quickly walks around the car.

Feeling that I'm about to cry, I quickly turn away and dash back upstairs, close my door, and race to the front window and look out.

But the blue Ford has already gone.

FIVE YEARS AGO

It was Labor Day, September 2, a Monday, five years ago, and I was twenty-seven years old and about to bring my forty-four-year-old mother and my forty-four-year-old father together for the first time in my adult life. All my life I had daydreamed about this moment, wondered if it would ever happen, and now that it was about to happen, I was so emotional, I was almost out of control. The night before, my father had flown into Chicago from Boston, where he worked as a real estate broker. I drove down to his mother's on Fifty-Fifth and Indiana Avenue to pick him up. Mother Zoe—that's what I call his mother, my grandmother—was sitting at the kitchen table with her cup of coffee when I knocked on the back door; and there was my father—whom I hadn't seen but once before—two years earlier when he came back to Chicago, that time, I think, because a brokers' convention was being held in Chicago. He was slender and brown and handsome and wore a beard and was smiling at me as I came in. Apparently ready to go, he was already holding a tan summer jacket across his arm. I blushed and felt something like a current of electricity shoot through my body as I simply lowered my head, hiding my joy, and walked straight over to him and slid my arms under his and around his body—which fitted mine nicely—and hugged him for all I was worth. I knew I was going to cry. Tears were already rimming my eyes. All it would take was a blink. And I wanted my face over his shoulder, so I'd be looking out the kitchen window, my back to Mother Zoe, when the tears came. But it didn't help and finally it didn't matter. I not only cried but also I sobbed, sobbed with joy and pain and love for this man I'd dreamed of and fearfully wondered about all my life. And here he was. Two years before, I had expected him to appear suddenly bigger than life, but when I came into Mother Zoe's house that time and saw him sitting at the dining room table with his mother, with his elbows on the table, he seemed so small, so fragile, so frail, compared to the giant I'd imagined. He was just a flesh-and-blood human being, a man, and one not especially imposing, just an ordinary man. But this time I didn't rush to him and hug him. I was too confused, too scared. He stood up and came to me and hugged me, put his arms around me and kissed my forehead. And, yes, this time, too, I cried. I cried but I pulled away in embarrassment, pulled back and went and sat down beside Mother Zoe, who patted me on my thigh. I was wearing jeans. I remember. Jeans and a blouse! And my curly hair was pulled back. I hadn't known how to dress for him. Before going down to Mother Zoe's, I'd tried on four different dresses and six pairs of jeans and told my husband, Austin, "If my father can't accept me in jeans, then, then—" but I couldn't finish the sentence. And I remember my husband—who, by the way, is ten years older than my father—saying, "Don't worry. He'll be happy to see you." But, you know, I was never quite sure that he was. Something about him seemed guarded. I'm still talking about that first time two years before. Sure, he hugged me, but it was a stiff hug. Maybe he was nervous, too. Maybe it was simply that he didn't know what to expect and was maybe even a little bit scared of me. Yes, that's what I felt. Felt that he was scared of me. After all he hadn't seen me since, since... Well, actually, I don't think he ever saw me after I was two or three years old. And I don't remember him at all. I know from what mother told me. They took him to court, you know. Tried to force him to marry or support her. But my mother, Pandora, was only sixteen. And my father, Barry Stanton, was exactly sixteen, too. Both of them still in high school! Messing around, they got me. And got themselves in a world of trouble. In fact, Mother got thrown out of school and Father joined the army. Mother's family said he ran away from his responsibility. That's the way they saw it. But I was talking about that first time seeing him and comparing it to seeing him this time. And this time I just walked right over to him and put my arms around him and he didn't feel like a stranger anymore. And I had gotten this fantasy version of him, this giant of a man, down to size. I was just hugging my father, just a normal human being, a man, and a handsome man with a face like mine. I could see myself in his face. Looking into his eyes, in a wonderfully strange way, gave me myself in a new way for the first time. I felt so close to him it was almost terrifying. When I hugged him I felt his heart beating against my breast and I held him close just to continue feeling his rhythm. Tears running down my cheeks, sobbing! I held him long and hard. But I started shaking and I pulled back and said, "I'm sorry, I'm sorry—" but I couldn't bring myself to call him Daddy or Father. I also couldn't call him Barry, just plain Barry. I didn't know what to call him. Anyway, the plan was he'd have breakfast, no, brunch, with Pandora—his old high school girlfriend—and my husband, Austin, and my sister Yvette, and my six-year-old daughter, Octavia, and me. Mother Zoe was still in her bathrobe, with her gray hair kind of standing out every whichaway. And just as we were leaving, Winona came down the hall into the kitchen and said, "Now, Ophelia, when are you bringing Barry back? You know we got plans for this afternoon?" And something in Winona's tone offended me but I held back and refused to lash out although I wanted to. He was my father. I had spent twenty-seven years without him and here was his sister—who grew up with him, who had visited him more than once in Boston—telling me to cut my time with him short, to bring him back, not to hog his time. I got so pissed I could have screamed but I didn't. I just looked at Winona standing there in her bathrobe with the corners of her big pretty mouth turned up like she was expecting me to give her trouble. And Mother Zoe jumped in and said, "That's right. And I sure hope you aren't planning to have your mother over there. I told you not to invite her. Didn't I?" And I couldn't remember Mother Zoe making such a request or demand till she said, "Remember, I said, just you and Barry, a quiet brunch together with you and your husband and your daughter, just to get to know your father." Then I remembered but I hadn't taken her words to imply that Mother wasn't to be invited. And anyway, what was this thing about, anyway? Mother Zoe hated my mother from the beginning; from the time she came home from work unexpectedly and caught Mother and her son making love on the couch. Mother told me all about it. Mother Zoe drove her out, shouting at her, calling her a whore, a tramp, a cheap little bitch. No woman, Mother said, was ever good enough for Mother Zoe's son. Mother said she thought he would turn into a faggot—her word—the situation was so bad. But why now, all these years later, did I have to be the victim of this shit, the victim of these ill feelings that existed between Mother Zoe and sixteen-year-old Pandora Lowell years ago? Why did the mess present itself just when I wanted more than anything in the world to bring my mother and father together and feel, for the first time, like I had a real family? So, I didn't say anything. I just nodded. I assured Winona I'd get her brother back before noon. And my father and I left. Octavia was waiting in the car in the back seat. And while we drove south—I live at Ninety-Fifth and Yates—I had the warmest feeling listening to my father talking with my daughter. He was asking her about her school, about what she liked to do, and being the smart kid she was, she kept telling him about a spelling contest she'd just won, and about her winning in the girl's footrace, and about her great math scores. They seemed to hit it off better this time than they had the first time when she was four. Back then she wasn't really that interested in him. But now she had a great curiosity because she had been made to feel his importance to her. Some kids had grandfathers, others didn't. In a way, it had become very important to her in the last year or so to have a grandfather. Having one—at least at her school, Martin R. Delany School, the best private school on the South Side—was a status symbol, especially since so many kids there don't. In fact, I had encouraged her to write to him in Boston and she did send three or four letters but he answered only once, and only with a postcard. I had to reassure her that her grandfather loved her—though I didn't believe it, didn't even believe he loved me, his own daughter—and that he was simply too busy to spare time to write often. Anyway, when we got to the house my sister, Yvette, was in the kitchen working on the muffins. She makes great blueberry muffins. We could smell them the minute I turned off the motor and the smell got stronger as we walked up the back walkway from the garage, and while crossing the patio, I slid my arm around my father's waist and hugged him to me. My father, I thought, my father, here with me. And I quickly kissed his cheek. And the minute we stepped up onto the back porch there was Mother sitting in one of the straw chairs waiting. And I thought of Mother Zoe and her warning and all I could hope was that my father would not tell. This was the moment. I had brought these two together for the first time since they were teenagers. I think the last time they saw each other was in a courtroom. When they both were not yet eighteen, mother was trying to get some money out of him, just before he joined the army and disappeared. But this was the big moment now. The one I had waited for. This was my moment. The three of us stood there. Octavia walked between us into the house and into the kitchen, following the smell of blueberry muffins. I watched my father and mother just looking at each other, looking fearfully. There was a distance of about five feet between them. He was trying to smile. God only knows what he was thinking. He didn't look happy to see her. In fact, he seemed a bit irritated. And she was giving him this cynical sideways look like she can get. It's a half sneer. I've seen it all my life. Then she did something she no doubt thought was a smile but it really didn't come out right. It was more a grimace. But she sort of slung her string bean of a body over to him and in a split second I thought she was going to hug him, thought he was going to respond by hugging her, but that's not what happened. She grabbed his beard and tugged at it forcefully, yanked it back and forth, and her mouth was twisted in an agonizing grin; and her eyes were blazing with contempt, though she was trying to laugh and to be playful. I'm sure she meant the gesture to be playful but it didn't come off that way at all. She yanked him too hard and he frowned and stepped back a couple of paces, pulling away from her. And she was saying, "What is this crap on your face?" And he was beginning to sneer. I saw just the edge of his canine. An almost imperceptible shudder moved through his face—his cheeks and his chin especially, and his eyes, like hers, blazed. And I wondered why I myself was feeling so elated, so up, so complete—for the first time—and why at the same time everything was obviously going wrong. These two people, I could see, should never have been brought together. Not only did they not like each other, they held contempt for each other. And though I had known that to be the case, I hadn't wanted to know it. And it gave me, for the first time in my life, a clear sense of the emotional foundation of my life. But even then, sensing this, I didn't want to face it, didn't want the full sense of it to reach my conscience. So I ignored it; pretended the hostility between them was not serious, not important, that, in fact, there was something deeper that held them together and that something was me, my presence in the world. Like it or not, I was their link. And I wanted them to like it. Oh, I so desperately wanted them to like it. So, grabbing Mother by the sleeve and my father by the elbow, I pulled them toward the kitchen, saying, "Come on, let's see what's cooking." And in the kitchen there was my sister and my husband and my daughter. My sister turned around from the stove as I introduced her to my father. Barry Stanton, and she reached out, smiling, and shook his hand. Yvette is a very pretty girl, with bright red full lips, and yellowish-green eyes.

She's tall and slender with naturally reddish hair. (People say we look alike. It's because we both look like Mother, whose is also red.) My sister was twenty-three then. And men were after her like crazy. In fact, she said, "I invited Robert over for brunch. Hope you guys don't mind." And though I resented the liberty she'd taken, I held back saying anything. Then my husband, Austin, standing in the doorway watching my father meet my sister, was smiling. Austin is such an elegant gentleman. He was nearing retirement, early retirement at that time. He was fifty-five and had been head of his own law firm, Tate, Jones & Bedford, on Seventy-Third and Cottage Grove, for the last fifteen years. He was now financially secure and wanted to stop work so he could go fishing when he felt like it, so he could be with his young daughter more and with me, too. Although he and I hadn't been getting along all that well lately, I still respected and liked him. He was like a father to me. In fact, it's true he had raised me, in a way. Taught me a lot! As he put it, he had made a "lady" out of me, sent me to law school and given me a comfortable middle-class life in a good South Side neighborhood. I now had a position in his firm and I was holding my own. And after passing the bar last year I defended my first client in a civil case, a woman fighting for child support. I was saying, "Austin Tate, my husband, meet Barry Stanton, my father," and I sounded awkward, but the moment seemed grand to me and I felt that a certain formality was needed. Now, my husband and my father were shaking hands and gazing into each other's eyes with tentative kindness. And at least their meeting was going well. Then Austin said, "Welcome to our home. How does it feel to be back in Chicago?" And my father was saying something but I was no longer listening to him because Yvette was having an emergency with the omelets she was making; breaking eggs into a big enamel bowl, she'd come across a bad egg, and she'd cried out as though bitten by a snake or as though she'd burned her hand on a hot stove; and I turned to her to help. And Mother all this time stood in the doorway between the kitchen and the back porch watching, I sensed, with a lingering though slight expression of contempt. And Octavia ran her finger around in the blueberry batter bowl, then, with her eyes closed in bliss, licked the finger. "By the way, we're eating out on the patio. It's nice out there this time of morning. You guys go on out," I said with a wave of the hand, "and get started. I want to get my camera, and show my father my office." And I took him by the hand and pulled him up the hall, then up the narrow stair to the second floor, where Austin's and my and Octavia's bedrooms were. And I led him into my little study at the back of the house, a place I was proud of. My law diploma was framed on the wall over my desk and I wanted him to see it. But I wasn't planning to point his nose in that direction. Yet I did stand with my back to my desk—my camera was there on the desk—and took my father by both of his hands and pulled him to me, so that he would be facing—over my shoulders—the vivid evidence of my accomplishment. Three things I was proud of,: this degree, my career, and my daughter. And I wanted my father to admire me for those three accomplishments. So I pulled him against my belly and put my arms around him and held him close so that our bodies were breathing together. Thinking back on that moment I know it was a strange thing to have done, but I felt so close to him; I needed to be so close to him; and I wanted him to feel what I was feeling. Touching him this way was the only way I knew how to reach him. Then I kissed him, fully on the mouth and forced my tongue into his mouth, kissed him the way I kissed my husband, kissed him deeply, so deeply he would have to feel how passionately I loved him, how deeply I felt for him, how much he meant to me. I held his head with one hand and held his back with the other; I lifted my stomach toward him and pressed harder and harder, and I felt him respond, felt his whole body come alive in my arms. Then I slowly let him go and nodded toward my diploma, and said, "See? I earned that all by myself?" And he took his glasses out of his jacket pocket and put them on and read the words, actually read the words, read them slowly, then he said, "I'm very proud of you, Ophelia." And I squeezed his hand. Then he said, "We have so much to talk about. I wish there was time—" and I said, "Now that we've found each other, there will be endless time. I want to know everything, everything you've ever felt and done, everything." And while he looked a little embarrassed by my passion, I picked up my camera and pulled him by the hand and we went downstairs and out to the patio where the others had gathered around the long table. Robert, Yvette's boyfriend, had arrived. Robert was tall like Yvette, and good-looking with curly hair. He was standing there by Yvette at the table as she set out the plates. Mother and Octavia were helping at the other end. After I introduced Robert and my father, Yvette and I brought out the various platters of eggs and bacon and muffins and, following us, Octavia brought out the jam tray and other miscellaneous condiments. Then mother went in and got the pitcher of orange juice. Now Austin was in his natural place, at the head of the table. I sat down to his right, my usual place, and when I saw my father beginning to sit between Robert and Octavia, I said, "Oh, no you don't." And I patted the seat next to me. "You're sitting right here next to me." And everybody laughed and he came over and sat down beside me. Then I said, "Let's all hold hands." I took my father's hand and my husband's hand. We all held hands and closed our eyes. Then Austin said grace, a short and to-the-point prayer of gratitude. I glanced at Mother down the table and she was looking cheerier than before as she reached for the muffins and held them in front of Octavia, saying, "Just take one at a time, now. Don't let your eyes be bigger than your stomach." And I remembered her saying those same words to me when I was a child and I had to choke back resentment. One thing I dreaded was her influence on Octavia. I felt that in many ways she had given me an unnecessarily hard time, had often struck me in rage for minor things, and had nagged me constantly when I was growing up. I felt in myself a tendency to treat Octavia this way and I was on guard all the time against the tendency. I meant to break the cycle. This was all the more reason why I was leery of Mother's presence around Octavia. Anyway, this was a happy moment and I wasn't going to let anything spoil it. I had put the camera down at the end of the table. "Robert, do me a favor. Please take a picture of my father and me together here like this at the table?" And I could see everybody glancing at me, understanding my eagerness, and sympathizing with me. I was acting frantic, acting like I thought he was going to suddenly disappear and I'd never see him again. And the fear wasn't unfounded. So Robert, a sweetie, got the camera and stood up and went into a crouch and snapped the picture as I leaned closer to my father, my face cheek-to-cheek with his. Later, after brunch, we took more pictures. And before I knew it, it was eleven-thirty and I shouted, "Oh, Winona's going to kill me! We've got to get you back!" So I ran inside, grabbed my purse and car keys, while my father shook hands with Austin and mother and Robert and kissed my sister on the cheek. Octavia hopped in the back seat and we drove back down to Fifty-Fifth and Indiana Avenue. Octavia waited in the car. And we walked into Mother Zoe's kitchen exactly at five minutes to twelve. Both Mother Zoe and Winona were dressed now and both were sitting at the kitchen table smoking cigarettes and drinking instant coffee. Giving me this severe look, her crazy look, the first thing Mother Zoe said to her son was, "You have a nice time?" And he said, "Yes, very nice." And she wanted to know who else was there. And my heart stopped. I tell you, my heart literally stopped because I had forgotten her concern. I started to say something but couldn't. Then my father said, "Oh, just Ophelia's sister and her boyfriend." And the relief I felt was obvious, maybe too obvious. I'd been holding my breath; then I let it go. And it was then, for the first time, that I thought to ask my father how long he was planning to stay, and he said, "I'm leaving in the morning, Ophelia. I've got to get back. I have an important transaction coming up. I'm representing both the buyer and the seller this time and it's a very sensitive situation. But I'm coming back when I can stay longer. Okay?" But all I heard was him saying he had to leave and it caused something in me to cave in and I couldn't hide my feelings. With all my might I tried not to start crying and shaking. Somehow I'd thought he would be around at least a week. At least! I sighed and said, "Can I take you to the airport?" But Winona answered for him, saying, "That's all right, Ophelia. I've already asked for the morning off so I can drive him out to O'Hare." And I said, "Oh, I see. Then I guess this is the last time I'll see you, at least for awhile. Huh?" I could feel the tears coming up again and I didn't want Winona and Mother Zoe to see me cry again so I said, "Come out to the car with me and say goodbye to Octavia. Okay?" And he followed me back out the back door, down through the backyard, out the gate, to the curb where Octavia was sitting at the wheel pretending to drive. By now I was shaking all over and tears were running down my cheeks and I didn't give a damn who knew it. I was miserable. He squatted down by the car door and spoke softly to Octavia for a minute or so, then stood up and I grabbed him and hugged him. I know I was being dramatic, too melodramatic. But I couldn't help it. It was how I felt. I didn't know how to feel or be any other way. I held him like it was the last time I would ever see him. And, like I said, that was five years ago.

SUMMER LOVE

SUMMER, 1941! It was raining that Friday afternoon, but the two bands were jamming up a storm, under the canopies. Pun, but not intended. The bands were trying to outdo each other, to see who could swing the hardest. One group was in powder blue, the other in metallic red jackets. They were alternately playing Artie Shaw numbers and Duke Ellington. One time the blue boys cut away and did a little tribute to Lester Young, an extended riff, but other than for that moment, both groups were sold on Swing.

We were all dancing in the playground, in the rain, but we didn't mind. We were doing all right. Actually, it was just a light shower. Nothing was going to spoil our farewell party.

Harlem was like that. Things went on as planned. The school building was on a side street, off 7th Avenue, about a five-minute walk from the Lenox Avenue subway stop.

Neighborhood people came out on the stoops to listen. Folks probably heard the music as far away as Broadway, west, and over east, as far as the Harlem River, and up on Sugar Hill and Morningside. Some of them came over to see what was going on. Some joined in.

Mrs. Ferguson had sent for the janitor to unlock the building. He lived in a building only around the corner. We kept the school building locked to keep the kids out when they were supposed to be out.

So we were dancing in the rain, and waiting for the janitor, and now he finally came, hopping along the sidewalk in his overalls, and smiling his missing-tooth smile, and waving the keys at us. I was dancing with Lana.

Even before the janitor got to the door, the kids, shouting and laughing, enjoying the shock of the rain, started converging on the entrance. Holding hands, Lana and I ran too.

I called out for the kids to line up and to stop pushing. Slowly they got in a sort of line and Lana went along the line. They liked her. A boy pushed the girl in front of him out of line, and Lana made him apologize; then Lana stood there till the girl regained her place.

Lana was pretty in her favorite color, yellow. She and I were summer social workers. We had been at it since the beginning of July and it was now near the end of August. I'd never met a girl like her before, a girl so sophisticated and intelligent, so poised and cheerful. She awed me. This was her first summer in Harlem. She was from Brooklyn, where her father was a big-shot insurance man, and her mother was an elementary school teacher.

No doubt about it, I was in love with Lana. She was my first girl since Lee Ann, last winter. Now I couldn't imagine what I'd ever seen in Lee Ann. Even the thought of her made me feel sad and doubt my own judgment.

But Lana! I can close my eyes now and see her beautiful face, framed with that long straight black hair—wet that day, wet and clinging to her exquisite face and long, lovely neck. I loved her peachy soft skin and those dark eyes of hers, always so full of laughter.

That was the summer I was nineteen. She was twenty-one. We'd started out with the understanding that ours would be only a summer romance. She would start her first year at Spelman (her second attempt at college) in Atlanta this fall. Except for Lana's presence in it, my life was a drag. My social work job with the kids was only a summer job. I was working mainly as a waiter and hating it. And I was thinking about joining the army just to get away from myself.

After the last of the kids entered the building, Lana and I followed. In the lobby she turned to me and said, "Chuck, I didn't know you were such a great dancer."

"I'm not. Not really. The rain kept me hopping."

She laughed. "My father can't dance at all. I used to try to teach him," she said, "but he is afraid for me to touch him."

That was a strange thing to say. I asked, "Why?"

"That's just the way he is."

I'd never met her father, but I knew he disapproved of her living with me and had from the very beginning, back in early July.

The musicians were coming in now, lugging their instruments, hovering over them, trying to keep them dry.

The kids were scattered all over the auditorium, socializing. But the nature of their socializing changed the minute the musicians got set up; and they got set up on the auditorium stage pretty quickly. They still kept their groups separate. The blue guys immediately cut into "Little Brown Jug," and some of the kids moved out onto the floor, trying to find the right steps.

Now the dancing resumed in earnest.

Lana and I, too, got into it and danced till we ached. At one point while we were dancing to a slow number, while she rested her cheek against my bosom, she whispered, "Chuck, we've got to talk. But not now." I held her close, wondering, hoping. Could it be that she had changed her mind about college? I held my breath at the thought. *She loves me. She's going to stay.*

Because we were in charge, we were the last to leave the auditorium that afternoon. By six the high school auditorium was just about empty; the blue and red musicians stopped, and started packing away their instruments. I had the checks for the guys in my wallet, so when I saw them getting ready to leave I hopped up on the stage and gave each of the bandleaders a check. The leader of the blue band said they had another gig that night at the Cotton Club. So they had just enough time to grab two or three hours sleep. I thanked them and shook their hands, shook all the hands and thanked them again.

Lana was beginning to get kids out of the building when I found her. She was out front by the doors checking off names as they left. Everybody had to be accounted for. We'd promised that much to the parents.

Then I noticed a stranger standing nervously just inside the lobby. He was a grown man in a suit and wearing a hat and tie. He looked like business. A white guy and he had a face like a funeral.

I went over immediately and asked him what could I do for him. He wanted to see my boss, Mister Wagner. He said he was from Harry Hopkins' office downtown. I knew what that meant.

We were either going to be funded again next summer or not. This was the New Deal in action. Everybody knew President Roosevelt was strong on these programs.

I told the man our coordinator, Mister Wagner, was due back at six but he wasn't back yet, not as far as I knew. I said, "Let me check the office just to be sure."

We walked across the lobby to the office door, but it was locked and the guy said he couldn't wait. But he handed me an envelope and asked me to pass it on to Wagner. "Is it what I think it is?"

He chuckled. "I think so. Your budget for next summer has been approved." He tipped his hat and walked across the lobby, and out past Lana who was getting the last of the kids out.

I felt a moment of ironic happiness. Ironic because chances were I wouldn't be there, and Lana definitely wouldn't. But it was good news anyway.

I had to work that night. Lana and I walked all the way home rather than taking the streetcar. We were feeling good. Our place was tiny, a kitchenette in a brownstone on Morningside Avenue just off West 123rd. It was actually my place before we met.

Lana fed the cat, Missy, then walked with me to Mama Sally's Soul Food Restaurant on Lenox Avenue near 127th. We kissed outside in front of the door and I watched her walk to the subway entrance. She had quite a style. Then I went inside.

Mama Sally was a big yellow woman, too huge to move around much, and she was behind the cash register by the door.

This was her usual place. She held forth here till about eight, when her husband, Bob, came in to take over the cash register.

Bob held it till midnight, closing time. Bob worked days downtown operating an elevator in a fancy hotel. He had three or four hours between jobs to do whatever he did with that time. Bob was a quiet man. He had recently returned from military training in South Carolina, where he served nine months practicing as an ammunition supply tech to a potential combat unit. Both he and Mama Sally were easy to work for.

The minute I walked in, Mama Sally said, "Chuck, your mama was by here this afternoon. Said for you to come see her first chance you get. She said your daddy died."

My daddy died? This was interesting but it was just information, really, since I had never known my father. He was supposed to be living somewhere down South. He and mother separated before I was even walking. She had a couple of pictures of him. In those pictures, he was a pretty man, as they say, sporty with his hat tilted at a hepcat angle.

I thanked Mama Sally and went on to the back to change. I knew my mother was at work right now. She was a nurse at Harlem Hospital. I'd been out of high school now for almost two years and she was still bragging to her co-workers about my grades at De Witt Clinton.

I remember her sounding like some liberal white person, saying, "Chucky is the only black boy in that class and he's the head of his class." I used to want to say, So what, mother? Don't say it like it's something remarkable. Why shouldn't I be the smartest?

Amos was in back changing into his uniform when I got back there. "Guess what," he said, "I've joined the army."

I gave him a big-eyed look. "You *what*?"

"That's right. We gonna be going to war any day now. There's no way we can stay out of it much longer, not with Mussolini and Hitler on the march. Did you hear that Germany just annexed Austria? They're now saying that if we get into the war, black boys are going to do some of the fighting too."

"What if you get killed?"

"Ah, I don't worry about dying, man. I'm just thinking about getting the hell of out Harlem, seeing the rest of the world. They say them French women are really nice."

I had my pants off by now and was stepping into the starchy white cotton pants of the uniform. I thought of Lana leaving for college. The army might just be the thing. I was sick of being a waiter. I had no money to go to college. Since meeting Lana, I had felt a sharp sense of my own poverty. At least by going into the army I might luck up on some way out of my situation.

The next day, at my mother's kitchen table, with her across from me, looking uncomfortable in her uniform, tired and resigned, I said, "But Mother, I have no money to go to Atlanta to his funeral." The funeral would be held the next day.

"I know," she said, "but his mother called. She wanted you to know, so you'd have a chance. It was good of her. She never liked me and I wasted no love on her. But she thought of you. And I give her credit for that."

"So it was a heart attack and he was fifty-three?"

"That's right. How is your girlfriend, what's her name?"

"Lana."

"Yes, I try to remember Lana Turner to remember."

I didn't want to talk about Lana with my mother. I knew how mother felt about Lana. They'd met once when Lana stopped with me at the hospital when I needed to borrow twenty dollars till payday.

That night in bed, I tried to articulate my feelings to Lana about my father's death.

"I can't hate him because he wasn't a person to me, only a photograph, a name, an idea. He is a hollow space in me. His death now simply means that space will never change. But he is not my fate." I didn't know what I meant by saying, "He is not my fate," but it sounded right.

Noon, Saturday, a week later. We were home together. I was sitting in the armchair, reading over my final report, due in to Mister Wagner Monday, when Lana came out of the bathroom after taking a shower. She was naked and dry.

"Chuck!" Lana said with controlled excitement, "Let's take the train down to Central Park." When she got an idea she was like a little kid, full of excitement, gleaming and glowing. "We could walk around the lake." She stretched her arms above her head and gyrated her hips a couple of times. "It's such a beautiful day. Why stay stuck up in this place?"

"Sure, Lana." I wasn't feeling as excited about the idea as she was but, hell, I thought, with as much cheerfulness as she had, some of it was bound to rub off on me, once we got started.

We came up out of the subway at 72nd Street and headed west toward the park.

Walking along, holding hands, Lana said, "Chuck, I don't know how to tell you this, but I've just gone through hell. I thought for three weeks I was pregnant. But luckily, I'm not! Thank God!"

I stopped, as they say, dead in my tracks. "Pregnant? But, uh, you're not?"

"I'm not. Never was." Her eyes were closed like a kid playing hide and seek; she shook her head.

I felt a sudden and surprising, ironic moment of joy. I might have been a father, the father of Lana's child. Lana would be a mother. She couldn't leave me. We would be inseparable. It was irrational, desperate, and maybe even perverse.

As we walked on, I said, "Did you do something to get rid of it?"

We had been holding hands. Now she let mine go.

She gave me an astonished look. She frowned. "I told you, I wasn't pregnant. But if I had been I would have had an abortion."

"What if I had wanted you to have it?"

"Chuck, don't be silly. We're not married."

I let it go right there, afraid to push further.

I thought of the famous Harlem abortionist, Madame Bridges, and shuddered at the thought of Lana in her hands. I knew of at least three young women, ex-school mates of mine, who'd died of massive infections of the womb after seeing her.

We walked in the crowd down Park Avenue till we came to the big entrance leading into the park. There, we passed the funny man with the sad monkey on his shoulder. He was grinding his ancient organ music box, which was painted with tiny happy and gay clown faces. We entered the park with its flow of people.

We'd been here together one time before, back in July, and I had enjoyed just walking around with Lana and sitting on the grass. We stepped around a big, black woman pushing a tiny pink baby in a silver stroller, then weaved our way through boisterous kids horsing around and kept stride with contented couples strolling, arm in arm. We moved deeper into the park, possibly headed for the magical presence of the lake.

At the lake, hundreds of people were gathered. We walked about through the sluggish but colorful crowd for a while, then turned back and took the main path on around till we came to a quiet area and a little bridge over a stream.

"Let's sit for a minute." I leaped up onto the stone ledge of the bridge. Lana held her hands out and I pulled her up. We turned around and were facing a peaceful stretch of hillside. The outer edges were graced with deep green shrubbery and thorny bushes in blasting white bloom. Children, smaller than any I'd seen in a long while, were running around, screaming in a circle, in the valley below, playing tag. I was reminded of ancient Chinese brush drawings of enchanted landscapes.

Then before I could say anything, Lana said, "What was Lee Ann like?" She glanced at me from her position with her chin on her knee as she gazed out upon the Chinese landscape.

"Did I tell you about her?" I was not ready for this.

"Don't you remember?" Her puzzled look disarmed me.

"I guess I told you a lot. We grew up together. Her parents divorced and she moved to LA with her mother. I got a letter from her last spring just before you and I met. She took a job in a shipyard making war ships. Said they're teaching her how to weld. She's not going back to school."

"Did you love her?"

"I think so."

"Why did it end?"

"At the time I didn't know what I wanted and she did."

"Was she the first girl you ever loved?"

"Probably. Why so many questions?"

"Just curious." Lana reached up and snapped off a tiny stem from an overhanging branch and suddenly started pushing an ant along the ledge, causing him to wobble and lose his concentration, his direction. "His leg is broken," she said. "I'm helping him walk."

"You probably broke it jabbing at him like that."

"Have you ever loved anyone else?"

"What? No. I don't think so. What about you? You never told me much about you and Louis."

"I don't want to talk about Louis." She threw the stem out as far as she could and frowned. "My father hated him. He threatened to transfer me if I didn't break it off. That whole year at Howard was hell." She looked at me. "Don't you want to do anything with your life? I've known you two months and I have no sense of what you want out of life."

The question unsettled me and I looked at her with my mouth hanging open. I was stalling because I truly didn't know how to respond. "Sure," I finally said. "I have ambition. I want to make a lot of money and—"

"Yes? And what?" Her dark eyes challenged me.

"And be happy." I hated the sound of my own defensiveness.

"How do you propose to make a lot of money, Chuck?" She squinted, turned her head slightly away from me without shifting her eyes. She folded her arms across her chest. I think she was holding her breath. Her lips were pressed tightly together.

I couldn't look at her. I, who had grown up being called "The Brain," now felt foolish. "I have a good head for business. I'm going to run my own business." I stuttered. "Probably a trucking business, or I might open a chain of restaurants..."

"In Harlem?"

I hesitated. Opening a chain of restaurants itself was so new that the possibility of *not* opening them in Harlem had obviously never occurred to me. I had no response. I was defeated. *She doesn't love me. Look how she's looking at me.*

She was smiling, and that made me feel even more discomfort. "Your ambition," Lana said, "is to make money but you don't know *how* you want to do it." She shook her pretty head. "Not very promising, Chuck. You have a good mind, you know. Too bad you don't have any burning passion to do anything but make money."

"Well," I said defensively, "that's why you're going to college, isn't it? To get an education so you can make money and be secure and happy. Isn't that true?"

A severe look emerged from her face, one I'd never seen before. "Not exactly. I'm going back to college so I can learn more about life, the world, history, and myself." Then her eyes grew large with something like astonishment—no doubt astonishment at my stupidity.

"How is that going to help you? I've never heard you say anything about what *you* want to do with your life."

"I told you two months ago when we first met that my ambition is to design clothes. I like beautiful things. One day I'll own my own design and manufacturing company." She looked out across the Chinese landscape with her nose held high.

I didn't want to, but I believed her. Just being beside her, hearing her talk like this, made me feel inadequate. Because I loved Lana, my secret longing—till this moment—was to somehow become good enough for her and to one day marry her.

I had not wanted to face it, but it was right up on me like a mad dog: she was born in a class above my own and acted like it, had the self-confidence I didn't yet have. But over the last couple of months I'd told myself that that didn't matter. I had a chance with her. This wasn't just a summer affair.

But now in Central Park, on a sunny Saturday afternoon, near the end of summer, I was being suddenly kicked back into reality. When I dared think about it, I knew Lana had never even said she loved me or that she wanted to continue any kind of relationship with me beyond the summer. As painful as it was, I was only her summer boyfriend.

Suddenly, Lana leaped down from the stone wall, and swept her hand across the rear of her wide yellow cotton skirt. "We'd better go back. I've got to study."

That night she left her diary in the bathroom. I'd never stooped to opening it before. Yet, as I sat there, with the door closed, I turned against my own sense of decency. I read the latest entry:

I know my brother is my father's favorite so the will of the son will be done on earth as it is in heaven daddy I love you and you don't tell the truth you didn't tell me that I could freeze to death outside your love and that I your firstborn your second-favorite is it because I am a girl could suffer so in the face of your rejection daddy you gave me repressive moralized crap daddy and I wonder what you would think if I got pregnant before marriage would you disown me you would wouldn't you you hypocrite you selfish cold hearted dog oh I want to be alone somewhere on a beach a warm beach lying on the sand with no worries but I never have a chance to do anything to comfort myself to be alone to be peaceful and now going to Atlanta isn't going to be any easier especially having to share a room with another woman I started to say girl isn't that funny maybe I still think of myself as a girl and perhaps I am in ways you never like about me so no wonder I became a tomboy trying to win your love but I am a girl even if I am not your girl daddy's girl I always envied girls who were daddy's girl oh I had a dream about you daddy and you and I were together on some strange beautiful beach and it was summer the end of summer really and I was in a bathing suit but you were dressed to the neck in a wool business suit and wearing a necktie and black shoes just as though you were about to go to your office and I begged you to relax and to undress and come swimming with me but you ran away back from the beach and disappeared into the trees along the parking lot

That night I lay in bed thinking about Lana's stream-of-consciousness diary entry. *I don't know the person who wrote those words.* This thought scared me.

Later, I had a nightmare. Lana was giving birth to me. I actually saw myself, a fetus, coming out of her, tearing away from her uterine muscles, swaying in a milky universe of pain and blood. I was looking out of her, wearing her clitoris as a baseball cap, and big hands were reaching in for me, grabbing, tugging, pulling, and trying to yank me out. I had teeth and my gap between them. I saw my woolly head emerge, stretching her to her limits. When the hands finally got me out, I felt a chill and woke, realizing I'd kicked the blanket and sheet off and had pissed in the bed. I was lying there in a pool of my own urine. Shame hugged me like a compassionate mother.

A Monday, mid-morning. Lana was standing at the front window looking down at the street, waiting for her father to come to pick up her trunk. He was going to drive her to Union Station. "I should help your father with the trunk."

"No, it's not necessary. It's not heavy." She swished over to the trunk and stretched her arms across it and lifted it from the floor. Such an elegant young woman. Classy is the word that comes to mind. "See? I can pick it up by myself."

She came back to the window, brushing her hands together. I looked at her. Had Lana just been slumming all summer? Was I part of her ghetto research, perhaps her guide to Harlem, part of her means to getting *down* to the disadvantaged among her people?

I stood with her awhile, too depressed to talk, then abruptly turned away and briskly walked into the dark bedroom and closed the squeaky door.

I stretched out on the bed, feeling the springs sink, the same springs that had sung to our love-making for two months, and closed my weary eyes. I didn't want to see her cold-hearted father, and I was sure he didn't want to see me. To him it was just as well that I never existed.

Then, at last, I heard his insistent knocking at the front door, and Lana calling out, "Just a minute," and the door opening, and his heavy, hushed voice, then the fumbling thud made by her trunks, the rustling of clothes. For a moment I almost got up to go help anyway.

Then the noise stopped and he apparently had taken the trunk down.

Now she came into the room and sat down on the side of the bed. She leaned over me and whispered, "Take care of yourself, Chuck." She kissed my salty lips.

Then she was gone.

Defensively, I fell asleep, and when I woke hours later, I was surprised to see daylight still in the room.

I closed my eyes again. I could see it now: in a month I might be somewhere in the South, crawling on my belly, with a carbine resting across my arms, perhaps not far from Lana, at Spelman.

One thing was clear to me: I had to change my life.

TRICIA (1)

THREE DAYS BEFORE CHRISTMAS, Tricia leads him right into the dining room and into the kitchen where she's busy preparing a capon with stuffing for the oven. "Pour yourself a glass of wine, Mark." She nods toward the wine glasses suspended on a rack above the big jug of cheap wine sitting on her kitchen island chopping block. "Pour me one too."

Not much of a drinker, he dreads jug wine, but not to offend her, he pours himself a half glass and slightly more for her. He feels loose tonight, maybe on the edge of happiness, not so tense. Too often, in his severe self-judgment, he's too complicated and mysterious; too hawk-like; too aware of his own persona. He believes self-consciousness robs him of simple fun and simple pleasure.

"Ian is downstairs," she says. "I don't know where Luzette is. *Zet! Ian!*"

The boy shows up first. He's wearing a bush haircut and he's thin with big sad brown eyes. Must look like his father. He and Mark shake hands as Tricia introduces them. The boy is shy. He can't look Mark in the eye. Mark senses the boy wants out of the kitchen as quickly as possible.

He slinks out, looking like one of those cartoon characters that manages to get up and wobble away after being run over and flattened out by a giant rig.

Now comes the girl, Luzette, younger, closer than the boy to her mother's light brown complexion, and the brown of her eyes are specked with yellow and at times green. She's pretty in an odd way and not as shy as Ian. Immediately she says, "Hello. I know who you are. You are Professor Smith. How are you, Professor Smith?" She's a little lady.

"I'm fine, and you, Luzette?"

"Very fine, thank you." She's playfully swaying her hips from side to side. "Mother is cooking dinner. Do you know, sometimes we send out for pizza. Sometimes we . . . we uh . . . "

"Go wash your hands, Zet. You can help me if you wash your hands. Scoot."

Luzette skips out of the room, almost falling on the edge of the rug in the hallway.

Tricia's hands are so busy in the dressing crumbs that Mark isn't sure if he sees a slight tremor in her fingers. Could she be *nervous*?

"There's a teenage girl, Mabel, who lives with me. She helps with the kids. I don't know if she's going to get back in time to join us or not. I took her in a year ago after her parents kicked her out when she got pregnant. She lost the baby but she's been here ever since. She's a big help to me."

As he listens he feels that somehow Tricia's life is so ready-made. It sounds like a soap opera. But, tremor or no tremor, he is surprised at how relaxed he himself feels suddenly, and it is not the wine. He has only pretended to sip it, and later he might have to explain why it has lasted forever.

Without losing the rhythm of her chopping of celery, Tricia shoots a glance at him. "You good at chopping garlic?"

"Sure." He's ready for anything short of a firing squad.

Tricia stops what she's doing, wipes her hands, glides across the kitchen to a side-counter, yanks open a big drawer, pulls out a folded red plastic apron, shakes the big thing open, and, grinning, comes at him with it like it's a cape and he's a bull. "Turn around." She ties the thing in a bow at his back. He can feel her knuckles pressing into his lower back. She giggles a couple of times.

She marches him up to the chopping block, where he places his wine glass, and she pushes the handle of a little silver knife into his hand. From a hanging basket she grabs two cloves and dumps them on the block in front of him. "Go for it. You're on." In the same breath, with her head lifted in the direction of the hall, she shouts, "*Zet! Turn off the water—you've washed your hands long enough.*"

Dinner? The dressing is delicious, the capon tough. The kids refuse to stay put. They grab what they want from the table and leave.

He says, "You have beautiful children."

The compliment, and maybe something else outside the astrology of his range, makes her grin. In a voice thick with wine and sentiment, she says, "I love them to death. They're my whole life. Everything I live for."

He wonders how important her academic career is.

She's frowning, perhaps following a thought or a feeling she can't quite get a handle on. "I would like to marry again someday if the right person comes along, but I'm not in a hurry. I'm still young." Her smile is one of hope and fear.

"How young?" His courage is up but not flying.

"I'm thirty-three. You?" Now with her eyes leveled against his in an unwavering crystalline focus, he knows she is bravely on top of the moment, calm in what might turn out to be crossfire.

"Thirty-seven." The words taste like sugarless cotton candy stuck to the roof of his mouth. And he's thinking, *this is the age that most becomes me; I shall never again be as coherently connected to everything else as I am at this very juncture.*

But she's talking and he's not listening, though he now picks up the thread of her words. "There's this friend of mine, Darcy Wheeler, who wants to marry me. Years ago we had an affair, but we ended it and settled for just being friends. He's been after me to marry him since Jordan and I broke up. With Darcy it would be too much like a business arrangement. I don't feel romantic about him. He's a nice guy, a big shot in the Internal Revenue Service, makes gobs of money, and owns lots of property. I would never again have to worry about tenure. I could even stop teaching if I wanted to. In fact, he would *want* me to stop. That's part of the problem with Darcy. He has no appreciation for my intellectual life, for my commitment to teaching. For him, a job is a job, never a passion."

After the kids go to bed, he and Tricia stretch out on the fluffy rug in front of the fireplace, breathing the smell of ashes and rug cleaner. He closes his eyes and listens to the crackle of the flames. Something as dense and deep and dark as plant growth far down in soil stirs in his groin; maybe it's desire, maybe desire and more. He's watching the flames dance from the gas spouts.

He watches her pour more of the bad wine from the nearby jug into their glasses on the fireplace ledge. He's *drinking* it now. The fire shimmers through the yellow liquid.

He knows what's coming. Now Tricia turns on her back and reaches for him. He pulls up on his elbows and they kiss. Her lips, warm and wet from the wine, feel tight and tense. It's a tentative kiss that warms up and sings like a fertile bird.

She unbuttons the two middle buttons on his shirt with her right hand and slips her hand inside. With the other she reaches up for his head and strokes his brittle short hair. Her right hand feels tense as it moves gently across the hairy surface of his chest.

He closes his eyes and feels a swaying, not unpleasant but a bit grimy, feels a tossing, as if his terra firma has been replaced by an escaped sailboat. It must be the wine.

Tricia whispers at his ear as she bites his earlobe, "You want to stay over?" It *is* late and there's some question about the dependability of his moorings, isn't there. Who can say for sure he's in shape to safely venture out into this bustling night? He's likely to zig and zag. "Sure," he whispers back with the insecurity of a boarding school boy on his first real hot date.

The minute he whispers this word, Tricia grins widely and sticks her tongue out, pulls him close again, and forces her tongue, a hungry seal, into his mouth.

And what he's feeling is unclear. But he cares about her pleasure as she pulls him fully upon her, stretching and retracting at the same time like some wonderful water creature.

And he knows he's here for a serious reason beyond sex. He's really looking for the right woman to spend the rest of his life with. But she has to be the right one. Tricia might be that woman!

Now that he's staying she has a childlike joy. "Let's take a shower together and wash each other's backs. Won't that be fun?"

Her sheets are pastel purple with big splotchy yellow flowers. They jump under, pulling the covers up quickly. They lie there, stretched out shoulder to shoulder. He knows where he is now. What he doesn't know is where tonight will *take* him.

Tricia says, "If you're wondering about the kids, don't. They understand that what I do once my bedroom door is closed is *my* business and not theirs. Okay?"

"Oh, sure." Without realizing it, he now knows he had been wondering, just that, perhaps fretting a bit about it, trying to locate and define this errant uncertainty.

Half the night they make love, working up winter sweat, with heavy breathing, the works, to the comforting hum of the central heating. He keeps varying the approach, the touch, the motion, watching her, changing himself to match her shiftings.

Around five he feels himself swirl away across a vast stretch of space. He knows he's dreaming and he's not in his own bed. A tiny, unidentifiable worry nips at the edges of his mind.

It's the day after Christmas. Mark is packed and his bag is by the front door. In an hour he's leaving for the airport. He has to fly to Washington, DC, for the Modern Language Association meeting where he will lecture on Jean Toomer. Toomer's life is a metaphor for Mark's own life, as touchable as the leather of his luggage.

The phone rings. He's in his kitchen standing by the stove. He picks up. Tricia says, "I just had to talk to you again. I'm going to miss you."

"I'll miss you too."

"Mark?"

"Yes?"

"You're not going to see Joan, are you?"

Joan is Mark's ex-wife.

Tricia and Mark have spent almost every night together since that first one lighted by firelight and later by another kind of heat. He says, "Uh, I have to, I guess, since I want to see my daughter while I'm there. But listen, don't worry. There's absolutely nothing left between Joan and me."

He's back from DC, and all has gone well. He and Tricia are in her bed with the reading lights on. He's looking through one of her glossy fashion magazines; she's plowing her way through a stack of student papers, suffering with drooping eyes, bored. She sighs again for the tenth time and says, "It's my own fault for asking them to write about themselves. *God!*"

"Tricia," he says without looking at her, "While I was at MLA I interviewed for another job. University of Maryland, College Park. This morning they called and offered me an appointment." Now he turns and looks at her.

She's also looking at him. She takes off her reading glasses. "I knew this was coming. Don't ask me how. I don't know. But I *knew*. You're leaving and you've been here only a year. So," she says, throwing the student papers on the floor, "does this mean the end of us?" She pulls herself up higher against her stack of pillows. "Or can I—*and the kids*—plan on joining you there?"

He hesitates, looks away, searches for his courage. "I guess I am a little surprised that you'd be willing to move there, give up your appointment, move the kids so far from their father, change their school."

"I know. It would be a big step."

By now he knows she's not going to fly into a rage. This

he has dreaded; but he is prepared to say, "I didn't go to MLA planning to interview. *They* approached me *after* my talk. And now they've made an offer I can't refuse. I'd go in as a tenured associate professor."

"Promotion *and* tenure! That's hard to beat," she says. She reaches over and touches his hand. "As long as I know you love me and want me, I'd be willing to do it, give up everything here and start new with you wherever you go. But you've never even said you love me."

He's baffled. Is this a confrontation? Sure, he's told her he loves her. Hasn't he? He, such a deliberate person, so out front. He says, "That's not true. I must have *said* it. You've just forgotten. I *do* love you, Tricia." And as he says it he means it, it's as sure as a doctor's appointment, something you can see entered into a ledger.

"And I love you, Mark." She leans over, and they kiss; then she resettles against her pillows. She sighs. "But it scares me so."

"What?" A scansorial bird climbing up the bark of a tree!

She closes her eyes. "All I can do is hope things will work out."

"And they will." But the minute he has put the lid on these words he feels some emotion escalate, flying up out of focus.

He and Tricia are in one of the newly renovated restaurants down at Pioneer Square, feeling cozy and warm with the sun coming in through the big plate glass. Eating mussels, sipping Fume Blanc. It's Saturday at noon, end of the first week of the year.

She's telling him about a guest lecturer in one of her classes and he is thinking how interesting it might be to share life with Tricia. She might turn out to be an improvement over Joan, who, unfortunately, was more interested in gossip magazines and sit-coms than books and ideas.

Then the image of Tricia's son, Ian, fades in and he skids to a halt as though having driven too fast toward a changing light. How, in this imagined ideal world, would he ever manage to *live* with that boy, with the boy's hostility?

The second Friday in March he parks his blue Subaru in Tricia's driveway behind her white-lettuce-colored Toyota. On the way in he notices new growth on the two oaks in her front yard and also on the spruce.

Inside, in the hallway, here's Tricia, with a head-rag around her hair, looking like an *Ebony* ad for Dutch Boy, in paint-stained coveralls. She's up on a shaky step ladder, paint bucket in one hand, dripping brush in the other, obviously painting the hall an off-white, painting directly over gold wallpaper, a relic of relocated lives.

"What ambition," he says. He means no irony but it's awash in his voice like the glaze of oil on water.

"Got spring fever early. I should be grading papers, but to hell with it." Her grin is wide as a view from a mountain ridge.

He walks over, she leans down, and they kiss.

"The way I figure it," she says, "if I'm going to sell the house I have to make it look pretty."

Sell the house? Best not to press for clarity. He knows, he knows. Send her a questionnaire? He suddenly feels odd, false, pretending to be smooth and honest while feeling like some sort of creature with weird, excessively developed pectoral fins radiating from his hipbones, scurrying about in the bottom of the sea. No conflict, please. But this is cowardly. And he knows it. "Where are the kids?" That's right. Change the subject.

She steps down and he takes her in his arms. "Zet's next door with the neighbor girl. Ian's with his father. He's gonna be away the weekend." She steps back. He feels her scrutiny; it's of the genus reproach. "Maybe I misunderstood *you*."

She looks worried or on the verge of rage. He can't tell whether she's about to cry or scream at him.

Again he takes her in his arms and the gesture hides his confusion. "Listen, don't worry." He's talking into her paint-smelling, beautifully curly hair. "I'm taking a year's leave. See if I like the DC area, the university. If, say, in six months I can't stand it, I'm coming back to UW. Meanwhile, you can come to D. C., to visit, say, on some long weekends. That way we can test being there together. That would also give us time to see if we can scare up a teaching job for you. Lots of schools in the area, if nothing turns up in the department."

When she pulls back and looks at him, he can see she's been crying. The rims of her eyes are red. She sniffs and smiles. "You're right. I can't just *up* and move on a moment's notice. Come on in the kitchen," she says, locking her arm in his. "Let's have a glass of wine."

He thinks there has to be some point at which two people get a handle on the peculiarities of their situation, which is always changing. He follows her deeper into the sanctuary of the house. On the way down the hall he leaves his jacket on the chair by the phone.

In the kitchen he leans his belly against the chopping block, hands in pockets, as she pours white wine from a half-empty jug and he says, "Last night I had a dream that woke me. Another man and I are in the open cab of an elevator. We are about to descend but suddenly the coils break and the elevator starts plunging to the bottom. I immediately leap up and grab the railing inside the shaft and hang there. The other man remains in the cab as it falls. Apparently he decides to take his chances that way. As I hang on, I am not sure I have made the right decision."

"*Ah hah*!" Tricia says as she finishes pouring the wine. He senses in her some kind of tortured victory, riddled with desperate hope.

"But that's not all. As I am about to lose my grip, the elevator returns and I scramble desperately, trying to climb back into the cab. I suspect I have only a few seconds to get in before the cab will once again move. I wake before I succeed."

Tricia brings his glass to him and clicks hers against his. She's grinning. "What are *you* making of that dream?"

His smile is defensive. "Nothing, in particular."

She takes a sip, smacks her lips. "Listen, I feel better already. You're brave to make a move again so soon. But you *do* have a big incentive: tenure. I know people our age who'd kill for tenure."

He takes a sip of the astringent wine. He says, "You're up for tenure. What if you get it?" He has his moorings now.

"I'll never get it here." She leans across the chopping block, balancing herself on her elbows, holding her face in her paint-stained hands. "Haven't published anything." She sighs. "I don't have an easy time writing. It's very painful."

In the night, after sweaty, springtime lovemaking, they are lying side by side in the dark, holding each other.

"I have this feeling, Mark, that I will never see you again. Please tell me I'm wrong."

"We'll be together again. Don't worry." Again he is dismayed by how like soap opera performers they sound.

"Are you sure?" Her head is resting on his chest. "Do you *really* love me? Do you care deeply?"

"Yes, and I care *very* deeply," he says, believing it, and pulling her closer. Her body heat reinvigorates him. She opens again to his almost desperate desire.

But after lovemaking, the uneasiness and the awkward, sad silence won't go away. And he knows the rest of the weekend will be this way. Lying here, he feels closed tightly, like a conch shell, in himself. His plan is to get started sometime next weekend.

Saturday morning. Standing at the kitchen phone, which is attached to the wall across from the stove, he dials Tricia's number. He left her place at six this morning, saying goodbye. "Hi. As it turns out, I'm not leaving today. Didn't finish packing. At the last minute the secretary called and I had to go back down to the university and finalize some paperwork she forgot to give me last week. I'll be leaving first thing in the morning."

"Mark, this only makes it all the more painful. In a way I wish you hadn't called. But I'd be mad at you if you stayed an extra day and hadn't. It's really *hard*, Mark."

"I'm sorry. I understand."

"Are you coming back over here, then?"

"Tricia—" He hates the whine in his own voice.

"Don't say any more, Mark. I'm going to hang up. This is too painful. Call me when you get to Maryland."

"First thing." His words feel like they're strangling him.

"I love you." Even as she speaks these words her voice seems to be receding, elusive, as though she's speaking more to herself than to him.

"Love you too." And out of which hemisphere of self does this tone of clipped reassurance arise?

She hangs up first. He makes sure of that.

Now it is his turn.

He hangs up and at that same moment catches a glimpse of his own exhausted reflection in the glass of the upper oven door. It's too hawk-like to believe this image is of his face.

TRICIA (2)

MOST OF THE TIME Mark isn't sure that he exists, which is why he grew up looking in mirrors. But right now, as Tricia leads him into her dining room and into the kitchen where she's busy preparing a capon with stuffing for the oven, he feels pretty confident that he's really here.

She says something to him in a gentle voice. She nods toward the wine glasses suspended on a rack above the big jug of cheap wine sitting on her kitchen island chopping block. Again, she speaks, in the same soft way.

Not much of a drinker, he dreads jug wine, but not to offend her, he pours himself a half glass and slightly more for her. He feels loose tonight, maybe on the edge of something new. Too often, in his severe private judgment, he's too complicated and mysterious, too hawkishly aware of his own persona.

This self-consciousness seems to rob him of simple fun, the aroma of pleasure, the texture of leisure. He also feels he's too ambitious, too ready to move on to the next conquest, the next job, as if driven by an inner demon. He wants to move on sometimes even before he's conquered himself or whatever it is he happens to be after in the present quest.

The boy shows up first. He's wearing a bush haircut and he's eight and thin with big sad brown eyes. Must look like his father. The boy and Mark shake hands as Tricia introduces them. He's Paul. Paul is shy. Can't look directly at Mark. Mark senses Paul wants out of the kitchen as quickly as possible.

He finally slinks out, looking like one of those cartoon characters that manages to get up and wobble away after being run over and flattened out by a giant rig.

Now comes the girl, Luzette, younger, closer than the boy to her mother's light brown complexion, and the brown of her eyes are specked with yellow and possibly green. She's pretty in an odd way and she's less shy. Immediately she says a few innocent playful words to Mark, and then blasts her mother with a request.

Tricia, in a moderate voice, blasts her back, showing who's boss.

Unshaken, Zet is playfully swaying her hips from side to side. She turns back to Mark and starts chattering away about that event a couple of weeks before that excited her so much.

Tricia, in a firm voice, tells Zet to do a specific thing.

Without hesitation Luzette skips out of the room, almost falling on the edge of the rug in the hallway.

Tricia's hands are so busy in the dressing crumbs that Mark isn't sure if he sees a slight tremor in her fingers. Could she be *nervous*?

But, tremor or no tremor, he is surprised at how relaxed he himself feels suddenly, and it is not the wine. He has only pretended to sip it.

Without losing the rhythm of her chopping of celery, Tricia shoots a glance at him. Her one simple sentence gets him up. He stands by her.

Tricia stops what she's doing, wipes her hands, glides across the kitchen to a side-counter, yanks open a big drawer, pulls out a folded red plastic apron, shakes the big thing open, and, grinning, comes at him with it like it's a cape and he's a bull. She tells him what to do. He turns around. She ties the thing in a bow at his back. He can feel her knuckles pressing into his lower back.

She marches him up to the chopping block, where he places his wine glass, and she pushes the handle of a little silver knife into his hand. From a hanging basket she grabs two cloves and dumps them on the block in front of him. Laughing, she gives him a directive. In the same breath, with her head lifted in the direction of the hall, she shouts.

After dinner and after the kids go to bed, he and Tricia stretch out on the fluffy rug in front of the fireplace, breathing the smell of ashes and rug cleaner. He closes his eyes and listens to the crackle of his own aliveness. Something as dense and deep and dark as plant growth, far down in soil, stirs in his belly. He watches it as though seeing it on fast-forward, coming up, manifesting itself across the cloud-packed sky of his mind.

He says in a kind voice what is on his mind.

She smiles and in her amiable tone responds.

His courage is up but not flying.

Now with her eyes leveled against his in an unwavering crystalline focus, he knows she is bravely on top of the moment, calm in what might turn out to be crossfire.

He asks a private question.

The words taste like sugarless cotton candy stuck to the roof of his mouth as he tries to dislodge them.

She tells him.

And he's thinking, *this is the age that most becomes me; I shall never again be as coherently connected to everything else as I am at this very juncture.*

But she's still talking and he's listening with misgivings brought on by what she is saying.

Seemingly out of nowhere she says something that puzzles him. He does not respond. Now in a silence he can't decide is easy or uneasy, they watch the ever-consistent flames dance from the gas spouts.

He watches her pour more of the bad wine from the nearby jug into their glasses on the fireplace ledge. He's *drinking* it now. The fire shimmers through the yellow liquid.

He knows what's coming and it seems as natural as the two equal parts of the aromatic kernel popping out of the seed and lying dry in the sun at the base of the tree, then burrowing itself when the storm hits with a constant and bright force.

Tricia turns on her back and reaches for him.

He pulls up on his elbows and they kiss. Her lips, warm and wet from the wine, feel tight and tense. It's a tentative kiss that nevertheless warms him and sings on its own.

She unbuttons the two middle buttons on his shirt with her right hand and slips that hand inside. With the other she reaches up for his head and strokes his brittle short hair. Her right hand feels tense as it moves gently across the hairy surface of his chest.

He closes his eyes and feels a swaying, not unpleasant but a bit grimy, feels a tossing, as if his terra firma has been replaced by an escaped sailboat. It must be the wine.

Tricia whispers at his ear as she bites his earlobe. It *is* late and there's some question about the dependability of his moorings. Who can say for sure he's in shape to safely venture out into this bustling night? He's likely to zig and zag, miss the harbor, so to speak, hit the rails.

He whispers back with the security of a boarding school boy on his first real hot date.

The minute he whispers Tricia grins widely and sticks her tongue out, pulls him close again, and forces her tongue into his mouth.

But he cares about her pleasure as she pulls him fully upon her, stretching and retracting at the same time.

And he knows he's here for some kind of serious reason, here because he wants something, maybe something lasting, hard to name but reassuring. He can't name it precisely. And he knows he doesn't have a clue to her, what she wants, if anything, beyond this night. He can only guess.

Now that he's staying the night she has a childlike joy. Her voice is like flowing water.

Coming out of the steamy bathroom the bedroom feels cool as a stretch of unspoiled coastline, palm trees swaying, seagulls riding the wind currents.

Her sheets are pastel purple with big splotchy yellow flowers. They jump in and shoot their legs under the covers. There isn't the slightest touch of steaminess in any of this. He's sure. He's very sure, as sure as a good horse trainer about his best horse.

They lie there, stretched out shoulder to shoulder. He feels no need now to consult a compass; he knows where he is. What he doesn't know is where tonight will *take* him.

Tricia says something that takes three sentences to complete.

He smiles.

After their making love and sleeping he wakes around five. He feels himself swirl away across a vast stretch of space where lines and colors keep moving darkly but have no meaning he can identify. Asleep again he knows he's dreaming and he's not in his own bed. A tiny, unidentifiable worry nips at his edges.

The day after Christmas: He has to go away on business. He calls Tricia with the news. Her response is reassuring.

He's back and all has gone well. He and Tricia are in her bed with the reading lights on. He's looking through one of her glossy fashion magazines; she's plowing her way through a stack of student papers, suffering with drooping eyes, bored. She sighs again for the tenth time and says what he expects to hear.

But he isn't listening carefully. He has something else on his mind. He wants to tell her something important. It will hurt. He says it without looking at her. She takes off her reading glasses. He can see the surprise, the fear, and the disappointment in her response.

He hesitates, looks away, searches for his courage.

They exchange careful words now, stepping around each other carefully. He knows she feels betrayed by the news.

But by now he knows she's not going to fly into a rage.

She reaches over and touches his hand. She says in a soft voice something that he likes and ends by saying something else he dislikes.

He's baffled. Is this a confrontation?

She leans over and they kiss, then she resettles against her pillows. She sighs, a scansorial bird stepping up bark.

But the minute he has put the lid on his next words he feels some unnamable emotion escalate, flying up out of focus, out of control. He feels a loss of *something* that is replaced by a sense of terror and crisis. It is a feeling that comes over him when he himself is in danger of completely disappearing. But in a short while the terror passes.

He and Tricia are in one of the newly renovated restaurants down at the Square. He feels cozy and warm with the sun coming in through the big plate glass. Eating mussels, sipping Fume Blanc. It's Saturday at noon, end of the first week of the year. Beneath his good feeling he feels guilty. Of what, he doesn't know.

The second Friday in March he parks his blue Subaru in Tricia's driveway behind her white-lettuce-colored Toyota. On the way in he notices new growth on the two oaks in her front yard and also on the spruce.

Inside, in the hallway, here's Tricia in paint-stained coveralls, up on a shaky step ladder, paint bucket in one hand, dripping brush in the other, obviously painting the hall an off-white, painting directly over blue and gold wallpaper, a relic of relocated lives.

He means no irony in what he says at this point, but it's awash in his voice like the glaze of oil on water.

Her grin is wide. It's early spring. There's fever in the air.

He walks over, she leans down from the ladder, and they kiss. Is she planning to sell the house?

She steps down. He takes her in his arms. She looks worried or on the verge of rage. He can't tell whether she's about to cry or scream at him.

When she pulls back and looks at him, he can see she's crying. The rims of her eyes are red. She sniffs and smiles. He knows she wants so desperately for this relationship to work, possibly end in marriage. How does he know this? He just does. He also knows that she loves him more than he loves her.

He thinks there has to be some point at which two people get a handle on the peculiarities of their situation, which is always changing. He follows her deeper into the sanctuary of the house. He leaves his jacket in the chair by the phone on the way down the hall.

In the kitchen he leans against the chopping block, hands in pockets, as she pours white wine from a half-empty jug. They talk and talk and talk, quietly, courteously, and amiably.

She sighs. She takes a sip, smacks her lips, languid eyes in a shipshape face. He too takes a sip of the astringent wine. He has his moorings now. She leans across the chopping block, balancing herself on her elbows, holding her face in her paint-stained hands.

In the night, after sweaty, springtime lovemaking, they are lying side by side in the dark, holding each other desperately. He knows she would give anything if he didn't have to go away to live in another city because he's found a better job.

But the uneasiness and the awkward sad silences won't go away. And he knows the rest of the weekend will be this way. Lying here, he feels closed tightly, like a conch shell, in himself. His plan is to be finished with his packing and to leave town next weekend.

Saturday morning. Standing at his kitchen phone, which is attached to the wall across from the stove, he dials Tricia's number.

He left her place at six this morning, saying the polite thing and what he needed to say.

Tricia answers the phone. Sweet sad greetings. Then she says how much she feels and what she is going to feel and what she will try not to feel.

He says it back to her, feeling badly because he's partly lying.

He hangs up and at that moment catches a glimpse of his own exhausted reflection in the glass of the upper oven door. It's too hawk-like to believe. But it is surely his own face; it proves he is real. No doubt about it. Behind him, looking over his shoulder is some sort of beast, a winged monster, with a hideous face, glaring at him in the mirror.

DRIVING EAST

THIS IS HOW IT WAS. And this is how it is.

I drove out from the East Coast to be with Elliott. I had high hopes. Late afternoons glowed orange-red. The morning countryside possessed me. The life I was leaving? My life on the East Coast was like a bad date. My time there had left me with deep disappointment.

Then there was the memory of that brief time with Elliott on the West Coast. Just think, a man who understood lungs, guts, ovaries, testicles, what the pancreas does, how the thyroid glands work. What more in life could a health-conscious person want out of a, well, say it, out of a husband. But could I be sure? Should I risk everything, go west, check out the possibilities; shake the dullness and disappointment; get a life, as they say, take a new lease; cuddle and be cuddled. Did I dare hope, to dream, to act on those high hopes? I liked the way Elliott pronounced my name, "May-gen." It was like the taste of good white wine, like excitement brought up to the level of verbal sculpture.

But it was a mistake. Coming out West, I mean. That was a year and a half ago. Where am I now? I'm heading back East, talking to myself, cajoled, Blues-drenched, green, no, yellow-green with disenchantment, wondering where my wonderment went. In the district of Hanging On, looking out across the lawn toward the landscape of What Next.

This time I was on my way to Boulder. It was there, while I was a wellness student three years ago, that I met Elliott on the mall. He was on a skiing trip with a group of other interns.

Going west to be with Elliott, I drove up to Ontario and across Canada—because it was a great chance to see a *lot* of Canada—through Manitoba, Saskatchewan, and Alberta. I swung down through eastern British Columbia to Seattle. Scared, being a woman and all, but it was also great fun to be out there on the road all by myself speeding along, a tiny piece of cartilage moving through a vast artery, with a new view every second.

Once we decided to live together, everything happened fast. Anticipating my arrival, Elliott moved from his mother's house and took out a lease on a ranch-style house with three bedrooms out in the northwest part of the city. A skeptic's dream, a house with a facade that said: no frills, no trills, you get what you get. In Yonkers I got my few possessions packed and called UPS and they swept them away in their big groaning, hissing truck, and I got going in my little Honda.

At first, during the first week or two, everything was fine. I set up a work area where I could paint. I'm a therapist and painting is my hobby. I figured this was a fine time to do some painting before I got real busy with my professional work. I figured it would take a while to get established, to build up a list of patients. So I set up an easel in the basement.

The first day, I walked through our rooms with him. They were still empty, yet filled with loud silences, busy emptiness. Then Elliott surprised me by stopping at the entrance to the smallest bedroom and saying, "I'll take this one for my study." How nice, after half expecting him to take the biggest one.

I liked the house all right. The kitchen window over the sink looked out on a fenced backyard of grass that needed cutting. We kept talking about hiring a neighborhood boy, but it was awhile before we did. When we finally got one, he was unreliable, wouldn't show up half the time, and when he did, he did a piss-poor job. Still the backyard was nice to look out on. Next to water, I like to look out at grass.

Now, heading for Boulder, I thought about Boulder and Lynda Carlyle. I thought about an incident. I remembered that time when Lynda's hand was sliding along my thigh. The motion was managed in a hesitant, questioning manner. I remembered how close I had felt to Lynda Carlyle only moments before, as though we were sisters in conspiracy, as though Operation Whole Body belonged only to us alone. Then I removed her hand. And that was the end of it. We never spoke about the incident.

But what went wrong in Seattle? In Seattle, I soon had to start meeting Elliott's colleagues and associates. That was hard. I didn't like many of them. I especially disliked the head doctor, grizzly

Doctor Larry Dayton who lived in a big house up in Riverton Heights. One night we were at his house for a retirement party for one of the older doctors. His cutesy wife was a Presbyterian minister. They were the most intolerably precious couple I've ever seen. They went about seating everybody with such formality that I suspect the others felt as uncomfortable as I did. If they didn't they should have. But it wasn't just that. The whole evening was like that—full of dainty stiffness. Elliott's other colleagues, Doctor Carl Modac, Doctor Paul Higgins and the head nurses, Elena Murphy, Doris Leach and Alicia Smith, and their families, were easy to take compared to the Daytons. But unfortunately we couldn't avoid them.

At one point during the evening of that retirement party Larry Dayton smirked at me and said, "I understand you're new to Seattle. Seattle is a good place to live and work. What kind of work do *you* do?" He was looking down his nose at me, head slightly drawn back like I smelled bad and he didn't want to get too close. I almost folded up right on the spot. I hated that question. And people were always coming at me with it but his approach was the most unsettling I'd had to face in a long time. Rather than telling him I was a therapist I said, "Oh, I guess you could say I'm at the service of humanity." And he of course took offense, which is the effect I intended to elicit.

Speaking of work, I did meet a woman therapist, Diane Pallas through Elena Murphy, a rough-edged, well-preserved older woman. Actually met her in a supermarket. She and Elena were together shopping. Diane's eyelashes were long, ornamental, and she clearly used rubber gloves to handle dishes.

"Megan studied with Lynda Carlyle," Elena said.

"Oh, I'm impressed," said Diane Pallas. "Carlyle is one of the best, I think. Did you like Boulder?"

"Loved it. When I'm old and gray it's the sort of place where I'd like to live."

"Have you found work here?"

"No. But I haven't tried—yet."

Diane smiled. "Would you be interested in joining my clinic?"

When a week later I told Elliott that Diane was considering having me join her practice, The Holistic Wellness Clinic, he hit the ceiling, "Are you crazy? Diane and her associates are a bunch of quacks."

That, of course, startled me and started me wondering if he thought less of me, too, because of my belief in holistic medicine, and because I don't have a medical degree. I have a certificate from Lynda Carlyle's Operation Whole Body Institute in Boulder.

As it turned out, Elena's other partner, Jane Farley, was so strongly against my joining them that the proposition was dropped pretty quickly. When I stopped by there a couple of days later, Diane wasn't in and Jane said, "Megan, don't get me wrong. I like you very much, but there just isn't enough work for us to take on another therapist. Diane and I are barely working part-time."

It was later that morning while we were walking in Lincoln Park when Elliott stopped. "Megan, I have to tell you, I'm not sure about us," he said without looking at me.

I stopped. He stopped. He looked away then down.

I watched him drag his foot in an arc, like a windshield wiper, in the sand. Then I turned away from him toward a giant tree. And I was tongue-tied. Earlier in my life, when I had more self-confidence, I might have simply said, "It takes courage to love." But with Elliott I had tried hard to be the woman I had always wanted to be: a sweet woman of moonlight and romance, a woman now given to walks on Mercer Island and in Seattle drizzle.

Now I drifted away from him and began walking along the gravel path ahead of him. I felt a tear start, then roll down my left cheek, then along the line of my nose. Well, I wasn't going to be sentimental about this. Tears fall in times of joy and pain. Sentiment clutches the heart of whole populations. I'd gotten through worse things. I told myself I wasn't going to let this get me down.

Not long after this devastating news, I was going through Elliott's shirt and pant pockets, as my mother always went through my father's, before dumping clothes in the washer. Once my mom washed a shirt of Dad's that contained a state lottery ticket. The blue ink ruined Dad's shirt, but worse than that, the ticket turned out to be worth about two or three hundred dollars. Dad had memorized the number but he couldn't prove it and when he presented the ticket they wouldn't accept it. So that's why I always go through pockets before I wash things.

This time I found a tiny folded piece of paper in one of Elliott's pockets. Thinking it might be something he needed, I saved it, put it on the dresser. This was in the morning. By mid-afternoon it crossed my mind again because I happened to be in the bedroom looking for the *TV Guide*.

On impulse I opened the piece of paper and held it toward the light. "Donnie 524-4206/ 12:30 Olympia Motel." Donnie? Olympia Motel?

When he came home that evening I confronted him with the note. He looked cornered for a moment then shrugged. "Okay. So you found out. What's the big deal?"

Elliott and I didn't have sex again after I found out about his affair with Donnie. I couldn't stand him touching me anymore. We rarely made eye contact either. I wasn't emotionally free of him but was getting angry enough to leave.

The next time Elliott left for San Francisco—a week after I learned of the affair—I was not in the mood to drive him to the airport. He called later and said, "Megan? I'm tied up here. I've got to stay over a couple of extra days."

"As usual," I said. I wondered if *she* was with him.

"What? Let's not fight, at least not on the phone. Okay?"

"Next time you leave, pack me in mothballs and throw a drape over my head." I hung up.

I packed, put my things in my Honda, and pulled out of the driveway that same day. And that was yesterday.

Now, straight ahead, in front of me, level with the highway, was the sun, a giant orange-red ball. It is slowly lifting itself up out of the earth, surrounded by the misty, wet blue stretch of land. It is my fidus Achates—if I can be Aeneas for this inspired moment.

Lucky me! I get a Blues station that's coming in clearly. The Blues makes me happy. That's the purpose of the Blues. Some old-time guy really knows his stuff, talking about Albert Ammons's ability at the piano, his tempo Blues, with eight to the bar as a working base. Then the disc jockey plays some Canju, Clarence Garlow, "Let The Good Times Roll."

Pretty soon I lose the station so I turn off the radio.

But the view in front of me matches my mood. I feel better than I've felt in the last year and a half. I'm leaving Seattle for good. Goodbye Elliott, hello Blues, hello Happiness, hello Boulder. True, I still feel a little nervous on the highway alone, but I'm not about to show it or give in to it. And I feel nervous about seeing Lynda again. But I must!

I keep moving at a steady pace, swinging slightly south for the first half hour of the morning, driving right through town after town, crossing the Cascade Range. People tell me I drive fast for a woman, but that's my style. Left-handed, I'm working both hands equally so as not to get tired too quickly.

Now it's not quite seven and I left the motel at six and already I'm feeling freer than I have in my life. Sure it's partly the symbolism—sun and motion and the deliberate changes, leaving Elliott—that's lifting my spirits.

Maybe it's also the symbolism of the drive. Moving from west to east is refreshing, driving into the sun. But somehow I have come through a bad spell—with Elliott and being out of work for a year and a half. Yet, I survived, and as odd as it sounds, I feel cleansed, ready to truly start a new life in Boulder. I always liked Boulder. My dreams took me there the first time when I was eighteen.

I was a student at the University of Massachusetts at Amherst when I wrote away to the world famous therapist, Doctor Lynda Carlyle, boldly asking her for her personal guidance. So friendly was her response that, after that semester, I dropped out of college and flew out to Boulder and became one of her few hand-picked students at her wellness institute, Operation Whole Body.

But I remember the day the letter came. Ten below! What excitement! I was walking from the campus post office, sifting through my mail, with the crunching hard snow beneath my boots, when I came to her envelope. I tore it open. With my parka holding back the free movement of my arms, I couldn't get it open fast enough. My knees felt weak. I was sick with joy, even before I read it. My heart was racing. Hands shaking. Ten below, and I didn't feel cold. In my excitement my hood had fallen down and I'd dropped my gloves.

A boy walked by and whistled at me but I didn't even look up.

I sat down on the curb, right where I stood, rather than crossing like anybody in her right mind might. I sat there, my rear soaking up the snow, and read each word over and over. Even the green inked-in corrections were beautiful. The boy called back over his shoulder, "Don't freeze it off. You're too beautiful to lose it." I was not yet old enough to be offended by this sort of comment but I was embarrassed.

That summer I took the AM flight out to Denver and a bus to Boulder to see the great Lynda Carlyle, a woman who had healed hundreds of sick minds and bodies. I knew about her from newspaper articles, and she had published in journals, and there was her own book, *Operation Whole Body.* She was only in her mid-forties.

Still, I was shocked by her appearance. She met me on the front porch of her school. A plain woman with short brown hair, she was tiny and spoke with a heavy British accent.

I don't think she had expected me to be African-American. I saw the surprise in her eyes. But she was clearly curious about me, this young colored woman who'd dropped out of college to be one of her disciples. She hugged me and right away I felt at home.

Lynda showed me into her crowded office. Self-help books and pamphlets and newspapers were piled everywhere. Her home and school shared the same house. It was a block east of the main post office.

She pointed to an airbrushed photograph of herself as a child. I stood close to the picture on the wall. It was of a girl with an angelic face. I looked again at Lynda and I could not see the child, but I trusted the innocent-looking wise child to still be there somewhere inside her.

Then we walked up the mall to Pearl's. The mall was crowded with couples, pretty girls, bums, hippies, intellectuals, poets, homeless people, hangers-on, and philosophers. Lynda ordered for both of us. She insisted I eat boiled potatoes and yogurt and a salad. It was a delicious lunch. What I remember most about lunch was Lynda watching me. At one point she said, "You are going to be happy here, Megan. And you will learn the art of healing."

Again I turn on the radio. It's a talk show. People are calling in to respond to the host's question: "What should the president do to end this most recent crisis?" I listen to the answers, asinine and sensible alike, for about an hour. Just as I'm about to change the station, the host says he's having a free-for-all. People can call in and ask or say *anything* they want. Yes, this is America.

I stay on Highway 90, and pretty soon, while turning the dial, I pick up a station where they got this black guy on talking about the Mississippi Sheiks, Rex Stewart's Big Four, Big Bill Broonzy. The host plays some Lemuel Flowler's Washboard Wonders ("Chitterlin' Strut") and some Washboard Sam doing "C. C. C. Blues." Turns out the guest got his start with Cadillac Slim and worked with Benny Carter and his Chocolate Dandies. He's just passing through and they had him on because, the host says, "Blues ain't all that different from Country and Western."

I'm going to be on 90 all day today and for most of tomorrow. My plan is not to drive for more than eight to ten hours each day. Sometime late tomorrow I should reach Butte, Montana. I'll stop there. Today I'm trying to push beyond Spokane, if possible, without getting exhausted. But at fifty-five, pushing it up occasionally to sixty and sixty-five, it's questionable. The muscles in my arms and legs are as relaxed as they can be, sitting like this. I feel lucky I'm not on my period. And I don't miss Elliott.

Exactly at 12:30 PM, I stop at a roadside fast food joint called Medicine Lake Grill. It's on the highway a little before you reach Spokane. It was filled with an array of brooding and laughing truckers and local farm workers. I sneak a look at what they're eating as I search for a seat. They're eating mostly burgers and fries, chicken fried steak and fries, fish and chips, cherry pie. A motley bunch, they glance at me sideways from under their baseball caps, looking at my legs, then my face.

I find an empty booth and order a hamburger because it's the best-looking thing on the menu. The waitress shows up in a polyester pink uniform and she's wearing purple rhinestone glasses.

When the hamburger is set before me, my health consciousness is shot for the moment; I overwhelm it with ketchup and hot sauce. Even someone like me might, once in a while, pig out. A trucker looking over his shoulder at me from the counter laughs, showing me his coffee-stained teeth.

My head feels remarkably clear. I remember Lynda's philosophy: live in the present, live in the present; stay focused. So, I'm focused. Not on disappointment. Disappointment is behind me. But even between disappointment and happiness, there is a thin wall of bone that's stronger than it seems, a kind of septum through which you can spin on into the next mood. So, I'm here in this booth, eating this greasy, delicious, Ketchup-covered hamburger.

But back on the road a half hour later, I start worrying about how staying with Lynda Carlyle is going to be after all this time, helping her run the school. There are other things about her I'd like to forget. She still thinks of herself as my mentor and teacher. Not sure I can go back into that kind of relationship with her. If I have to, will I be able to change the terms of the relationship? Can we be equals and business partners? Or, as before, will I be the student and she the teacher?

I almost make it to Missoula before stopping. At Superior, I pick up my dinner of fried chicken and biscuits and gravy. I buy a bottle of seltzer water and a bottle of warm Coca-Cola (the only kind I can find). I check into a little cowboy motel, get a bucket of ice from the machine outside my door, and call it a night. Once my door is locked, I'm an individual again, realizing that out there, on the road, though happy, I've been a nameless selfless entity.

But when I turn on the TV, I feel myself begin to disappear again, sucked up by the braille-like surface of the thing, but I go on watching, watching news and sitcoms. I eat and drink Coke and water till I'm sleepy. At ten I turn off the light. I return to myself to sleep with myself. It's going to be a long night.

The bed is lumpy and I keep shifting around on it till I find the most acceptable position. I'm conscious of the human traffic going and coming half the night in the rooms on both sides and above. No way around it, I'm going to be exhausted in the morning. Next time I'll pay more and stay in a better motel, one with thick walls.

During the brief time I sleep, I'm in a dream with Elliott, who's complaining because I'm not walking fast enough. We seem to be going somewhere important to him. I give up and sit down on a park bench and watch him disappear down the street.

At daybreak I'm up and on the road. I'm feeling surprisingly well, and after I drive past the Helena area I'm heading almost completely south for about an hour toward Butte, moving through a giant area, the colors and patterns of cranial nerves. It's so beautiful, with its nerve system of trees, highway, sky, farms, and vast stretches of land and shrubbery like brain tissue. Suddenly, I burst into song, which surprises me. I'm singing, "Everybody Needs Somebody to Love," doing damage to it for twenty minutes or so before I cut into "That's Life." Then I shut up and turn on the radio.

Out here these stretches are long and lonely-looking. They are the hot color of opened sweat glands with the blood wiped carefully away. But the sky is tall and clear. The stretch between Butte and Bozeman is big with clearly defined land and farm lines. It's white as bone, pink-tan as the lips of a squirrel monkey. I love being under this incredibly bright sun as it begins to command its place in the sky. It is all very soothing. I've made all the right moves. And the landscape seems to compliment me.

I stop for lunch in Bozeman. I later walk around, looking in the shop windows at the expensive lady cowboy hats and dresses and the saddles and the spurs. I feel good knowing that nobody knows how to reach me—not my father, who's retired and living in Palm Beach; not my mother, who's in Yonkers, where she lives (three blocks from my old place) with her second husband, Bill, and no doubt still worried about this move I've decided on. (She was worried about my going to Seattle to be with Elliott too.) When I told her I was going to Colorado to resettle, she said, "Don't count your chickens before they hatch." This is her way of warning me not to depend too much on Lynda Carlyle. Mother never liked my involvement with the Operation Whole Body Institute.

Nobody here in Bozeman knows me. I can move through without having to talk to anybody. I browse in an antique jewelry shop for a half hour.

I take it very easy between Bozeman and Yellowstone, reaching Yellowstone in the late afternoon. I see no yellow in Yellowstone; instead, I see veins of red, veins of silver-green; I see the earth itself as brown-black skin. I see a sky the warm texture of the epidermis. I see highway patrolmen lying in wait for speeders. They're like living cells shooting out of nowhere with their sirens. I'm not exceeding the speed limit by more than a few miles; I can easily drop down if I see a cop. Here, I want to be extra cautious. Although being a woman helps, because of my color, I can't drive by unnoticed.

I leave 90 after Bozeman, taking a little road toward the park. I pick up 90 again for a brief time. And I head toward Utah, but soon the road gives way to 25. I take 25 on into Utah. This is all new to me; so I trust the map spread out on the passenger seat.

But for now, in Yellowstone, the tourists are milling about in their bright polyester pinks and yellows. I stop at Morris Junction and buy a bottle of spring water from a tourist shop. The place is crowded. I get out of there as quickly as I can.

It's six before I check into a motel at Cody. It's Tuesday night and the town is nearly closed down at sunset. Keeping my room key, I drive to a supermarket and buy a bottle of seltzer water and a six-pack of Coke. By seven-thirty I'm in bed, with a glass of Coke on ice, and watching TV. I wiggle my toes with joy.

At noon the next day, I cross the border into Utah, still heading southeast toward Twin Falls. In some stretches, the landscape is the colors of cartilage and bone; in other stretches, it's bright green, then dull green. I stop at Bliss, Utah, and pull into the parking lot of Debbie's Place. A waitress, with a nametag that says her name is Christine, takes my order of fish and chips. I watch her write. She's left-handed. I feel affection for that left hand as it moves the pencil across the pad. Then, over her shoulder,

Christine calls back to the kitchen, "Chips!" She's got it down to a science.

It's Wednesday afternoon. I'm on the road still driving toward Boulder and my new life. I don't expect to pull into Lynda's gravel driveway till Friday morning. I can already see her. She's wearing sunglasses. She's standing in the yard, under the big walnut tree. Its limbs are like capillaries; both she and the tree are waving to me. As I pull into the driveway, the sun is shining on her brown hair. And, with her arm stretched up above her head, she's waving to me. And she is smiling.

THE LAKE

ONE NIGHT SANDY WAS OUT LATE at some sort of "mind and body" improvement session, or, so she said, and Joe was in bed, reading a murder mystery, when the phone rang. The voice was male and it said, "If you eat Chinese pussy you'll be hungry an hour later," then he giggled and hung up. A sour feeling rose from the bottom of Joe's stomach and settled at the root of his tongue.

Obscene calls had come before but none had ever been so personal, so specifically meant for him. It frightened him and made him mad. It had to be someone who knew them. Or maybe a stranger, possibly someone in the neighborhood who'd observed Sandy and him going and coming, possibly even someone in the building; or someone at his job at the law firm. Also, Joe couldn't help wondering if his own recent infidelity had something to do with the obscene call.

Joe and Sandy left New York City at five in the morning, and got into the little town at about six-thirty. With the windows rolled down, Joe immediately felt the coolness from the giant trees. He pulled into a gas station right at the mouth of town and a young man came out and filled it up—just like in the old days. And he told Joe how to get out to the cabin on one of the Fulton Chain Lakes. The guy said you got to watch for the dirt road on the right. It was hard to spot but if you look for an old road sign on the left that said, "No Hunting," it would be just a few feet beyond that sign.

They took the paved road the guy indicated and drove straight out there in about twenty minutes, except that the first time Joe missed the dirt road because he didn't see the "No Hunting" sign since it couldn't be seen coming in. But after awhile, Sandy said, "I think we've gone too far," and agreeing with her, he pulled into somebody's driveway, and turned around and headed back. Coming back, they spotted the sign at the same time and sure enough there was the dirt road—hidden by trees and bushes. But once you focused on it you could see where vehicles had been down in there. He carefully eased the new Honda down the difficult, narrow, bumpy road, inching along, trying not to damage his new car.

This was going to be great! A whole week with no computer, no telephone, no cell phone! Although they both had them, they'd agreed to not turn on their cell phones for a week.

Finally, there was the yellow cabin sitting on four-foot blocks, right there on the lake, pretty as a picture postcard. Joe turned off the motor and they got out. The key was under the loose floorboard where the owner, by phone from the Bronx, said it would be. They let themselves in. The old battered door opened into the lopsided kitchen. Though standing at an angle, Joe felt good already. This was going to be rustic but great. Sandy was looking just a little skeptical.

"Don't you like it?" Joe said.

Her laugh was restrained. They were standing between two stoves, an old electric gas range and a wood-burning stove. "We haven't seen it yet," she said, opening the oven of the wood-burner and looking in. "Filthy oven," she said, then glancing over at the electric stove.

Joe shrugged and went back to the car and started bringing in their things—two large suitcases, bags of cooking utensils, a few books. Sandy took the utensils and started putting them away. Joe took the luggage to the musty bedroom, placed them on the bed, unzipped them, and started hanging things in the tiny closet. He could hear Sandy in the kitchen banging the pots and pans, clicking the dishes as she stacked them.

When the closet was full, Joe looked around helplessly till he spotted the dresser. He loaded most of the other stuff—bed linen, underwear, socks, and so on—into the dresser drawers. But there were still about ten various dresses on hangers in one of the suitcases. They'd definitely brought too much stuff. Frustrated, he dumped the empty suitcase on the floor behind an old rocker, and took the half-empty one to the living room. The living room was ratty and smelled mildewed. He plopped the suitcase down on an old piano stool against the front wall. Then he looked out the window at the calm lake.

Suddenly—with great urgency—Sandy called, "*Joe!*"

He shot back there. "What's wrong?"

She was standing rigidly in the middle of the floor and pointing at the drainboard. "*Look!*"

Joe looked at the drainboard but saw nothing unusual about it. "What?"

"Don't you see *them*?"

"What?"

"Those *mice* turds! *Yuck!*"

He stepped closer and did see the tiny balls along the backside of the drainboard, and, yes, they were definitely mice turds. He started to laugh but didn't; instead, he said, "We'll have to pick up some traps in town."

Again she said, "Yuck!" making a face.

Joe's smile was glued on as he tried to console her, placing his arm around her shoulders.

She said, "You mean we've got to deal with mice the whole time?"

He kept his arm around her. "Come on, Sandy. We came up here to relax and to have fun—do some horseback riding, swimming, boating, bike riding. What'd you expect in the country? Mice are bound to be in an old place like this. You said you were all for it."

"Yes," she said, leaning her cheek against his chest, "but I didn't count on *mice*. I hate mice."

He took her fully into his arms and kissed her on the mouth. Gauging how he felt about her at this moment, Joe decided he didn't detest her, didn't love her, but somehow was stuck with her like he might have been stuck with, say, a smoking habit that he both hated and loved. He kept telling himself he was stuck with Sandy because somehow it made what he was doing—staying with her—make sense. If he was not responsible, because of forces beyond his control, then it was okay. But lately he'd also begun wondering why in hell she was staying with him and the only conclusion he could reach was that she too was locked into some kind of sado-masochistic bonding with him.

Later they drove into town. Joe drove slowly through the main street till they spotted a hardware store. People walking along the street stopped and stared. He parked across the street, and they crossed the street, aware that a group of idle old men, sitting in front of the hardware store, was watching them with great interest. Joe could imagine their thoughts: struggling to make sense of a black man and a Chinese woman together.

In the hardware store they picked up five mice traps, paid the clerk at the checkout counter, then walked down the sidewalk to the general store, got a shopping cart, and started moving up and down the little aisles, picking up milk, Corn Flakes, olive oil, a few bags of frozen green peas, a bag of unsalted peanut butter, Cheddar cheese, and at the fish and meat counter, they selected two salmon steaks for tonight.

The woman at the check-out counter, as she rang up the stuff, couldn't keep her eyes on what she was doing because she was so busy looking from Joe's face to Sandy's and back again, like somebody trying desperately to read two road signs on a rainy night at a dangerous crossroad. Joe could see the simple-minded bewilderment in her eyes.

Back at the cabin Joe set two of the five traps, then he and Sandy, holding hands, went exploring around the yard. The grass and weeds had been recently cut. There was a little unpainted landing dock that jutted out into the gently swaying blue lake. The air was cool and clean. An old rowboat was docked at the landing. They could do some rowing.

Over to the left of the yard was a woodpile with an ax leaning against a big chopping block. Over the phone the owner had told Joe that sometimes at night you needed to build a fire. It was already after eight but still light and warm.

After dinner, they crawled between their own familiar crisp sheets, under a stack of old blankets and quilts they'd found in a footlocker that stood in front of the couch, serving as a coffee table. It took a little while for Joe's hands to warm up. But this was fun. An adventure. Sandy whispered, "I love you so much, Joe. Let's not hurt each other any more. Okay?"

He said nothing. It wasn't that he wanted to hurt her or that he didn't love her. He knew he had deliberately suspended himself from commitment and strong emotion. He told himself he wanted to be free of the hold he knew she held over him.

Then Sandy whispered, "What's the matter?"

"Nothing."

"You don't love me, do you?"

He forced himself to say, "Yes, I love you."

"You don't *sound* like it." Then, after a long pause, she said, "We're never going to get married, are we?"

"I don't know," he said with conviction and relief.

She sighed. "Let's be monogamous. Okay?"

"I thought we already were."

"You know what I mean. I mean, no more swapping like we did that time, no more lying, no more cheating. Okay?"

"Sure," he said, feeling heartsick, hating her for forcing this conversation he wasn't ready for. He himself felt victim enough of what he imagined to be her lying and cheating to feel that this was yet another charade to cover her own ass; but worse than that, he didn't trust her, or himself, or believe a word of what she was saying. In the pit of his mind he felt alone with nobody to trust or turn to. He was forever on guard in a dangerous terrain and she was only the most present and visible danger—a narcotic in which his spirit drifted like flotsam.

She kissed him and he tried to shake off the coldness he felt and return her kiss but he was shuddering, not from the cold but from inner coldness. He felt her hand making him hard. Joe listened to his own breathing increasing steadily.

His heart was broken into two parts as he felt her tongue moving down his chest, down his stomach. Night-callers outside. He heard somebody on the lake rowing in the dark. The owner said the locals had tried to forbid motorboats but hadn't had a lot of success. Suddenly Joe stopped Sandy and gently turned around in the bed, throwing the covers back. She took him in her mouth, and, sixty-nine style, he smelled her lower steaminess. With the first touch of his tongue she gasped. There was enough desire and good will in him to make it mutual.

Later, she said, "I have good news. Rhonda told me Friday I will be promoted to assistant editor as of September first."

He absorbed the rush of excitement, conflicted with modesty—false or otherwise, he couldn't tell—in her voice. "That's *great,* Sandy. But I thought you were *already* an assistant editor."

"I'm an editorial assistant. Assistant editor is an official position." She paused. He imagined she was smiling to herself, pleased and fearful at the same time. He felt a true moment of genuine tenderness for her. She said, "Just think, I'm an *editor* at the world's most famous fashion magazine. It's ironic because I don't especially care about fashion."

"But you always wanted to be a journalist."

"That's true." She fell silent again. "Rhonda wants me to start travelling more, too. Right after vacation I have to go to Boston to interview Poppy Holly."

"Who's Poppy Holly? Sounds like a made-up name."

"It is. You don't *know* who Poppy Holly is? Poppy Holly is simply the world's most famous fashion designer of women's casual wear in the world."

"Oh."

*

They woke Sunday morning to the smell of the mildew and lingered in bed, screwing around, and when they got up Joe drove into town for *The New York Times*, then spent the morning on the porch reading it piece by piece.

In the afternoon, when it had warmed a bit, they got into the rowboat and rowed out across the lake. From the lake, the yellow cabin, with its screened porch, looked quaint.

The next morning they were out on the front porch drinking coffee and listening to the quarreling birds in the trees. Two tangled in dexterous flight, then cut out across the lake. One was crying victory or defeat. It was hard to know which.

After breakfast he and Sandy got dressed in their new tennis outfits and got out their tennis bags and rackets, got in the car and, going through town, drove out to the tennis courts. Neither one of them could play. They were hoping for lessons.

Joe asked the woman behind the desk in the recreation grounds office about the possibility. She gave them a faint smile, then pointed across the room toward the exit to the tennis courts. "See that tall gal out there? Her name is Cheryl. She teaches tennis. You'll have to make an appointment with her."

Joe gazed at the tall blond woman. She was talking with a fat teenage girl who was swinging her tennis racket along her thigh and looking away from Cheryl. The tennis instructor seemed to be trying to reason with the girl, and the girl was hurt and angry. Joe and Sandy approached Cheryl and the girl. They then stopped respectfully a few feet away.

Cheryl turned and said, "You people want to see me?"

And that was how Joe and Sandy got started.

At nine the next morning Cheryl came across the parking lot toward the court where Joe and Sandy had been waiting maybe five or six minutes. They were standing outside the first court. With her was a guy as tall and as blond as she. Both were dressed for tennis and carried long tennis bags. Cheryl—who, Joe noticed, had a weathered face and hands—introduced her husband Ralph, who gave them an easy but lazy smile. Cheryl explained that Ralph would work with Sandy and she would work with Joe. "Okay, Joe," she said, "let's get started." And she led the way onto the first court.

Sandy and Ralph walked over to the next one.

Cheryl hit the ball back and forth across the net with him for about five minutes. For the next two hours it was a real struggle for Joe, but he learned more in those two hours about playing than he had ever thought possible. Near the end of the lesson he was playing so well that he began to feel cocky.

Cheryl walked toward the net and called him over and, with hands on her hips, squinting from the sun, she said, "Joe, you could be turned into a good tennis player with practice. You have excellent reflexes and you make constant contact with the ball."

They both glanced over at Sandy and Ralph. Sandy hadn't hit the ball more than twice in two hours. Joe thanked Cheryl, glancing again at Sandy and Ralph. Ralph was impatiently saying, "Take it easy, slow down; watch the ball; take your time." And she kept swinging past the ball. Then suddenly, again, she connected, but it seemed to be an accident because her eyes were closed. It was as though she thought the ball was going to hit her in the face and she whacked it away—to the left, out of the court. Then the lesson ended.

Driving back, Joe felt excited. He looked over at Sandy. "Hey," he said, "cheer up. You'll get better. It takes time."

"I'm just a klutz," she said with a smirk. "The only sport I was any good at was volleyball. I like volleyball."

Joe tried to imagine Sandy as a teenager hitting a ball with her fist. He saw her in pea-green shorts, the sun falling down across the playground, girls on the other side of the net, and those around her screaming and laughing, running for the ball, as Sandy knocked it back across the net.

That afternoon they drove over to the horseback-riding stables and parked in the shade under an ancient giant tree. Pat, the instructor, wanted to know if they'd ever been on a horse before. Sandy's answer was no. Joe said, "Two or three times I've been on a horse, but I can't say I know how to ride."

"City folk, huh?" Pat said, smiling.

She was a freckled redhead, very horsey and big-boned, in a plaid shirt and jeans.

Pat walked them down to the stables where three or four horses were tied at a railing outside the fence. A boy was there leaning against the fence, carving a piece of wood with a pocket knife.

"This is Thunder," Pat said, holding the bridle and patting the brown horse on his white-spotted face.

Thunder looked like a Kladruder—but one without spirit.

"Her name is ironic. She's gentle. Joe, why don't you take Thunder? Billy, help Joe up."

The boy came over and held the reins while Joe got into the saddle.

Then Billy helped Sandy up on a horse Pat called Meatball. Meatball was a Palomino. Sandy grinned down at Pat. "Why you call her Meatball?"

"I don't know. There were two previous owners."

Billy said, "Cause she stupid."

Then Pat got up on her mount, and looked over at them. Her horse was a brownish-black Nonius with a lot of energy and spirit. He kept moving about, shaking his head, ready to go. Pat was stroking his neck, calming him as she waited for the boy to turn Meatball around to face the path that led out across the valley.

They then got started. Pat let them go ahead of her, Joe directly in front of her and Sandy in the lead. Pat said, "Okay, Joe—you too Sandy—just give your mount a nudge with your heels to direct him out the path. I'm right behind you." And they got as far as the clearing when Pat called out to Sandy, "Pull in on the reins, Sandy! Pull in gently to slow her down."

Meatball stopped. Pat moved her horse between them and stopped. "Okay. Watch me, both of you. Hold the reins like this and he'll stop. Then gently move them to the side like this and he goes to the left. See? This way and he goes to the right. Got it? When you want to turn around, go like this, just directing the reins gently. No fast motions. Just take it easy." And she turned her horse completely around. "Now," Pat said, "if you want him to go forward, just press your heels against his sides like this. Got it?"

They both nodded yes. Joe's horse was restless. Joe thought: Restless like me. He kept dancing around and around. "Thunder is a bit crazy," Pat said. "You have to let him know who's boss. Just be firm with him. Okay, let's go. Head out, Sandy."

And Sandy, on a very passive horse, started moving along the path. "Okay," Pat called out, riding ahead of them, "watch me. Do everything I do."

Now she was ahead of Sandy, leading the way. They reached a narrow path across a half-burned meadow heading for a green and wooded area.

When they reached the blue shade of the tall trees, Thunder got spooked and wanted to turn around. Joe kept directing him forward but he was stubbornly determined not to go a step farther.

Pat had stopped and was looking back at Joe and Thunder. "That's right. Just keep at him till he understands you're the boss. You're doing fine. He'll turn right here every time and trot back to the stable if you let him. Why, I don't know, but he tries it every time."

Joe tightened the grip of his thighs on the horse's ribs and directed his head forward toward the trail. Thunder didn't like it but he had no choice. That was clear from his frantic sidestepping in an effort to turn around. Joe now wished he hadn't said he'd been on a horse before.

But he was managing now to keep Thunder on course till they reached a fork in the trail. At this point Thunder went wild, kicking and turning, acting like a wild horse.

Pat trotted back and reached over and pulled the reins. "Thunder!" she shouted. "Behave yourself!"

But Thunder was now reacting more to the closeness of Pat's horse. They'd worked their way off the trail into the underbrush.

Joe, at this moment, in fear and determination, felt more intensely alive than he'd felt in ages. He backed Thunder away and got him back on the trail and up to where Sandy was waiting peacefully on Meatball about fifteen yards up. But Thunder was still high stepping, wanting to gallop. Joe gave him some slack, then moved forward, but only a bit, pulling back enough to slow him down, to keep him at a trot.

They turned around soon after that.

On the way back Thunder was no trouble. Pat said he liked it when he was headed home. She was riding behind Joe.

Sandy was behind her. Pat called out, "I think he respects you now, Joe!"

They took another riding lesson Friday morning, but this time Joe was on a horse called Boston Blackie, and Sandy again got Meatball. Joe liked Boston Blackie better than Thunder because he was easy to direct and he moved gracefully. He obeyed the rein signals.

The next day, at one-thirty, Joe and Sandy were out on their dock waiting for the boat race. It was supposed to start at two. Heavy, pregnant clouds were lingering overhead. At five-to-two it started raining and it looked like it would be just a typical afternoon shower. But it actually rained for three hours and the dank smell of wet earth and foliage consumed the afternoon. It was a good bet that the race had been cancelled.

Then Sunday afternoon they went to the bike rental place and stood among hundreds of silver and black handlebars. Joe signed for two mountain bikes, his red and white, Sandy's green and white. The clerk couldn't stop gaping at them. Joe imagined they looked to him like two creatures from Mars.

Leaving the car in front of the supermarket, they headed out of town on the bike path. Joe knew Sandy had had a bike as a kid but she never became comfortable on one. Joe kept glancing back at her. She was wobbling along and he worried about her falling and seriously hurting herself. It was also clear she had no confidence in her own ability to stay on the thing and to keep it moving forward. She rode like she was at the mercy of the bike. Finally, she came to a stop by a tree. Joe stopped and looked back.

When she attempted to dismount, she lost her balance and fell over into the grass. Sandy went one way and the bike the other. Joe leaped from his bike and ran back to her. "You okay?" She lifted herself up and said she was fine, but she looked embarrassed as she brushed at the grass stains on her elbow and knee.

9:30 AM Monday morning, Sandy was already sitting stiffly up on Meatball waiting for Pat to take the lead. Joe was waving goodbye. On Pat's advice they were taking lessons separately. His would be at noon, noon to one.

Sandy waved back as she followed Pat out into the meadow. Joe thought: there goes the woman I sleep with—a stranger with a familiar face.

It was one of those clear mornings full of solid blue light; and Joe hopped back in the Honda and drove over to the tennis court. On the way he looked at his hands on the steering wheel. All his life he'd seen these hands. They were familiar yet the hands of an unknown person, someone who might slip away from him, away from his consciousness without notice.

But this was no day to think such dark thoughts. It was a beautiful day full of the light and fresh air. As he parked, he saw Cheryl knocking balls across the net then walking over and knocking them back the other way. Joe was early. His new lesson time wasn't till 10:30 AM. It was five after.

They greeted each other and he told her he'd come early to practice a bit before they got started. Cheryl said there was no one ahead of him so they might as well get started. She said, "Ready?"

"Hot to trot all over the lot," he said, grinning.

"That's the spirit."

While they were warming up, Cheryl said, "You and Sandy been together long, Joe?"

His defenses immediately shot up. The relation was such a wreck he didn't want to talk about it. But why was Cheryl interested?

"About five years. Why?" he said, knocking the ball back to her.

She rubbed the edge of her eye. "No reason."

Joe grunted and returned her serve.

First thing Tuesday morning Joe and Sandy got in the car and drove down to a little shack of an office on the dock of a neighboring lake. Sandy waited outside while Joe went in and talked with the old man in charge.

The guy was really old but rugged-looking. He came out with Joe and he was scratching at the red blisters on his bald head. He was constantly chewing on a toothpick and adjusting his suspenders as though they irritated his shoulders. He handed Joe a set of keys and pointed to one of the seven or eight motorboats docked only a few feet away. When the old man saw Sandy his eyes stretched. Then he gave Joe another close look, twisted his mouth, spat on the ground, and walked over to the boat. "Here, let me show you how to operate this thing," he growled. "This is the safety switch."

Joe got in the boat and put the key into the ignition.

Joe turned on the motor. As the old man was explaining a few things, Joe turned off the motor. Finished explaining, the old man walked away, glancing back with a sneer, as Joe helped Sandy in.

Now Joe got the hang of it and they got in and were ready to go. Joe pulled the starter out a few times and the motor kicked in.

Joe guided the motorboat out to the deep part of the lake; then he moved it smoothly down the lake out of view. He thought he might return alone. It was risky; but it was a possibility. It would be the absolute way out. He kept telling himself accidents happen. He then felt ashamed of himself for having such a toxic thought.

INNOCENCE

NYDIA AND I ARE WATCHING TELEVISION when a news bulletin comes on saying that somebody just shot a government official in Los Angeles. The official was making a speech. A "suspect" was seized on the spot. The suspect says he is innocent despite the fact that cameras caught him in the act. So many televised deaths lately, I am too numbed to react. A further loss of spirit is what I feel.

I wake up in a sweat. It's one-fifteen and Nydia is still not home. I get up and go to the kitchen for a glass of water. I check my email. Nothing but unwanted crap!

In the living room I sit on the couch to drink the water. While sipping water, I turn around and look out the window at the dark city with its sprinkle of lights scattered across my vision.

Then I glance down at the street. The cars, lined bumper to bumper, are dark and silent. Then I notice the burning red tip of a cigarette glowing in the car just below on the other side. I stare at the red spot till I make out the figure of a man sitting at the steering wheel. Beneath the glowing cigarette something seems to be bobbing. I stare at the area till it becomes clear. It's somebody's head moving up and down.

I get the binoculars from the closet and, standing on my knees on the couch, focus them. This is perverse, but what the hell. I can now see the moving head clearly. It's a woman.

When she lifts her face the streetlight catches it. My heart seems to come to a full rest and moves up into my throat. I refuse to believe what I am seeing.

At that moment the door on the driver's side opens. I had not seen him approach, but another man in shadows opens the door and I can see the streetlight glowing on the barrel of his silver pistol. He pulls the trigger. I am surprised by how faint the sound is. Then it comes again. Then two times more. He closes the door back, turns and—still a shadow—hurries down the street back toward Eighth.

Had the gunman not arrived, what would have happened?

Possibly this: I watch till the woman finishes. She kisses the man on the mouth. They talk for another five or seven minutes, then she climbs out of the car, checks the contents of her purse, glances up and down the street before crossing over to this side. While crossing she glances up at this window but obviously she can't see anything.

Then, I think, possibly it is Nydia. And she comes in and we have this conversation:

"I saw you," I tell her while she is taking off her clothes.

She looks shocked then tries to appear calm. "What did you see?"

"I saw what you were doing in the car."

She waves me away. "There you go again with your jealousy."

"I got the binoculars."

"How *low* can you stoop?"

But if it was Nydia then I had to be the gunman. I am not ready to be the gunman.

The morning TV news has the story: two bodies, a woman's and a man's, each shot through the head, found in a parked car in the Village off Eighth Street. What a relief! What sadness!

This is early Sunday morning. We're in the living room. I'm standing, looking down at Nydia.

"I'm leaving," I say. I'm surprised to hear myself say this. I realize at this moment how desperately unhappy I am, how desperately unhappy Nydia must be. I have no idea where I'm going.

She says nothing to my announcement. She is sitting slumped over on the couch. She begins to cry.

"You keep the apartment, if you want it." Apartments are hard to find in New York and I feel like I'm being very generous.

She stops sobbing and says, "Who gave you the right to judge?"

I'm in California. I answer the phone. It's Nydia. I don't remember giving her my new number. Could I have called her at a moment of weakness in the middle of the night? "Hi! Just want you to know I'm on my way to California," she says. " I'm not going to let you dump me." She hangs up.

Before I know it, Nydia is walking beside me on Fisherman's Wharf. Her request. We've had lunch and this morning I had my feet measured at the sandal shop. Now, at three, we should be able to pick up my sandals.

She looks different, better. I wonder why I left her. What was it about her that bothered me so? Oh, yes. I didn't love her. Or was it that I shot her and her lover and had to get out of town? Need I say anything about the quality of my memory?

The sandal shop is crowded so we have to wait a whole hour before the guy can go to the back to see if they are ready.

I have a little green convertible MG now. With the sandals in a plastic bag, we hop in and head for the hills. "I love it out here," says Nydia. "Let me drive."

I get out and walk around to the passenger side. She climbs over the stick. She blushes and giggles when she notices me watching.

I get her going in the right direction and once she's got it, she hits the gas; in fact, she scares me. The cops out here don't play that shit. Anybody black or in a sports car already has a highway patrol demerit—driving while black.

Sure enough we're pulled over and as the officer writes the ticket I keep my mouth shut. I figure it's the only way to stay alive when you're in this situation.

My new house is far back behind a swirl of palms.

We get out and while walking up the long flagstone path to the deck stairs, a stranger waves and calls out, "Hi! Didn't mean to startle you. I'm your neighbor. I'm Maxwell. My house is over the hill there. You can't see it from here." He's holding out his hand.

We shake. He's a healthy brown—that kind of brown California white men love to sport.

I tell him my name and say, "This is Nydia Wilson, from New York." He holds her little hand a moment longer than is polite. I can see Nydia gets the message. Whether or not she wants it I can't tell.

I unlock the house. "Can I get you something, Maxwell, a drink?"

While I work in the morning, Nydia goes for long walks on the beach. This morning, two weeks after her arrival, I can't get anything started so I decide to go catch up with her, to walk with her.

I set out across the sand following the tracks of her tennis shoes. They seem unusually far back from the edge of the water, which isn't especially dangerous-looking this morning.

Then the prints cut back away from the ocean up a dune and over it. I follow. At the top I see what must be Maxwell's house, a modest one with bay windows and a wrap-around deck perched on stilts.

No Nydia yet in sight.

You already know what's coming. I walk on down the sand and up to the house. In the front yard I stop. All is silent except for the sound of sea gulls and the distant beat of the ocean. I shudder as I walk up onto the porch.

Just as I am about to knock I hear a loud gasp from inside. I think oh well, why should I be surprised. Another gasp, a whimper, a moan, all punctuated by grunts.

I start to go back across the sand but once I'm in the yard I decide to make sure. I tip alongside the house and look into the first window. This is a crime, I know. A dining room. I walk around a pile of debris to the next window. A pantry. Then the kitchen. There! On the kitchen floor Maxwell and Nydia making those noises. Need I say more?

I refuse to watch.

I turn to leave but then a muffled scream pulls me back. I look again and I realize I am seeing a man killing a woman. I am witnessing a crime—murder! The woman is not Nydia. She's pink, not brown. But the man is Maxwell. He has a kitchen knife and he is driving it repeatedly into the woman's upper body. She is beginning to make fewer sounds.

Running back across the sand, I see Nydia strolling along the beach. I catch up. I know she has a cell phone. But I'm too out of breath by the time I reach her to tell her what I want. I want her to call the police but I can't get the words out.

They simply won't come. Nydia reacts to my distress by holding me in her arms. I weep with the pain of my distress. She begs me to tell her what's wrong but I can't.

Back at the house, feeling calmer, I call the police and spill my guts.

Nydia and I gaze out the window toward Maxwell's house, waiting.

Three hours later three policemen come to my door and say, "You imagined the whole thing. Mr. Maxwell is fine. No one was murdered. No blood is on his kitchen floor."

Before leaving they give me a warning about trespassing on my neighbor's property. "If it happens again, Maxwell will file charges."

Now that Nydia is back in New York, I am alone here again and winter is coming. But it is not as before when I was unaware that another house was just over the hill. Oh, I knew a house was over there but I didn't know about it. Now it is a sinister house of uncertainty. And anyway, how can I trust the police?

When I walk on the beach—wearing my heavy sweater—in the afternoon I am apprehensive. I dread coming face-to-face with my neighbor Maxwell. How can I be sure he is so innocent? How can I be sure I am so innocent?

MY MOTHER AND MITCH

HE WAS JUST SOMEBODY who had dialed the wrong number. This is how it started, and I wasn't concerned about it. Not at first. I don't even remember if I was there when he first called, but I do, all these many years later, remember my mother on the phone speaking to him in her best quiet voice, trying to sound as ladylike as she knew how.

She had these different voices for talking to different people on different occasions. I could tell by my mother's proper voice that this man was somebody she wanted to make a good impression on, a man she thought she might like to know. This was back when my mother was still a young woman, divorced but still young enough to believe that she was not completely finished with men. She was a skeptic from the beginning; I knew that even then. But some part of her thought the right man might come along some day.

I don't know exactly what it was about him that attracted her though. People are too mysterious to know that well. I know that now and I must have been smart enough not to wonder too hard about it back then.

Since I remember hearing her tell him her name, she must not have given it out right off the bat when he first called. She was a city woman with a child, and had developed alertness to danger. One thing you didn't do was to give your name to a stranger on the phone. You never knew who to trust in a city like Chicago. The place was full of crazy people and criminals.

She said, "My name is *Mrs.* Jayne Anderson." I can still hear her laying the emphasis on the Mrs., although she had been separated from my father twelve years when this man dialed her number by accident.

Mitch Kibbs was the name he gave her. I guess he must have told her who he was the very first time, just after he apologized for calling her by mistake. I can't remember who he was trying to call. He must have told her and she must have told me but it's gone now. I think they must have talked a pretty good while that first time. The first thing that I remember about him was that he lived with his sister who was older than he. The next thing was that he was very old. He must have been fifty and to me at fifteen that was deep into age. If my mother was old at thirty-five, fifty was ancient. Then the other thing about him was that he was white.

They'd talked five or six times, I think, before he came out and said he was white; but she knew it before he told her. I think he made this claim only after he started suspecting he might not be talking to another white person. But the thing was he didn't know for sure she was black. I was at home lying on the couch pretending to read a magazine when I heard her say, "I am a colored lady." Those were her words exactly. She placed the emphasis on "lady."

I had never known my mother to date any white men. She

would hang up from talking with him and she and I would sit at the kitchen table and she would tell me what he had said. They were telling each other the bits and pieces of their lives, listening to each other, feeling their way as they talked. She spoke slowly, remembering all the details. I watched her scowl, and the way her eyes narrowed, as she puzzled over his confessions as she told me, in her own words, about them. She was especially puzzled about his reaction to her confession about being colored.

That night she looked across at me, with that fearful look that was hers alone, and said, "Tommy, I doubt if he will ever call back. Not after tonight. He didn't know. You know that."

Feeling grown-up, because she was treating me that way, I said, "I wouldn't be so sure."

But he called back soon after that.

I was curious about her interest in this particular white man, so I always listened carefully. I was a little bit scared too because I suspected he might be some kind of maniac or pervert. I had no good reason to fear such a thing except that I thought it strange that anybody could spend as much time as he, and my mother, did talking on the phone without any desire for human contact. She had never had a telephone relationship before; and at that time, all I knew about telephone relationships was that they were insane, and conducted by people who probably needed to be put away. This meant that I also had the sad feeling that my mother was a bit crazy too. But more important than these fearful fantasies, I thought I was witnessing a change in my mother. It seemed important, and I didn't want to misunderstand it or miss the point of it. I tried to look on the bright side, which was what my mother always said I should try to do.

He certainly didn't sound dangerous. Two or three times I myself answered the phone when he called and he always said, "Hello, Tommy, this is Mitch. May I speak to your mother?" And I always said, "Sure, just a minute." He never asked me how I was doing or anything like that, and I never had anything special to say to him.

After he had been calling for over a month, I sort of lost interest in hearing about their talk. But she went right on telling me what he said. I was a polite boy, so I listened despite the fact that I had decided that Mitch Kibbs, and his ancient sister, Temple Erikson, were crazy, but harmless. My poor mother was lonely. That was all. I had it all figured out. He wasn't an ax murderer who was going to sneak up on her one evening when she was coming home from her job at the office and split her open from the top down. We were always hearing about things like this, so I knew it wasn't impossible.

My interest would pick up occasionally. I was especially interested in what happened the first time my mother herself made the call to his house. She told me that Temple Erikson answered the phone. Mother and I were eating dinner when she started talking about Temple Erikson.

"She's a little off in the head," Mother said.

I didn't say anything but it confirmed my suspicion. What surprised me was my mother's ability to recognize it. "What'd she say?"

"She rattled on about the Wild West," said Mother. "And about the Indians, and having to hide in a barrel or something like that. She said Indians were shooting arrows at them, and she was just a little girl who hid in a barrel."

I thought about this. "Maybe she lived out West when she was little, you know? She must be a hundred by now. That would make her the right age."

"Oh, come on now, Tommy!" Mother laughed. "What she said was she married when she was fourteen, married this Erikson fellow. As near as I could figure out he must have been a leather tanner; but seems he also hunted fur and sold it to make a living. She never had a child."

"None of that sounds crazy." I was disappointed.

"She was talking crazy, though."

"How so?"

"She thinks Indians are coming back to attack the house any day now. She says things like Erikson was still living; like he was just off there in the next room, taking a nap. One of the first things Mitch told me was his sister and he moved in together after her husband died; and that was twenty years ago."

"How did the husband die?"

She finished chewing her peas first. "He was kicked in the head by a horse. Bled to death."

I burst out laughing because the image was so bright in my mind, and I couldn't help myself. My pretty mother had a sense of humor even when she didn't mean to show it.

She chewed her peas in a ladylike manner. This was long before she lost her teeth. Sitting there across the table from her, I knew I loved her, and needed her, and I knew she loved and needed me. I did not yet fear that she needed me too much. She had a lot of anger in her too. Men had hurt her bad. And one day I was going to be a man.

When I laughed my mother said, "You shouldn't laugh at misfortune, Tommy." But she had this silly grin on her face; and it caused me to laugh again. I think now I must have been a bit hysterical from the anxiety I had been living with all those weeks, while she was telling me about the telephone conversations that I wanted to hear about only part of the time.

It was dark outside; and I got up when I finished my dinner and went to the window and looked down at the streetlights glowing in the wet pavement. I said, "I bet he's out there right now, hiding in the shadows, watching our window."

"Who?" Her eyes grew large.

She was easily frightened. I knew this and I was being devilish, and deliberately trying to scare her.

"You know, Mister Kibbs."

She looked relieved. "No, he's not. He's not like that. He's a little strange but not a pervert."

"How'd you know?"

By the look she gave me I knew now that I had thrown doubt into her and she wasn't handling it well. She didn't try to answer me. She finished her small, dry pork chop, and the last of her bright green peas, and reached over and took up my plate and sat it into her own.

She took the dishes to the sink, turned on the hot and cold water so that warm water gushed out of the single faucet, causing the pipe to clang, and she started washing the dishes. "You have a vivid imagination," was all she said.

I grabbed the dishcloth and started drying the first plate she placed in the rack to drain. "Even so, you don't know this man. You've never even seen him. Aren't you curious about what he looks like?"

"I know what he looks like."

"How?"

"He sent me a picture of himself and one of Temple."

I gave her a look. She had been holding out on me. I knew he was crazy now. Was he so ugly she hadn't wanted me to see the picture? "Can I see the pictures?"

"Sure." She dried her hands on the cloth I was holding, then took her cigarettes out of her dress pocket, and knocked one from the pack, and stuck it between her thin pale lips. I watched her light it and fan the smoke and squint her eyes. She said, "You have to promise not to laugh."

That did it. I started laughing again and couldn't stop. Then she started laughing too, because I was bent over double, standing there at the sink, with this image in my mind of some old guy who looked like the Creeper. But I knew she couldn't read my mind, so she had to be laughing at me laughing. She was still young enough to be silly with me like a kid.

Then she brought out two pictures, one of him and the other of his sister. She put them down side by side on the table. "Make sure your hands are dry."

I took off my glasses, and bent down to the one of the man first, so I could see up close, as I stood there wiping my hands on the dishcloth. It was one of those studio pictures where somebody posed him in a three-quarter view. He had his unruly hair and eyebrows pasted down and you could tell he was fresh out the bath, and his white shirt was starched hard. He was holding his scrubbed face with effort toward where the photographer told him to look, which was too much into the direction of the best light. Beneath the forced smile, he was frowning with discomfort. There was something else. It was something like defeat or simple tiredness in his pose, and you could see it best in the heavy lids of his large blank eyes. He looked out of that face at the world with what remained of his self-confidence and trust in the world. His shaggy presence said that it was all worthwhile, and maybe even in some way he would not ever understand, also important. I understood all of that even then, but would never have been able to put my reading of him into words like these.

Then I looked at the woman. She was an old hawk. Her skin was badly wrinkled like the skin of ancient Indians I'd seen in photographs and westerns. There was something like a smile coming out of her face; but it had come out sort of sideways, and made her look silly. But the main thing about her was that she looked very mean. On second thought, to give her the benefit of the doubt, I can say that it might have been just plain hardness from having a hard life. She was wearing a black iron-stiff dress, buttoned up to her dickey, which was ironically dainty and tight around her gooseneck.

All I said was, "They're *so* old." I don't know what else I thought as I looked up at my mother, who was leaning over my shoulder, looking at the pictures too, as though she had never seen them before, as though she was trying to see them through my eyes.

"You're just young, Tommy. Everybody's old to you. They're not so old. To me, he looks lonely."

I looked again at him and thought I saw what she meant.

I put the dishes away, and she took the photographs back, and we didn't talk any more that night about Mitch and Temple. We watched our black-and-white television screen, which showed us Red Skelton acting silly for laughs. So we laughed at him.

Before it was over, I fell asleep on the couch, and my mother woke me when she turned off the television. "You should go to bed, Tommy."

I stood up and stretched. "I have a science paper to write."

"Get up early and write it," she said, putting out her cigarette.

"He wants me to meet him someplace," my mother said.

She had just finished talking with him and was standing by the telephone. It was close to dinnertime. I'd been home from school since three-thirty, and she'd been in from work by then for a good hour. She'd just hung up from the shortest conversation she'd ever had with him.

I had wondered why they never wanted to meet; then I stopped wondering and felt glad they hadn't. Now, I was afraid, afraid for her, for myself, for the poor old man in the picture. Why did we have to go through with this crazy thing?

"I told him I needed to talk with you about it first," she said. "I told him I'd call him back."

I was standing there in front of her, looking at her. She was a scared little girl with wild eyes dancing in her head, unable to make up her own mind. I sensed her fear. I resented her for the mess she had gotten herself in. I also resented her for needing my consent. I knew she wanted me to say go, go to him, meet him somewhere. I could tell. She was too curious not to want to go. I suddenly thought that he might be a millionaire, and that she would marry him, and he might eventually die and leave her his fortune. But there was the sister. She was in the way. And from the looks of her she would pass herself off as one of the living for at least another hundred years or so. So I gave up that fantasy.

"Well, why don't you tell him you'll meet him at the hamburger café on Wentworth? We can eat dinner there."

"We?"

"Sure. I'll just sit at the counter like I don't know you. But I've got to be there to protect you."

"I see."

"Then you can walk in alone. I'll already be there eating a cheeseburger and fries. He'll come in and see you waiting for him alone at a table."

"No, I'll sit at the counter too," she said.

"Okay. You sit at the counter too."

"What time should I tell him?"

I looked at my Timex. It was six. I knew they lived on the West Side; and that meant it would take him at least an hour by bus and a half hour by car. He probably didn't have a car. I was hungry though, and had already set my mind on eating a cheeseburger, rather than macaroni and cheese out of the box.

"Tell him seven-thirty."

"Okay."

I went to my room. I didn't want to hear her talking to him in her soft whispering voice. I had stopped listening some time before. I looked at the notes for homework, and felt sick in the stomach at the thought of having to write that late science paper.

A few minutes later my mother came in and said, "Okay. It's all set." She sat down on the side of my bed and folded her pale hands in her lap. "What should I wear?"

"Wear your green dress and the brown shoes."

"You like that dress, don't you?"

"I like that one and the black one with the yellow at the top. It's classical."

"You mean classy."

"Whatever I mean." I felt really grown-up that night.

"Here, Tommy, take this." She handed me a ten-dollar bill she had been hiding in her right hand. "Don't spend it all. Buy your burger and fries and keep the rest to just have. If you spend it all in that hamburger place, I'm going to deduct it from your allowance next week."

When I got there I changed my mind about the counter. I took a table by myself.

A cheeseburger, fries, and a Coca-Cola cost me three dollars.

I was eating my cheeseburger and fries and watching the revolving door. The café was noisy with shouts, cackling, giggles, and verbal warfare. The waitress, Miss Azibo, was in a bad mood. She had set my hamburger plate down like it was burning her hand.

I kept my eye on the door. Every time somebody came in I looked up; every time somebody left, I looked up. I finished my cheeseburger even before my mother got there, and, ignoring her warning, I ordered another, and another Coca-Cola to go with it. I figured I could eat two or three cheeseburgers and still have some money left over.

Then my mother came in like a bright light into a dingy room. I think she must have been the most beautiful woman who ever entered that place, and it was her first time coming in there. She had always been something of a snob, and did not believe in places like this. I knew she had agreed to meet Mister Kibbs here just because she believed in my right to the cheeseburger, and this place had the best in the neighborhood.

I watched her walk ladylike to the counter and ease herself up on the stool, and sit there with her back arched. People in that place didn't walk and sit like that. She was acting classy and everybody turned to look at her. I looked around at the faces, and a lot of the women had these real mean sneering looks like somebody had broke wind.

She didn't know any of these people, and they didn't know her. Some of them may have known her by sight, and me too, but that was about all the contact we had with this part of the neighborhood. Besides, we hardly ever ate out. When we did we usually ate Chinese or at the rib place.

I sipped my Coke and watched Miss Azibo place a cup of coffee before my mother on the counter. She was a coffee freak; she always was; all day long, long into the night, cigarettes and coffee, in a continuous cycle. I grew up with her that way. The harsh smells are still in my memory. When she picked up the cup with a dainty finger sticking out just so, I heard a big fat woman, at a table in front of mine, say to the big fat woman at the table with her that my mother was a snooty bitch. The other woman said, "Yeah. She must think she's white. What she doing in here anyway?"

Mister Kibbs came in about twenty minutes after my mother, and I watched him stop and stand just inside the revolving doors. He stood to the side. He looked a lot younger than in the picture. He was stooped a bit though, and he wasn't dressed like a millionaire, which disappointed me. But he was clean. He was wearing a necktie, and a clean white shirt, and a suit that looked like it was about two hundred years old; but one, no doubt, made of the best wool. Although it was fall, he looked overdressed for the season. He looked like a man who hadn't been out in daylight in a long while. He was nervous, I could tell. Everybody was looking at him. Rarely did white people come in here.

Then he went to my mother like he knew she had to be the person he had come in to see. He sat himself up on the stool beside her, and leaned forward with his elbows on the counter, and looked in her face.

She looked back in that timid way of hers. But she wasn't timid. It was an act and part of her ladylike posture. She used it when she needed it.

He ordered something to eat, and my mother ordered too. I don't remember what. They talked and talked. I sat there eating, and protecting her, till I spent the whole ten dollars. Even as I ran out of money, I knew she would forgive me. She had always forgiven me on special occasions. This was one for sure.

She never told me what they talked about in the café, and I never asked, but everything that happened after that meeting went toward the finishing off of the affair my mother was having with Mitch Kibbs. He called her later that night. I was in my room, working on that dumb science paper, when the phone rang, and I could hear her speaking to him in that ladylike way. It was not the way she talked to me. I was different. She didn't need to impress me. I was her son. But I couldn't hear what she was saying and didn't want to.

Mister Kibbs called the next evening too. But eventually the calls were fewer and fewer till he no longer called.

My mother and I went on living as we had before he called the wrong number. And after a while, we never talked about him or his sister again.

THERE IS HOPE

A TALL SLENDER WOMAN steps cautiously into my office. She's dressed in quiet blue. "Welcome to SUNY-Ithaca. My name's Hope Breman. My office is next door. I teach composition. You're Professor Smith. Right?"

"That's right." I stand and shake her hand.

"If you need any help finding your way around just let me know. I'm always here. Resident slave, you know." She laughs.

"Thanks." I like her, like her smile, her laugh, her self-irony. "Are you free for lunch sometime?"

"Almost every day. Just name a day," she says.

"Tomorrow?"

"Tomorrow it is. Noon? Noon it is. I'll drop by your office at, say, quarter to? We can walk over to the campus restaurant together. Big exciting adventure."

In the campus restaurant, Hope and I move in the noisy, crowded line, pushing our hard plastic trays on the cast-iron railing and selecting what we want from the steaming-hot trays behind the cloudy, poorly lighted display windows.

Hope selects the grilled beefsteak and fries. Although feeling shy in doing so, I select only mashed potatoes and string beans. Hope immediately says, "That's *all* you're eating? I wish I could eat wisely like that. You must be *healthy*."

The food servers spoon the portions up into our plates and we move on. I feel comfortable with Hope, like her easy-going, self-deprecating manner, and I don't want to know what this says about me.

At the end of the line a woman cashier sizes up the contents of each tray and says, "Together?" Yes, together. And I pay. We find an empty seat by one of the tall windows looking out on a lawn and a walkway. And there really is the feeling—or am I misreading the moment? —that we are *together.*

I watch Hope's long neck as she talks. Her eyes stretch and she constantly moves her head about on the stem of that long, interesting neck. Many would think Hope's neck ugly because of the veins and the way the bones show through the smooth tightly stretched skin.

She's telling me in distressed syllables why she is so miserable teaching composition. It's a thankless task. "The University doesn't value it and it is the single course every student needs most desperately."

She says she can't get herself hired on any kind of secure footing. She has no medical benefits. The English Department treats her and the twenty or so others teaching composition like second-class citizens.

It's a familiar story. I push my mind against the huge problem and it resists. I can't even think of a consoling thing to say. I want to shift, talk about something else. What *else* is going on in her life? Is she married, does she have children?

Suddenly I break my own rule and ask, "Do you have children?"

"Yes, a daughter, Alva. She's fourteen, a terribly troublesome age."

I'm still wondering if she's married but leave it untested. I don't say anything about my own fifteen-year-old son, Albert, who is home right now probably watching television. His main interest at the moment is rap music and he spends too much time glued to the cable rap station. He hasn't yet gotten to know any of his schoolmates. Knowing Albert though, hanging out with the guys is not far off. But he may have to pay some dues first.

Hope's cutting into her beefsteak. It resists like the sole of a house shoe.

Before I know it, Hope has chosen me as her confidant. She chews a little bit, then holds her fork and knife suspended and talks with poise and practice. Alva was born out of wedlock while Hope was an undergraduate. She and the girl's father tried living together for a brief time. They were both college students at Chapel Hill. He ended up another black male statistic, strung out on drugs and burned out before he was twenty-one. She went on to graduate school, supporting herself and her daughter. She moved to Ithaca five years ago and this is her second job, a step up from the community college in Albany.

At the present time she is sharing a house with another composition teacher, Farrell G. Johnson, who is on his first three-year contract. My budding romantic interest in her begins to dry up.

We finish lunch and walk back. She has office hours all afternoon. "Let's do it again sometime."

"Oh," she says as though I have misunderstood something, "absolutely. In fact, I'd like to show you around. We can drive down to Elmira to see Mark Twain's house, and his grave; stuff like that. Are you free this weekend?"

Without thinking about it, and partly in desperation, I say, "Sure, I'm free," all the while thinking that I might put Albert on the commuter flight Friday night and let him go down to New York to spend the weekend with Drusilla, my ex, who right now works in a law office typing from nine to five, and works nights in off-Broadway plays when she can get the work. This would be his first trip from up here.

Before, when we lived in The District and I was teaching African-American lit at The American University, all he had to do to get there was hop on the commuter train and round trip wasn't all that expensive. Making him move up here, despite the plus to my career and income, was one of the more painful things I've had to do. But I have custody, I care, and I think he's going to be better off here anyway.

In Washington, he was around kids who sold and used drugs. Although he himself never even dabbled, he was out there on the streets where he was as likely as any other kid to suddenly stop a whole spray of bullets.

Lately he's been after me to let him go back to Washington to visit his friends, but that's one request I will not give in to. So letting him go see his mother—although he normally does it—feels like some sort of compromise.

Saturday is a sunny day. In Elmira, Hope and I tip through the Twain museum, then drive up to the Quarry Farm place and park on the road and snap a picture of it. Later, Hope wants me to take her picture in front of Twain's tall gravestone. "I wrote my dissertation on Mark Twain," she says proudly and defiantly.

I am properly impressed as I press the little rubber button on her camera.

After dinner in an Italian restaurant, on the way back I have the feeling we are tired and peaceful together. I mention Albert for the first time, that I sent him to see his mother in New York.

"So you're *unattached*?"

"I guess you can say that."

She is resting her head on the back of the seat and her eyes are closed but I know she's not sleeping. Suddenly she says, "I wish we could just drive on like this forever, not go back to Ithaca."

Keeping my right hand on the steering wheel, I reach over and touch her hand that is resting in her lap. She gives me a look full of sadness, fear, and promise, and, if I'm not misreading her, trust.

She turns her head and looks at me. "So, now I know you have a son and an ex-wife. Beyond those facts, all I know about you is what I read on the bulletin board in the hallway: hot-shot new associate professor just appointed with tenure, direct from American University, with a book coming out from UMass Press, will be teaching Afro Am in the English Department."

"That's about it."

"Don't answer if the question is too personal, but . . . Why did your marriage end?"

"You don't want to know," I say. "It's a boring story. Look, there's a motel. Let's stop and make love."

"*What?*" Her eyes stretch a tiny bit but she's really not so shocked by my casual proposal. But she's measuring me with a steady gaze.

"Let's stop at that motel and make love. We're going to miss the exit. How about it?"

She looks straight ahead. "Why the hurry? I want to know you better, feel *closer* to you."

The exit is coming up in a few seconds.

Her long hands are folded on her lap. I reach over, intending to press my hand against hers, but she meets me halfway and suddenly I'm driving with my left hand only and holding hers with my free hand. She squeezes me. "Okay," she says, just as we reach the exit.

I'm already in the right lane so I abruptly turn off, shift down, and coast to the stop sign.

As I pull away from the stop sign, Hope says, "I'm on my period. Is that all right?"

I squeeze her hand. "No problem."

I go in and pay for the room and with the key in my pocket, I get back in and we drive around to the back of the line of strung-together rooms and park in front of our door, number 35.

I lock the car and look at my watch. It's a little after seven. I wonder what Albert could possibly be up to at this very minute. Drusilla would right now be backstage getting ready for an eight o'clock opening. Maybe she took him with her. Although Albert never has trouble keeping himself entertained, I worry about him anyway.

On the crisp white sheet, Hope's long thin brown body is as alive as an electric storm. She's good to look at though she seems sexless.

"I never come," she says, lying beside me, "so don't *expect* it and don't feel bad. Okay?"

I gulp but manage to say, "Okay."

*

When she tells me to drop her off a block from her house, I suspect she *is* involved with Farrell. As I pull over to the curb on a side street, I try to imagine him. He's probably white. He has a handlebar mustache and a loud shrill voice. He likes to break things and shout when he's angry, which is every day. He professes to love Hope, his dark goddess, *and* to love her daughter, although she is not his own.

She's about to get out. She kisses me quickly and leaps out. We've made no promises.

Sunday night, I pick up Albert at the airport, and Hope and I meet again Monday for lunch. She's wearing dark glasses.

I select the tuna melt. It's the least lethal-looking thing on display. At the end of the line I fill a glass full of water from the spout.

I follow Hope to a remote table.

Once we're settled at a table some distance from the nearest cluster of students, with the thumb and index finger of each hand, she gently lifts her glasses from her face and gives me a pathetic smile. Her right eye is swollen and half closed, bruised purple, and the other one is only slightly less damaged.

"Farrell was drunk and he slugged me repeatedly when I got in."

I'm horrified. "Did you call the police?"

She laughs. "What good would that do? Around here they call this sort of thing a domestic squabble."

"Has he done this before?"

"Oh, sure." She puts her glasses back on. "He drinks a lot. He's an alcoholic, no doubt about it. When he's really out of it,

I try to stay out of his way. I disappear. We have separate rooms. And Alva has her own room, too."

"Why do you stay?"

She looks down at her sad-looking fried chicken and baked potato, picks up her fork and rakes the peas around a bit, then puts the fork down on the edge of the plate.

"Habit? Many reasons, I guess. He *is* nice to Alva. I *am* locked into the house with him; we're buying it together. That was a mistake. But I don't see any easy way out. I'm not giving it up. I've worked hard to own my own home, and now . . . "

"He won't move?"

"He has no desire to leave me. Why should he? I take his shit, give him sex, and cook for him—not all the time—but sometimes. I tell you, Lester, my self-esteem hit rock bottom a long time ago. And what's so painful about the whole thing is I *know* what I'm doing to myself."

"You need help."

"I'd be the first to admit that." She sighed. "And what's so crazy about the arrangement is he can do anything he wants. A month ago I walked in and caught him in bed with one of my best friends. Needless to say, she's no longer a friend. I told him you and I went up to see Twain's grave and had dinner in Elmira. He didn't even ask any questions. Just the fist right in the eye."

"And what did you do?"

"Huh? I told him if he does it again, I'm leaving. But I've said that before. I don't mean it and he knows it."

"Are you telling me you're going to go on like this?"

"I want to make *him* leave. I've even offered to buy his share, though I can't afford it. If he ever consented I wouldn't know how I'd manage but I'm determined not to give up the house. I've put a lot of myself into that place. Plus Alva needs a permanent home. I'm not going to disrupt her childhood the way my own was."

"You should leave him. I can't see how holding on to the house is worth the price you're paying. What if he knocks your eye out or causes brain damage or accidentally kills you?"

"I've thought of all the risks involved. But emotionally I'm unable to make that move right now." She takes a sip of her Coca-Cola. "There are times when he's really *caring* when he's sensitive to my feelings, times when I swear he loves me, treats me well."

Hope and I plan to get together Friday night. She is supposed to go to a movie with a girlfriend. The girlfriend, if necessary, will cover for her later. Hope covers for the girlfriend by lying to the girlfriend's husband, when necessary, when the girlfriend wants to spend time with one of her many boyfriends.

I tell Albert I'm going to a faculty pow-wow at a colleague's home. He is sulking as he does his homework at the dining room table. I've told him not to turn on the TV till he finishes.

This time I pick her up on a street corner near campus. It's already dark. We drive to a nearby motel out on the highway.

The lovemaking is again disappointing. Later, I'm lying beside her wondering why I've come back a second time. Obviously something in me thought the first failure was just bad luck, bad timing, and that the chemistry would improve. Now I wonder.

I'm thinking what a mess her life must be. I thought *my* life was a mess. I remember the day I met her, remember liking her self-deprecating manner, her self-irony. Now I wonder about the depth of both. One can be *too* self-deprecating. In her it must be related to some form of masochistic self-destruction.

If I ever fantasized about a life with Hope—and maybe I have—that fantasy has gotten itself up on a velocipede and wheeled away into the sunset. But I feel sorry for her despite the fact that she doesn't seem to feel sorry for herself.

While we're lying here she says, "When will I meet your son?"

This takes me by surprise. I wonder do I really want them to meet? It doesn't seem to matter a lot one way or the other. More importantly, do I want to even continue seeing Hope in this way? A part of me is already wondering how to change the terms of our relationship, how to transfer from this physical intimacy to a more trustworthy friendship. But maybe it's too late. What follows breaking off could be disaster or silence or hostility or some combination of the three along with what might pass for friendship. "Albert is a killer-diller. You'd like him."

"I bet I would. So, when do I get to meet him?"

"Before long."

That answer seems to jar her. She sits up and props herself against her pillows. "I'm going to take a shower."

She's out of bed and I'm admiring her slender body, as she walks to the bathroom, passing the television set, when she stops, turns, and says, "You don't really want me to meet your son, do you?"

"Listen, I haven't even thought about it till now, till you brought it up. I've had no opinion about it."

"Why not? If you cared about me and respected me, wouldn't you want your son to meet me?"

"Hope, this is silly, I mean—"

She glares at me one last time before disappearing into the bathroom and slamming the door.

What's the big deal? If she wants to meet Albert, she can meet Albert. I pick up the remote and click on the set. I come in on a sit-com, click again till I hit a news channel. I lie here in a stupor watching the images of deceit and corruption, greed and power.

Hope comes out with a big yellow towel wrapped around her breasts and hips. The contrast with her cinnamon color delights me as much as I can be delighted in my present apprehensive mood.

"What are you watching?" She's coming toward the bed.

"Listen, Hope, I have no objection to you and Albert meeting. If you have time we can go by my place right now."

She sits down on the side of the bed, with her body facing the TV, but she's looking across her shoulder at me. "You sure you don't mind?"

"Not at all. I'll get ready." I lean across the bed toward her and reach past her for the phone. "I'd better call. Let him know."

She's now watching the screen. While I'm dialing she picks up the remote and clicks the picture off.

"Al, this is Hope Breman, the friend I mentioned on the phone. She teaches up at the university with me."

They are shaking hands.

We're standing in the living room. From where I stand I see the dining room table and his schoolwork spread out under the chandelier light. He looks presentable in a white pullover and jeans. He's put on his sneakers. Normally he'd be walking around in his socks. I often complain about the smell of his socks.

While they're shaking hands I notice how handsome my kid is, as he's grinning, showing his dimples, handsome despite his hair which, is cut in the current fashion of many of his culture and generation: bushy on the top and almost bald around the sides and back. But to my eyes it's an ugly style no matter where it originated, ugly as sin. In my time we wore huge afros for the same reason, the bushier and taller, the more glorious. These things were ugly to my parents' generation.

Behind him I see that the TV is on although it's on mute. The cable station, as usual. A rap group of five or six young black men are jumping and wiggling about on a stage and singing too, as images of a scantily dressed young woman of indistinguishable racial background flash across the screen.

I wonder if Al's finished his homework. A few days ago he told me he's met a couple of guys at school who want to form a rap group with him. "This is something new, Dad, entirely black and invented by my generation."

I remember laughing and saying that rapping was hardly new and that the dancing looked to me like a continuation of what, in the twenties, thirties, and forties was called Flash Dancing. His response? He got very indignant so I dropped the subject and didn't bother to go into this business about cultural or racial memory. You can't teach anybody anything till they're ready.

I've poured Hope and myself some of my best Cabernet Sauvignon, clicked off the TV, and the three of us are sitting in a sort of circle—Hope on the couch, Al in the armchair, I'm on the loveseat—in the living room's sitting area.

She's asking Al questions about school. He has answers that are not too cryptic. He seems to be warming up to her pretty quickly. While they talk I realize I'm holding my breath, then I let go and try to breathe naturally.

Suddenly there's a pounding at the front door. It confuses my heart before it does my mind. I was just beginning to relax. Who could it be this time of night? A neighbor coming to borrow sugar? Somebody going from door to door pushing his own agenda? "Excuse me." I glance at Hope and think I see a flicker of apprehension but I'm not sure how to read it.

I stand close to the door and ask, "Who is it?"

"Open up! It's the police!"

I glance back toward the living room and Hope has come to her feet and is stepping backwards across the rug. She stumbles but does not fall. The pounding comes again.

And I open the door just as Hope shouts, "No!"

And a big blonde white guy with a handlebar mustache stands there in a menacing way, obviously drunk, his spring jacket open, with a belly protruding over his belt. He belches once before stumbling into the room, knocking me aside with a thick arm.

What happens next is totally confusing. I see Albert running toward the kitchen. Hope runs through the dining room and apparently into my bedroom. I'm trying to restrain the guy but he's twice my size and he manages to knock me aside for the second time as he stumbles off after Hope, tracking mud across the floor. No doubt he came across the wet lawn or had been out at the window looking in.

I rush to the living room phone and dial 911, whispering in a shaky voice, "A man's just forced his way into my house and is threatening to kill a woman." I give the address. The woman on the other end wants more details but all I say is, "Hurry! Get somebody out here!" and hang up. Then I hear Farrell bellow.

When I get to the bedroom doorway I see Farrell's stuck in the window with his head and upper-body completely outside. The window has apparently fallen on his back and he's groaning and cursing but he isn't moving very much from his hips down. His butt faces me and he is practically on his knees. Immediately I suspect his back has been fractured by the falling window.

And Hope, bless her heart, has escaped through my bedroom window. She is probably at this moment running blindly across dark backyards because I hear a symphony of neighborhood dogs baying and barking and yelping.

This is a month later. Hope and I are in the school cafeteria having lunch together. "Well," she says, "I'll have to sell the house, but that's okay. I'll buy a smaller one."

"Do you know where he is now?"

"No, but wherever he is he's in a wheelchair. Probably at his mother's in the Bronx."

"I wasn't expecting that lawsuit," I said.

"That was a crock. Hurt on your property. So, what? He was there with criminal intentions. That's not any different from your shooting him as an intruder, which he was. No. There was no way he could make that lawsuit against you stick. He was attempting to do bodily harm to me, possibly to you too. My lawyer told me the judge would throw the case out of court. She could see through him a mile away. How's Al?"

"He's down in the city visiting his mother. Spring break, you know. Says he's got an appointment with a theatrical agent."

Hope smiles to herself. "What would you do if he really becomes a big-time rap star?"

I sigh and close my eyes. "I'd probably quit working and manage him."

"You wouldn't!"

"Just kidding." I look at my watch. "What's up tonight?"

"I have to help Alva with homework. But tomorrow night—?"

WEAVER

IN THE NAME OF CHRIST, listen to me, Lott, you a white man just like me. I told you before; I did what I had to do. She knew comic books was wrong. I had told her. God's word! And I know I can talk to you. God knows if I can't talk to you I can't talk to nobody. Nobody but God himself! And I know you a Christian. It shows in your face. So, I'm not worried. It's all now really in the mighty hands of the Lord. Always was, always will be. I did what the good Lord wanted me to do. But you say I can't go in court and speak the truth. But God's truth is greater than man's court. Well, I tell you, Lott, I don't know how to lie because the almighty God, in all his power, lives in me. I can't lie. I never learnt. And you've told me over and over what to say and what not to say and I've been praying to the Lord for guidance. I'm going to try to find God's way of saying it, I swear, without lying, without going against what he wants me to do. Now, this judge, Chase, you say he's an unpredictable man, and he hates niggers. So, he might be on our side. But you see, Lott, that's not what I want. I know niggers don't stand up before the Lord as well as we do but I tell you, Lott, they as much the children of God as any of us white folks. Look at me, I live amongst them! All these years out there on the South Side, with Mary Alice! What? Near ten years. People thinking I was some kind of white nigger. They didn't know what to think half the time. Me in a basement with a black woman! But the spirit of God in me transformed that place. Still, my own mama would've turnt over in her grave. But the niggers never bothered me. Never! I preached the pure work of God to them dumb niggers when I could and I tell you Lott sometime I saw the light in them black faces come on and that's how I know they—in spite of the liquor and the dancing and the fighting—as much God's own as anybody. Mary Alice too! But she didn't try much. I kept after that woman all the time, made her get down on her knees spring and winter, summer days, fall nights, all the time, to pray good with me. I tried, Lott, I tried, I tell you, I tried my best to break the evil in that woman, tried to get her to come to the bosom of the Lord. And God knows for a long, long time I believed it was about to happen. At first I was gentle with her, trying to get her to see that life has to be lived by the word of God and that the cursed world is full of evil, that we are all born nasty and mean and damned; evil, and have to be reborn. It took a long time to get her to just see God's simple and beautiful truth. Three or four years before, she started listening and understanding. For a long time I saw progress and thought well, well she's going to be born again in the grace of God. I had her getting herself neater, you see. Watching what she said! Keeping the place cleaner, scrubbing the floor; and learning how to handle the money better! Like my daddy, before me, I was always a man to bring my paycheck home. It's the woman's place to know how to stretch the dollar. But God knows, Lott, I had to teach that woman everything from scratch. She had her ways but they was not the ways the Lord would approve of. Her ways was colored folks' ways; and I know to a certain extent people bound to be the way they born to be. Yet and still, she needed to be taught how to ration things. With God's help, I made her a better woman. I taught her to count out things and to be thrifty. The Bible tells us to be thrifty. To be wasteful is a sin. Now you'd think a black woman would've already knowed that wouldn't you? But she didn't know much, coming from Georgia like she did, when she was seventeen, staying with her aunt, having that baby a year later. And you know the state took the child from her by the time she was twenty. Gave it to another family. God works in mysterious ways. So, it was best. Mary Alice never was cut out to take care of nobody, not even herself. God rest her soul, I had to take care of her. A grown woman of twenty-eight and she didn't know first thing about thrift. I had to tell her how to dress to go to work. You know she ran a switchboard all the time. They liked her voice. She had this music in her voice, you see, and a good way with words. So she got jobs as a switchboard operator pretty quickly. Soon as she'd lose one she'd find another. And she did have her high school diploma. That helped too. God knows, in today's world education means a lot. But I'm getting off the track here. Now, I know you're concerned about our going into that courtroom. God knows I tried to save her black soul. But, you see, Lott, I know now, you got to have faith. You believe in God, don't you? I thought so. As God is my judge, everything is going to turn out all right. No man can judge me when what I did I know is right. Right even for Mary Alice. She's gone on now. It's all in his hands. I did his will and I can't turn back and say what I did was wrong. I gave Mary Alice plenty of opportunity to change her ways, plenty of chances to let the light of God into her soul. But you see, Lott, she didn't have no soul. She may have one now though. Only God knows what death did to her. I'm sure she is better off. And it wasn't just that she was the descendant of Cain, black—though God knows she had to work harder to cleanse herself, there was a darkness all around her and a pit of evil in her. I had just come in from the graveyard shift at the stockyards, tired, you see. Did I tell you this before? Okay. A couple of boys from my crew was on the same streetcar going home. They had been teasing me all the way home, like they usually do on the assembly line, talking up Truman because they knowed I didn't think much of him cause he wasn't a man of God. So they had kind of ticked me off on the streetcar, kidding me about my faith. Even teased me about living among the niggers; me getting off at State Street; and them staying on, going on across town. I tell you sinners have no idea how terrible they look in the eyes of God. And the things they say! But I put their words out of my mind and went on home. And there was Mary Alice lying on the couch, with a mouth full of Baby Ruth, and looking at a comic book, like she didn't know no better. I'd told her no comic books in this house! I'd told her time after time not to read comic books, told her how evil them things was. And I stood there in the doorway just looking at her; and I felt so hopeless, like all the years I'd put into trying to train her, to get her to be a better person, to be a child of God, to walk the straight and narrow, to pray for God's grace. All of it hit me; all the years I'd pounded the rules in her, all of it hit me, hit me hard, my failure at it hit me real hard, Lott. I looked at her and I heard God speak to me. Heard God speak clear and unmistakable! He spoke in my ear: You must do what you must do! She will not change. That's what I heard and I didn't say a word. Not a single solitary word. With his sweet voice in my ear, I just walked right over to her and my hands felt the cool damp skin of her neck; and the Lord gave me the strength to squeeze her neck until she stopped jumping and jerking and gagging and choking and kicking and struggling and trying to tear my hands away. I just kept right on at her. And sure as my name is Harold Weaver, and as sure as I'm fifty-eight years old tomorrow, February twenty-eight, and as sure as I'm sitting right here in Cook County jail, God was right there with me, Lott. Plain as you before me now! And like I told you before, I had no choice.

GIRL IN A BOAT

I'M A PRETTY GIRL. Everybody says so. But sometimes I don't think I'm pretty at all; and being pretty never made me happy. Except once, a year ago, for a few days, when I was eighteen.

It was a small house and very cold at night. And because of this fact, Belle and I slept together; or, I suppose you can say we slept together because, under the circumstances, it was the practical thing to do. As I say, nights were cold, and there was only one good bed. But she never touched me sexually. Never! I swear! I know people might find that hard to believe; especially the people at school who know about Miss Belle Marie Livingstone, math teacher. And you can believe there was plenty of talk!

I never engaged in such talk. I'm not a bigot! Besides, Belle (and we called her Belle in the classroom) was always extremely nice to me. She was not only my favorite teacher; she was one of my favorite people in the whole world.

Now that I can look back to last summer with some objectivity, I am sure I feel no regrets—although at the time I thought I would. There's nothing really to regret. It was quite an experience—at first—being there at her summer home. The house set at the bottom of a steep private dirt road. Beyond the yard was the lake. As I said, at first I loved it there. I loved just sitting on the screened porch listening to the summer sounds of insects, such as crickets and grasshoppers, and birds too, making their calls, and singing their songs.

I must have felt loved, and that was something I felt I needed, especially last summer after the breakup with Billy, my boyfriend of almost a year. He was a nice boy but he didn't try to understand anything about me. I understood him; but he made no effort. Besides, all he cared about was video games. I got sick of his video games!

And Mother! Oh, don't get me started on Mother! To be perfectly honest: Mother didn't love me and I didn't love her. Besides, she doesn't need me. She has her boyfriend. They live together in Evanston, and I guess they're happy. I see her once in awhile. Actually, Moira, my roommate, thinks she is wonderful. She and Moira get along just fine.

My father died when I was five. He died in a car accident. I don't want to talk about it.

Anyway, Belle was the sweetest person I'd ever known. She made me feel pretty—especially when she touched me. She would comb my blond hair. I'd sit on the floor between her knees, and she would slowly comb my hair with a big black comb. I loved it.

I wanted to be a singer. I posted a lot of my songs on YouTube. I had a fan base there. You can probably still hear them. And Belle encouraged me, told me I was good, something mother never said. Each morning, before Belle was out of bed, I went out on the lake in the boat and sang to myself, loud and clear; and I felt beautiful and happier than I had ever felt before.

As I said the house was not large. It was a log cabin and at night we heard the wind singing through the cracks. While lying awake, I made up many songs in the night. They were songs about love, heartache, finding the true, everlasting love.

There are so many delightful things I'd like to say about Belle. For instance, how she carefully braided my long blond hair. How she washed my back as I sat submerged in the tub of warm water. How she cooked. How she laughed. Her laughter was music, simple, charming music.

She was, I think, beautiful. She was a thin lady with rosy cheeks and green eyes, the color of the Illinois sky on a good summer day. Her curly hair was a kind of metallic red. I loved touching it, running my fingers through it.

To my surprise, one morning, Belle told me that Mrs. Fuller, a teacher who had the division room next to Belle's, back at the high school where I was a senior, was coming up to see her, to spend a week or two. Mrs. Fuller usually taught summer school, but had declined this summer, at the request of her family doctor. I didn't know her well. I'd never taken a class with her, but I'd heard nice things about her. Kids said she was an easy grader, and a good teacher. If those two things can go together!

I was surprised because at the outset, Belle had informed me that she and I would be here alone together. I remember now that I felt betrayed and angry when Belle told me the news. Heck, I wanted Belle to myself!

Why did Belle want to spoil all our secluded fun by allowing such a person as Mrs. Fuller to appear? I didn't feel that I could voice any objection. I was only a guest there myself, a girl, a student; a student with one foot already out the high school door; a student already accepted in college. It was just too depressing to think about.

We had three days before she would arrive. Dreading that day, I now felt an overwhelming urge to be alone a great deal. I no longer really wanted to sleep with Belle. I had, before, enjoyed it. Now I resented her. And I didn't care if I was selfish.

The morning for Mrs. Fuller to arrive came, and I got into the boat and went sailing. Some of the fishermen were just coming to work. Of course many had started at three or four that morning. In a whisper, I spoke to one in passing. He only nodded. For them talking is bad luck.

I drifted along. Under the boat the lake rested. In my mind the lake was my romantic sea. The sun was coming up and falling across the shimmering water. The cesspool odors had now gone. For days they had been in the air. This morning there was a delightful freshness about everything, which made my grief ironic.

I began to sing, and my voice rose from a tiny sound to a loud echoing one. And I am sure I bothered the fishermen but I couldn't help it. I sang a song I myself wrote and less than a couple of seconds into it, I was weeping. I hadn't cried like that since my father died.

As I wiped away my tears, Mrs. Fuller's face leapt into my mind. Perhaps I should have spoken up, voiced my objections. Belle might have respected my wishes. But I doubt it. Who was I, anyway? Just a girl, a nobody.

When I, at last, got up enough courage to bring the boat in, to pull it ashore and tie it up and lock it to the tree, I think I must have felt less sorry for myself as I walked toward the cabin.

Nervously, I opened the door, and let myself in. I'd been out for about three hours. Then softly, I closed the door.

At first I saw nothing unusual. Everything was as it was when I left that morning. Then I took a step forward and almost stumbled over a suitcase, which had an umbrella propped against it. The suitcase had glued to it many colorful vacation tags. The bed springs in the bedroom suddenly moved under the weight of more than one body.

Belle, in a moment, stuck her head from the bedroom. Then came, beside hers, the anxious face of Mrs. Fuller. "You're back already, Sandra?" said Belle.

"Yes, I just came in. How are you, Mrs. Fuller? It's nice to have you with us." I was uncontrollably cold.

"I'm just looking forward to relaxing," she said with a nervous laugh.

Then they closed the door behind themselves and I could hear, from the bedroom, their muffled voices whispering.

After I used the bathroom, I walked back out on the porch and sat down in the rocker, trying to collect myself, trying to reason things out, trying to invent excuses for Belle, for *them*, but there was no use. Everything was clear.

A moment or two later Belle came to the screen door and said: "Sandra, show Joan around, I'm going to prepare lunch."

Mrs. Fuller came out and stood looking through the screen. The whole porch was screened.

Reluctantly, I stood up. "You want to see the boat?"

"Sure. I'd like to see the lake. If it's not too much trouble."

Belle said, "It's only a few steps in that direction behind that stand of trees."

Mrs. Fuller followed me down the path to my secret sea,

our lake. There were ten or twelve little children now playing in the white sand, and she raved about how healthy they looked. The kids were from the house farther down the lake. They often wandered along the edge of the lake like this.

As I led her back along the path to the cabin, Mrs. Fuller said the tall trees reminded her of the trees of Georgia where she was born. I slapped at my thigh. I was wearing shorts.

Behind me I heard her say, "Are those bites on your legs?"

"Yes. The mosquitoes here are bad."

That night Belle asked me to sing for Mrs. Fuller and her.

"I don't feel like it, Belle."

"But you always feel like singing, Sandra. What's the matter? Something bothering you, dear?"

"I don't feel very well. I think I'll go to bed."

There was a beastly silence in the room, which must have weighed a ton. I suddenly realized I didn't know where I was going to sleep.

But I stood up anyway. "By the way, where am I sleeping?"

"We can all sleep together—for the warmth," said Mrs. Fuller. She chuckled.

"No, thanks," I said. "I'll sleep on the rollaway."

The rollaway was in the small bedroom, which Belle used as a storage room. I'd simply move things back to make room for letting the bed out.

I was aware that Belle was giving me this disgusting look. But I didn't care.

That night, stretched out on the rollaway, with only one blanket to cover me, I wrote a hasty letter to my mother telling her I'd be coming back to Chicago. Then I realized that I'd get there before the letter. So I stuck it under my pillow, to be torn up and thrown away in the morning.

Before falling to sleep, I checked my Facebook page. Lately I had been keeping up with my friends. I clicked several "likes" and closed the computer.

"But why must you leave now, Sandra?" Belle was sincerely surprised. She was about to drive me to the station. It was a Sunday morning.

"Yes, we'll miss you terribly."

"You don't really have to go now, do you?"

"Yes, I must. I've enjoyed every minute of it, Belle. And I appreciate everything you've done for me. Thank you so much for inviting me up here. It's a lovely place."

Poor Belle. She looked so hurt—or maybe disappointed in me. I couldn't tell which.

On the station platform Belle said: "Don't mention to any of the other kids at school that I invited you up here, Sandra. You understand. And don't talk about this summer, honey. It's our little secret. Okay?"

"Of course, Belle."

And I thought about her last words all the way back to Chicago and what I had promised. I felt sad—the whole summer ruined like that. But, like I said, I don't regret having gone.

GELASIA'S PROBLEM

SOMEBODY SAYS SOMETHING from the doorway. I swivel around from the desk full of backed-up trucker's reports and it's the new girl, Gelasia. So I respond with a smile and a friendly greeting.

And she comes in looking shy with her hands in the pockets of her overalls. She has a burnt spot on her leather apron. And just out of habit, I glance down at her steel-toe boots.

She's wearing an army jacket. It is chilly in the shop so I can't say I blame her. This time of year it's warmer outside than in the shop. Today it's at least sixty-five in the shade and it's March. But this is Nebraska. Why, some people run around in T-shirts and shorts, others wear overcoats or jackets.

I'm not big on words but I say something else to her, trying to be friendly, waiting for her to tell me what she wants.

Her kneecaps look thick and red through the holes in her work overalls. She's been down on her knees burning or welding. And her helmet is sitting back on her head and she's lifted the goggles back too. She speaks again, slowly, telling me things I did not expect to hear today.

And I was just beginning to think how much I like this new girl. She reminds me in a way of myself when I was her age. She sighs. She stops talking then starts again. It's going to be a bad day. I can tell. Then again she stops talking.

So I tell her a few things, repeating what I told her the day I hired her two weeks ago. But I have the feeling she's not listening to anything I say.

I can see the girl is hurting so I say more. I think she might be ready to quit on us and I'd rather not see that happen because she's not a bad worker. I try to explain why things are as they are and why people do what they do. I can see that she is not listening so I stop talking.

So we step out of the little cubbyhole of an office Darby and I share and cross the bay, avoiding the glare of Luke's and Phil's rods, walk the stretch under a crane line, and open the heavy iron door to the cafeteria.

Sun's coming in through the cafeteria windows and it's eleven-thirty. Netty, a black woman, and Elroy, her husband, run the cafeteria. They say something to us and I say something back.

The coffee is self-service so Gelasia and I fill our cups and I wave to Netty behind the counter; Gelasia and I find a table by the window. Three or four truckers are in here working on their reports and drinking coffee. The table is dirty as usual, grimy from the crap that floats in from the shop through the broken windows, the door being opened a million times a day. I take a napkin out of the dispenser and wipe a spot clean for our cups.

Gelasia sits across from me and leans forward. I know she's a hillbilly. Smart but uneducated. She props her elbows on the table. But the coffee is too hot to touch just yet.

I pick up my coffee cup with both hands, sniff the steam lifting from it, and carefully bring the edge to my lips, ready to blow. With the tip of my tongue I test the coffee's temperature. It's cool enough for a tiny sip, which I take. I'm watching her all the time and suddenly she's got this secret smile with a downcast, funny gaze. I ask her something. She tells me the answer without looking at me. And I think it's possible she's lying.

She's now trying her coffee. I say something else, trying not to get too personal; she ducks her head and responds quietly. But I believe only about half of what she is saying. She tosses her curly hair out of her face and gives me a hot movie star look, sucking in her cheeks. I take a sip of coffee and try to put her at ease by telling her specific things I think she might find interesting.

Quitting time, I agreed to drop Gelasia off. She hasn't gotten a car yet; she says she came on the bus. I don't think she can drive. She usually rides with Gladys but Gladys is off today.

Gelasia directs me to her place on D Street between Second and Third. She opens the door but doesn't climb out right away. One leg is outside and her lunch bucket is on her lap but she's looking at me. She says something I don't expect. I feel something in me pause but I respond as calmly as possible.

I drop her and I drive home and forget about Gelasia. By ten-thirty I am sawing logs. Now, the phone starts ringing, messing up a nice dream of myself as a little girl playing in a meadow near my grandpa's and grandma's house. And I hear myself mumble something like hello and suddenly there's the thick, choked response of somebody crying.

Must be the wrong number. But the crying continues, messy and throaty. And she suddenly catches her breath, holds it, and lets it out with a big sob, then another.

Suddenly the crying is stopped by a hollow bang as the thick weeping stops again. The person responsible for it hangs up. Well, I'm stunned; with shaking hand, I slowly return the receiver to its cradle.

The way I get to sleep is to turn my back to it. The people upstairs are still listening to television, some late horror movie. Normally she's shouting, calling him a redneck and usually slamming doors and banging things around and he gets drunk and he calls her a slut and a whore then storms out. They have three small kids up there in those two tiny rooms. So, when the television is going and they're not talking I feel lucky.

But suddenly my phone is ringing again. With the receiver to my ear I hear weeping. It's the crying woman again. She calls my name and starts talking between sobs. Now I know. Of course it's Gelasia. She tells me between sobs what has happened to her. And I am very upset hearing it. Then suddenly she screams and the line goes dead.

I slide out of bed and reach over and turn on the bedside light. It stings my eyes. Halfway to the bathroom I stop. What in hell is going on?

In the bathroom I throw water on my face and wipe with the towel, trying to dispel my grogginess. In the mirror my eyes are as red as a vulture's. Hell, I know what I'll do. Find her number and call her back; tell her to call the police.

I look through the phonebook for her listing, but she's not listed. Of course she wouldn't be. New in town. To hell with this, I'm going to call the cops. As much as I dislike any contact with the police, I pick up the phone. I speak with a woman at the station. I hang up and get dressed.

Outside, I sit in my Bug with the motor idling, letting it warm up, not daring to start it a minute before I hear the motor start racing. She might die completely if I start her moving too soon.

When the car is ready, I pull out of Hanover Drive and the Jackson Place Apartments complex and circle around and out to Jackson Road and down Washington Boulevard. I'm wondering what the hell am I doing out this time of morning, at my age, my body aching, cramps, my period about to start, I think, and menopause not far off, though it's a beautiful night. Just go. Figure it out later.

Gelasia opens the door and she looks horrible. Her hair is in a tangle, eyes red, and cheeks puffy. She can barely focus as I step inside and stand with her in the half-lighted hallway. We exchange a few tight words.

She places her index finger over her swollen lips, turns, motions for me to follow and she leads the way on tiptoes down the hall, passing an old staircase, toward the back.

Though the wooden floor is squeaking, I follow Gelasia quietly past a series of grimy doors all the way to the back where one lone door stands ajar.

She steps inside and pulls me in. In one corner it is a bedroom with a single-sized bed and a straight chair and a tiny table on which sits her cheap hair dryer. In another, it's a sitting room mostly taken up by this big old armchair with a reading lamp beside it; in the third, its a kitchen with an old tiny green and white General Electric two-burner stove and a tiny table with one wrought-iron chair with painted plastic back and seat; and in the fourth corner, where we stand, it's the entryway to the other three.

But I'm interested in the quilt hanging on the wall over Gelasia's bed. It's one of those wool dyed ones with reds and yellows and bright purples and all decorated with flying fish and long spears. It must be one of those good Indian rugs. And I wonder where this poor polecat of a girl got such a pretty thing.

And I notice Gelasia is fumbling as she turns a dead-bolt lock in her door. But it's not till this moment that I know she's drunk. I watch her finish locking the door; then, to my great surprise, she turns around and throws herself against me, wrapping her arms around me, holding me.

Well, I can just about sink through the floor. And I feel her hands locked together at my back. Her face is against mine. She sobs, and I feel her body against my own. And she smells like she's consumed at least a gallon of cheap jug wine. And I'm wondering what's up. Did she lie to get me here?

I take her by the shoulders and gently lift her back just an inch or so. And I want to know everything all at once. She looks horrible but maybe nothing happened. Can I believe what she said on the phone? Will the police show up? What will I say to them? Gelasia does look like something happened to her. Just looking at her you can see that. And she is hysterical.

I turn from her and walk across the room into her living room area and turn and face her. She hasn't moved but we're only about ten feet apart. I ask her a question. She does not answer. I then tell her about the police. She suddenly looks unhappy with me. And she begins to cry again.

Then she starts slowly walking toward her bed. At the bed

she stops and throws herself on it, face down, holding her face. And her shoulders shake with the sobbing. I go to her and I pat her on the shoulder, trying to calm her down. And her arms sneak around me again and she asks me a question I can't answer. Meanwhile, I move her arm away.

But I take off my jacket and sit with Gelasia till daybreak, listening to her talk and sob. And after a couple of hours or so she seems to sober a bit. And every time my mind wanders, her voice pulls it back. She talks for a long time, talks passionately. And in the meantime morning approaches.

Finally, her room is lighter. And I lean across the bed and lift the edge of the shade back an inch. And outside in the brighter light of a foggy morning I see a stunted bare tree undaunted by human abuse and the blind window of the house next door.

And Gelasia pulls herself to the side of the bed and drops her feet to the floor. And after sitting like this for, oh, a couple of seconds, she says something different in a clearer voice.

Then I remember I'd promised Darby I'd come in this morning, Saturday, for a couple of hours to help him with the backed-up road paperwork. The truckers make such a damned mess half the time we have to rewrite the reports. And mostly Darby gets stuck with doing it and I know that's not fair.

Now Gelasia stands up. But she wavers a bit before walking across the floor and into the tiny bathroom and closing the door. And my sense of being out of place has dropped off a bit. But I am angry with her and I feel guilty about being angry with her. She's told me everything and I still feel like I know nothing, nothing about what happened, and nothing about her. And I'm angry with myself for staying up all night, letting this girl make me do that.

And we're now sitting at Gelasia's tiny kitchen table. The coffee is bitter, bitter like raw beetroot but I take a few sips before putting it aside. And she says a full sentence in a voice clearer than before. And I want to go, yet I'm still here.

Later, while she's in the shower, I fall asleep right there in the chair. And for a while I'm aware of the splash of the shower water but then those sounds later get mixed up with a water pipe that's broken in my mother's kitchen, and I'm scrambling around, desperately trying to find a way to stop the burst of water.

Now I wake and Gelasia is back in the room fully dressed like she's ready to go to work. I get up and walk over to the bed and pick up my jacket, put it on and walk toward the door. Then she asks a question but I'm finding it harder to listen to her word for word. And my response clearly isn't what she wants to hear. A cynical smile jumps around in her cheeks and eyes.

The following Monday after work, she stops me in the parking lot and says a few pinched-off words. then walks on to Gladys's car. I don't even respond. Just look at her. I still don't know if she lied to me about Friday night.

Tuesday morning. Gelasia doesn't show up. And her time card sits in the out-slot along with Gavin Clark's. Gavin's in the hospital having a bypass. When I get to my car around six-fifteen I see what looks like a flat at the back right rear. I take my pump out and hook it up and pump and pump but it does no good, the pump is useless. A couple of line guys, Karl and Quinn, walk by and start teasing me about being winded. And I'm thinking maybe I can get over to the repair shop at the gas station on G Street. But I listen to see if I hear air escaping and can't hear any.

I know it's the wrong thing to do. I drive slowly and carefully over to the shop; I pull up to the air pump, get out and take the hose and fill up the tire. Again, bending down, I listen for escaping air. Nothing.

When I pull up to my front door, Gelasia is sitting on the steps of my apartment building. She's wearing jeans and a leather jacket and a splash of scarlet lipstick across her mouth. This is a new look. I get out and face her. I say something, she says something back. It suddenly occurs to me that she might actually not remember anything about Friday night. I ask her a question. She's hemming and hawing now. She whispers back something as though she's lost her voice.

But I don't know what to say to her or what to do about her. And I start up the steps and she's behind me. And I realize I could have prevented her from entering but I didn't. So, I must be nuts too. And at the door to my apartment I say something else to her.

She doesn't have an answer. I try again. This too is met with silence. I unlock my door and turn to her. She suddenly turns and flies back down the steps. An hour later the phone rings and she says a few words quickly then hangs up. I rest the phone in its holder.

Later that night while I'm watching a sitcom again the phone rings. I hesitate, let it ring four times before I pick up. I say something and I hear breathing and more breathing. I hang up.

Wednesday morning. I don't expect her. If she comes in I swear I'm going to get Darby to fire her. But if she doesn't ever show up again, all the better. I talk with Darby and it's all set. I don't have the nerve. I'm authorized to do it but I don't have the guts. Darby can do it without thinking about it.

Mid-morning I go to the women's room and wouldn't you know it, there she is dressed like some hooker who's never been near a church. Has Darby spoken with her yet? I can't tell. Maybe she's snuck back. She's looking very grim. Something in her face makes me shiver; my whole body reacts. I imagine she's going to stab or shoot me dead on the spot. I want to turn and run. But I don't dare. And she stares at me with a sneer. And I try not to show my fear.

Now suddenly she leaps to her feet and strides to the door, stops and stands there with her right hand clenched around the dirty doorknob. She looks back over her shoulder at me. She says, "Too bad you didn't have the guts to be a real woman."

And I say, "What do you mean?"

And she turns and slams the door on her way out and I never see her again.

DRIVING KENNETH HOME

"Need a lift, buddy?" says Leo.

"I live pretty far out—out on Fairmont Avenue," says Kenneth, grinning but looking hopeful.

Leo nods for Kenneth to hop in. It's a cool but sunny late November afternoon. And while driving, Leo falls into his usual on-the-way-home lull, listening to talk radio. The host right now is asking some jerk why he hates homosexuals. The jerk says because they're unnatural and the host says that's not a good reason, you need a political, not a moral, reason. And Leo turns off the radio and glances at Kenneth.

"How do you manage without a car?"

But Kenneth seems off somewhere, gazing ahead at the avenue as they head north through the rush-hour traffic, hitting every stoplight.

"The bus is pretty dependable," Kenneth finally says. He glances at Leo and smiles.

After the long drive out Rose Avenue to Serafina and all the way west on Serafina out to the Roland Park area, they come to Fairmont Avenue. Slowly, Leo turns into the street.

"Right up there. The brown apartment building," says Kenneth. And they come to a stop in front of the building, which is exactly like all the other two-story dull brown brick structures. They stretch out for the entire block.

Leo pulls over to the curb and turns off the motor.

"Hey! Wanna come up for a beer? I mean, you drove me all the way out here, I feel sort of like I owe you one."

Leo can tell by Kenneth's expression he expects to be rejected.

But what the hell, why not? He says, "Sure."

Upstairs, Kenneth throws his parka down on the chair by the door and says to Leo, "Just leave your coat there. It's okay." And Leo takes off his down jacket and drops it on Leo's.

Kenneth locks his hands together and blows into them.

Then Leo, following Kenneth, wanders into the living room area with its nubby and lumpy furniture. "You live here alone? What's this—a one bedroom?"

"Yeah. I'm a bachelor. I mean, I just recently separated. My wife and kid are in Iowa, Grand Rapids. You married?"

"Nope. Not any more. Divorced five years ago. Nasty court battle. My wife got custody of our two kids, both girls. Now I get to see them maybe once a year if I'm lucky. She left Nebraska three years ago, moved back South to be close to her mother." Leo laughs.

Kenneth's place is one big room with a stark kitchenette off to the side. A small hallway leads to what Leo imagines is the bedroom and the bath. But it's not a bad place for a guy alone just starting out as a welder trainee.

Leo sits down suddenly in one of the two chairs at the kitchen table. He throws one leg over the other, and folds his arms across his big chest. He tucks his hands in his armpits to get his fingers warm.

Now Kenneth comes over and places his right hand on Leo's left shoulder and Leo looks up into his wide face. It's a map Leo can't read. "Dark or light?"

Kenneth reminds him of one of those so-called expressionless masks he saw in a shop window downtown.

"Huh? Oh. Whatever." He slaps his own thigh and grins at Kenneth, then starts playing with the opener on the tabletop.

Kenneth walks over to the refrigerator, opens it, bends down, and in one hand lifts out a couple of bottles of dark, gives the door a soft touch and it closes. He brings the bottles to the table and plops them down, pops them open with the opener, hands one to Leo, then sits down adjacent to him in the other kitchen chair.

"I can scare up some grub," says Kenneth. "That is, if you don't have to go."

"Don't want to put you out, dude."

"No trouble at all. Gotta cook for myself anyways. I'll just fry up some burgers and potatoes, slice some tomatoes, open some green peas and we're in business."

"Sounds good to me." Leo dislikes the tremor in his own voice. Suddenly he says, "Damnit! Isn't this what a guy suppose to do with a chick?"

They both laugh. And Kenneth says, "Turn on the TV, if you like. I usually listen to the six o'clock news."

"Sure." Leo walks across the room, turns it on, and comes back to the kitchen. "I'll help you, dude. My hands get restless watching other people work."

Now the two men are in Kenneth's little kitchen, and Kenneth opens two more beers while the burgers and fries are popping in the skillet.

Suddenly Leo notices a tabby wrapping itself around Kenneth's leg. He's surprised to see a single guy with a cat.

"Hi, Poodle," Kenneth says.

"Did you say Poodle? You *named* a cat Poodle?"

Kenneth laughs. "Yes. What's wrong with that?"

"Nothing, I guess. It does look a little bit like a poodle."

Now the telephone rings and Kenneth excuses himself and goes to the wall by the refrigerator and takes it off the hook.

Leo reaches down and tries to pick up Poodle but she scoots away. She stands by Kenneth looking back at Leo, who suddenly hops up and goes to check the skillet.

He lifts it from the flame and shakes the meat and potatoes around, then returns it to the burner. He looks around for a fork to turn the meat with, but there's nothing, so he opens one of the drawers Kenneth is pointing to while talking on the phone.

He turns the meat then the potatoes, one at a time, then goes back to the table and picks up his bottle of beer and turns it up to his mouth and takes a big swallow. Satisfied, he checks his cell phone. Nothing urgent!

Kenneth is talking in a slow, low-keyed voice, and Leo thinks, must be a woman, that's the way men talk to women.

But now suddenly Kenneth's voice lifts in intensity, like somebody shouting across a difficult distance in fear of not being heard. Leo thinks he must be talking with his ex-wife because he hears him ask about the kids. Just something in the tone. It reminds Leo of his own voice when he talks with Laura. Now Kenneth is saying, "Snow, huh?" and, "She did? I knew she would." And so on. "Yes, I've thought about it, Sally." And: "Yes, I'll let you know. I've adjusted a little bit better to it now." Then Kenneth says, "So long, Sally."

Free of the phone, Kenneth comes back to the table and picks up his bottle of beer and takes a drink. "My ex-wife."

Now Poodle walks slowly across the floor and stands at the front door, looking back at them.

"Huh? Ah, no. Excuse me. I have to let her out." And Kenneth goes over and opens the door; Poodle dashes out then Kenneth closes the door.

He comes back to Leo with a preoccupied but somehow innocent look. "Funny thing." He laughs as he again takes up his beer and walks over to the stove and turns off the fire, removing the skillet from the burner. "Sally and I grew up together. Seems like we knew each other real well in high school, but after that it all got confusing." Meanwhile, Kenneth is taking plates down from the cabinet.

Leo grins. "Talk about a coincidence. I met my ex-wife in the eighth grade." He chuckles. "We went to different high schools, so I never dated her."

"How'd you get together?"

"She'd already been married and divorced when we got together. That was back in Chicago. I grew up back there."

"Oh. From the big city, huh?"

"Yeah."

"Sally and I grew up in Waterloo. We were twelve and the nuns didn't stand for any kissing. The Devil made people kiss. But we were sweethearts anyway." He laughs. "It was some time before we got to know how sweet our hearts were." He laughs again.

The two men take their plates out to the sitting area and sit in the two armchairs facing the television, with their plates on their knees. They watch the screen and chew. They see images of war in a remote small country. They see images of poverty in a remote starving country. They see images of an earthquake in South America, bodies being dragged from the rubble.

Sometime later, after finishing another beer, Leo suddenly takes out his cell phone and checks the time. He says, "Christ, I've gotta get outta here." He leaps up and shakes himself.

Kenneth walks him to the door and watches him slide his arms into his down jacket.

With his hand on the doorknob, Leo looks at Kenneth and says, "Nice spending some time with you, dude. Maybe we ought to do it again sometime."

Kenneth nods. "Anytime, dude."

The next morning, Leo walks into the locker room and over to the urinals and there is Kenneth standing there taking a leak. Leo stands at the stall next to him. They mumble a greeting. They then both look up at the concrete wall just ten inches away from their faces. "Hey, man," says Leo, "Thanks a bunch for dinner last night. That was real great of you."

"Anytime," says Kenneth, zipping up and stepping back from the urinal. "I enjoyed having you over. I forgot how nice it is to not eat alone."

CHICAGO HEAT

HELLO? MAMA? It's me, Floyce. Me and Hank just got back from the courthouse. You won't believe it. Something terrible has happened. They kept Harley. And it looks like my husband is dead. The police was just here and they took my husband out of here all covered up on a stretcher. They asked me and Hank all kinds of questions. And we have to go to the police station tomorrow morning because I got to sign some piece of paper. But, mama, we didn't even know Medwin was dead. After the trial we drove home like that with him sitting up in the front seat, kind of all slumped over but still sitting up. And I could've sworn he was just sleeping. And you know, sometimes I have trouble waking him up. He just won't wake up. And I thought this was just another one of them times. 'Cause Medwin was messing up! You know, I told you before that Medwin had been abusing his medication lately, and it wasn't the first time he had passed out and come back hours later. So, that's why we thought he was passed out again. But he had to have died while we were in the courthouse. Can you imagine that? Sitting out there in that hot car all that time in this Chicago heat just 'cause he didn't want to see Vernon. And

August in Chicago, as you know, is hell. He wouldn't even come in to Harley's trial. But I guess he didn't have any love to lose on Harley or Hank, for that matter, the way they treated that poor man. It was like Medwin and Hank had never been friends. And you remember it was Hank who introduced me to Medwin while they were in recovery in the VA hospital. When was that? Already nearly ten years ago. My, how time flies. And you know, Hank brought Medwin home with him, playing on my sympathy, with all this mess about the poor man didn't have no place to live. Hank kept saying did we want to see his friend, Medwin, homeless, out in the streets? And knowing I had a sympathetic heart! So there was Medwin staying with us. Hank's friend, but a man almost my own age! And, you know, you remember, at first it was all right because it was just Hank and Medwin being friends and sitting around in the front room, watching television all day, and taking their medication and drinking beer. But when Medwin come justa noticing me and everything, reaching out and touching me when I walked by, no, boy, no way, Hank didn't go for that. Not with his mother! Not his friend and his mother! He couldn't handle it. But you know, Mama, love is strange, a strange thing. You can't stop it. Once it starts it just gets its own fire and keeps spreading. And there wasn't nothing Hank could do. He's my son and everything and I love him, but he sure did show his ass. I tell you, Mama, that boy gave me a hard time. Did I say boy? Shoot! Hank was a grown man! Grown as he would ever be. Hank was a grown, grown man! And is a grown man. And there ain't no way you can tell me he didn't know what he was doing, so evil and all, abusing Medwin, calling him poor white trash. You remember. I told you about it back then. It got so bad I had to put the boy out of the house two or three times.

He got to going off his head, talking about how he was going to kill Medwin. I tell you about the time I had to pull that boy off Medwin? Trying to choke him to death. Right across the bed! And poor Medwin was just lying there, gasping for his life, all red in the face. Mama, it was something terrible. And you know my own health started failing me back then. That was the beginning of my downfall, my trouble. I was always healthy before then. You know that. Went to work every day of my life. Never missed a day. But the stress and the strain my son put me through for the last few years has just about killed me, mama. I myself now have to take medication. Me! I never took medicine in my life before all this mess. The doctor got me on three different kinds of pills. Gave me all kinds of tests. Now they are trying to say I got something called schizophrenia. Well, I know you know more about this sort of stuff than I do. Well, yes, I take the medicine. They say it's supposed to calm me down, keep things from getting on my nerves. But I have to take all kinds of other little pills too. I don't know what most of them are for. But, Mama, I tell you, I'm not going to let these boys kill me. No, no way! They just about finished me off but I'm not going to let them put me in my grave. And Hank himself is so sad about his brother. But you know, Mama, Hank ain't much better off. He just sits around moping. Won't do nothing but watch television and sleep. Ever since he got out of the Marines, ever since he got back from duty in Germany, that boy ain't been the same. You'd think he saw action or something and got—what do you call it?—combat fatigue or shell-shocked. And now his younger brother, his baby brother, oh Lord! Harley's in prison just 'cause he got mixed up in the wrong crowd, running around with dope dealers and now they got him for first-degree murder. But I believe Harley, Mama;

I believe he wasn't holding the gun. He's just that stupid. Stupid enough to be out there with a bunch of losers, not holding the gun, and end up being the one they nail. You told me yourself you believe these other boys, Kelley and Pablo, had the gun. And I know you're right. He's got a very gentle, very kind heart. But since the police can't find the gun they can't prove anything. Now, you know they told the police they drove out to the lake and threw the gun in the lake; but Harley told me they didn't do that. They still got the gun hid somewhere. What? Oh, yeah. That's why I called you. Isn't it? Well, it's all just so shocking and new to me I can't get my thoughts straight, Mama. Let's see. What happened in court? What happened with Medwin? Like I said, well, first of all, Medwin didn't want to go into the court building because Vernon, the father of my sons, was there. And Vernon took a full day off from his job at the Stockyards to be in court with his son. Good gracious! But, Mama, Vernon is still handsome. You know I still have feelings for him? You can laugh if you want to but it's true. Yeah, I know. I know I'm too old for this kind of foolishness. But honey, believe me, I kept looking across the courtroom at Vernon. Even with the gray hair, he looks great. I said to myself, Go on, Vernon, with your fine self. But seriously, Mama, I guess it's like they say. You never get over your first love. And you see that's why Medwin didn't want to come into the courthouse. He got this thing about Vernon; what Vernon used to mean to me, Vernon being the father of my boys. And I mean, they were always reminding him that he was just Hank's used-to-be friend and not a stepfather to them. They refused him as a stepfather. And they told him he better not think of himself as their stepfather. And calling him names! It was a shame, Mama. I tell you. Anyway, that's why Medwin didn't go in. He said he'd just sit there in the car and wait for us. But you see, he didn't know, we didn't know, the case would drag on all day into the afternoon. You know, starting out at nine in the morning, like it did, we thought it would be over before noon. Then it looked like it was going so slow. We went in there, Hank and me, my sister and brother, their kids, all of us were there, all of us. By the way, Vernon said his mother,asked about you, asked about your heart condition. I told him to tell her you're doing as well as can be expected at your age. I'm sure glad you didn't try to come to the courthouse. Your heart couldn't have stood it. But that place was packed. There were people I didn't know; people came out of curiosity, I guess. Who? Oh, yes. The clerk's whole family was there. That's right, Valora. Yes, his name was Gilroy. You heard it on TV. His wife, Ella, they call her; she was there and she was called up to take the stand. And, you know, Mama, I swear I don't even remember much of what she was saying except she kept going on and on about what a wonderful, generous man her husband was. She said he always tried to help street kids like these boys who killed him. She called my son a street kid. And she cried too. And Harley's criminal friends, Pablo and Kelley, were there, in custody, but they were not on trial, just there as witnesses. They're supposed to be having separate trials. And you know, I told you before that I thought Angelo Passano, Harley's lawyer, was really great. He did the best he could, but it was a hard case. That judge—what's his name, some sort of old funny-sounding name? Judge Yurek Tancik—he was dead-set against Harley from the beginning. The only thing I know now that Angelo did wrong was advising Harley to waive his right to take the stand. That was a terrible mistake. Harley might be free this afternoon, instead of sitting in Cook County Jail, if he had told the jury what happened. But I don't blame Angelo. Angelo did what he thought was right. He trusted the jury. And Harley trusted Angelo. He followed Angelo's advice! Told the judge he didn't want to testify! Huh? Oh, the prosecutor's name was Dan Creaver. Same one they had at the pre-trial hearing. Remember? Now, you know, I sat there all morning and half the afternoon listening to this Creaver arguing to put my son away and listening to Angelo defending my son's innocence—and I tell you, Mama, that prosecutor did not make any sense, not to me. I mean I don't see how the jury bought his line. He just didn't present a story that added up to anything like the basis for some conviction. That's what Hank said. And I believe him. And Hank, you know, has studied them law books. He's read up on a lot of things. Hank has a good mind on him but he just won't do nothing with it. Anyway, after hearing Angelo and Creaver we thought surely that jury would say not guilty and let Harley walk out of there. But instead they said, "We find the defendant guilty as charged." And then the judge turned to the police officer standing by the exit, and in this calm voice, like he was bored half to death, said, "Officer, take the prisoner into custody, please." And I almost died. Mama, I tell you, my heart stopped. And it still ain't started beating right again yet. But, anyway, that judge—before you knew it—he was calling the next case. The sentence won't be till a couple of weeks from now. You see, all these Chicago prosecutors want is to get some kind of conviction, set their books clear, honey! They don't care nothing about justice. It's like Hank says, all they want is a conviction. Hank says once you get caught in the Chicago criminal justice system, charged with something—anything!—your ass is mud. If you're black you can forget it. Your life is just about over. That's what Hank says all the time. Huh? What'd you say, Mama? Oh, yes. Isn't that something? Dying like that. Just up and dying! Dying in the heat. And us driving home with him sitting up like he was still alive.

BOURBON FOR BREAKFAST

A TALL, BIG-BONED WOMAN, with a gray sweater thrown across her curved shoulders, comes toward her with her hand extended.

They shake. Edna thinks her own hand in the woman's looks like a child's.

The big woman says, "Edna Nowell? Yes, I thought so. Thanks for agreeing to meet me here in Philly. Sorry I wasn't able to fly you up here or meet you in the capitol. You know my mother lives in Seattle? You'd have to move out there."

"I understand, Mrs. Stevens."

"Call me Ann."

"Ann it will be. The ad was very clear about that. Let me also say that I think you were wise to run your ad in a national medical journal, and to ask for written responses, and résumés rather than phone calls. So many people use local newspapers for such matters. That would seem to severely limit choices."

"Yes. And thank you. And your résumé is upstairs in my room. I was just going over it before you arrived. How was your drive up?"

"Fine. And yours from Norristown?"

"Except for having to dodge the trucks, not bad." Miss Stevens sighs and looks down at Edna. "Well, I don't know about you, Miss Nowell, but I never like to fight the early crowd for breakfast. Any objections to waiting till later?"

"Not at all."

Without saying anything, Ann Stevens starts walking and Edna walks with her, and they end up standing in front of the elevators. All the while, Ann Stevens is talking, saying she read Edna's résumé and was impressed. "Were you *really* born in the South? You don't have a southern accent?"

"Yes, Atlanta."

One of the elevators comes down from the third floor, and the brass plated iron door opens. The lighted cubical with soft music is empty, and they step in. Ann Stevens presses the gold star on the little pink button for the fourth floor and the door closes. They stand with their backs to the wall; Edna is looking up while Ann Stevens is looking down. Edna is thinking, the blazer would have been better, the blazer and the black and white dotted halter with the fitted bodice.

Out of the corners of Edna's eyes she can see Ann Stevens is looking up at the circular display of floors listed.

Now they step out onto the fourth floor, and start down the hallway. Ann Stevens is saying, "It's not that I don't appreciate your work record, you've certainly had the training and experience, but—" She stops, mouth open.

They stop in front of Ann Stevens' door. Oh, God, thinks Edna, don't start like that and not finish the thought. Standing behind Ann, Edna quickly checks her cell phone. No calls; thank goodness!

As Ann Stevens opens her room door she glances back at Edna. For the flicker of a moment Edna wonders if her hair is neat, if any dead skin might be on the tip of her nose, or worse, something visible hanging from just inside.

Ann Stevens glances slightly down and away from Edna as the door opens and she says, "It's just that I don't *understand* why you worked at three different jobs in one year. I must admit *that* worries me a bit. So, you see, it's not the *work* itself. I suspect that you are a competent nurse, and that my mother would get expert attention in your care."

"My patients died," Edna says suddenly, abruptly, and with too much anger; then trying to soften it, she smiles and says, "They *just* died. But they were seriously ill."

"Yes, terminal," says Ann.

"I don't use the word terminal, Mrs. Stevens. No human being, in my opinion, is ever terminal."

They are now inside the doorway.

Ann Stevens' eyes stretch a tiny bit as she gazes into Edna's face. Edna looks back but refuses to hold the gaze.

In the room, which is dark and smells vaguely of an unmade bed, Ann Stevens throws the light switch rather than opening the drapes. And Edna's bewilderment increases. She wants the heavy red drapes open. Let in the January light! It's morning! Air out this room!

"Come on in," Ann Stevens says, as she walks over to a round table flanked by two armchairs. "Have a seat. Here's a glass. Let's have a drink."

And Edna suddenly wants to duck, as if somebody has just thrown something at her. A drink this early in the morning!

And an image of her father down in the kitchen in the pantry nipping and smacking his lips before anybody else is up. Now she notices a half-finished fifth of Jack Daniels on the table. Is Ann Stevens serious about drinking hard liquor before lunch? If so, why does she need company to do it? Or is this a test?

Two glasses are on the table. Ann Stevens pours liquor into each glass.

Edna sits down across from Ann Stevens and they are both within the light's area of radiance. They are facing each other across the table.

And Edna is thinking, What if I tell the truth, that I don't drink, wouldn't I be better off, or would I offend? She feels a generous surge of insecurity.

Ann Stevens pushes one of the glasses toward Edna and picks up the other. Edna watches her take the first sip. "Aaaa, that's good stuff. Hope you like bourbon. Deba drinks bourbon, you know."

"Deba?"

"Oh, sorry. Everybody calls Mother Deba."

Edna suddenly feels trapped by the new information: *Deba drinks bourbon, you know.* Could this mean she'd be dealing with a drunk invalid day after day? Somebody who is falling down in her bedchamber, crawling about in her own vomit, peeing anywhere? Maybe this is not the job she wants after all. Or does Ann Stevens mean that her mother is a sociable drinker, one who drinks the golden liquid, bourbon, only occasionally in the polite company of others. Or does Ann mean that her mother has a tiny nip before or after dinner, or at bedtime, producing nothing noticeable in her behavior?

She decides Ann's not faking it, she seriously wants to drink bourbon before breakfast and that's her business; but the thought of having to take one sip of the stuff makes her sick. Will Ursula "Deba" Stevens want from her more than nursing care? Will she also expect a drinking partner?

Ann Stevens closes her eyes as she takes another sip. Her whole upper body seems to relax. "Miss Nowell, I should tell you, Deba has very special needs in a nurse." She puts down her glass. "The previous permanent nurse didn't work out because she didn't well enough understand those needs. Mother needs somebody who isn't squeamish about a bedpan, a nurse who knows how to treat bedsores and enuresis. You *do* know what enuresis is, don't you, Miss Nowell?"

"Of course." Involuntarily, Edna suddenly reaches for the glass of bourbon, brings it halfway to her mouth. She catches a whiff of it, and then puts the glass down. She wonders if Ann Stevens' mother will have thickening of the middle muscular layer of her bladder tissue, thickening around her urethral opening. Can't urinate and can't hold it. Poor woman, her last patient, Mrs. Wellington, in Silver Spring, had an awful bladder problem. "Most elderly patients, Miss Stevens, wet in bed if they are not supplied with a bedpan or diapers. By the way, when I spoke with your mother last week, she mentioned the analgesics she's on."

"Oh, yes. Hypothetically speaking, if you were tending her you'd make sure she takes *only* aspirin, no codeine, no matter what she would say." Nervously, Ann Stevens picks up her glass.

Edna slowly crosses her legs. "One thing is not clear to me, Miss Stevens. Does your mother have any serious illness?"

Ann Stevens laughs. "Not unless you count old age as a serious illness. Oh, she has a touch of arthritis in her fingers."

"But no heart trouble?"

"No heart trouble as such. She's felt some numbness in her lips and down her left arm, and occasionally she feels a heavy dull pain in her jaw and neck, but—"

"Sounds like angina. But her doctor has never characterized these symptoms as heart trouble?"

"Hey, wait a minute," says Ann Stevens, "who's interviewing *who,* here?" Her laugh is short and stiff and staccato.

Edna blinks. "Sorry." She sits back.

"No problem. I understand. You need to know what you're getting into. And we need to know *you*. Mother did have an operation five years ago for pancreatitis."

"And she *drinks*?"

"Oh, not much. Doctor Winford says a shot or two a day won't hurt her. She has such little pleasure in life. The whisky makes her happy. Doctor Winford is a dear, dear man. Been Deba's doctor for thirty years."

Edna takes a tiny piece of notepaper from her purse. "Am I correct in understanding that she doesn't go outside the house any more?"

"That's correct. Oh, she'll go to the back porch in the summer but not down into the yard. She goes out only when the van comes to take her to the clinic or the hospital for tests. Are you having second thoughts?"

"Pardon me? Oh, not at all. Only trying to get the full picture. When I saw your ad in the journal I had no idea what was involved; then when I spoke with your mother last week, I learned only so much."

"*So*, this interview is turning out to be as useful to you as it is to us." Ann Stevens leans back against the back of her armchair. "But tell me, Miss Nowell, about your personal interests, habits, things like that. Your résumé tells me everything I need to know about you, professionally. And it's an impressive record, excellent letters of recommendation. But since you would be *living* with my mother, I think I have a right to know a few things about you."

"You certainly do. On my days off I like to go to movies. But I'm also interested in ancient medicine, so I spend a lot of time at the library reading."

"Ancient medicine?"

"Yes, it's sort of a hobby of mine. I've read the *Tacuinum Sanitatis*. It's a Middle Ages handbook on health and well-being. You know, the tacuinums of various cities such as Paris and Vienna, Rouen and Rome. It was based on the Taqwim. I'm interested in Medieval manuscripts, primarily. I'm especially interested in those relating to the health problems of women. I've been to Sicily to study some of them. I've filled ten notebooks with folk prescriptions. They're fun to read."

Ann Stevens' eyes stretch. "I hope you're not one of these, uh…people who is into herbal medicine and all of that mind-over-matter stuff." Here, she seems to catch herself, but it's too late. She says, "I mean, do you believe in *modern* medicine?"

Edna feels her anger rise as she struggles to hide it. She keeps eye contact with Ann Stevens. "Miss Stevens, in my profession as a nurse, I follow the advice of the patient's doctor. Folk medicine is strictly a hobby of mine; but for your information, there's a lot of wisdom in the ways of the ancient world, especially in medicinal remedies for human and animal ailments."

"Such as?"

"Well, we certainly know the curative effects of certain teas and things like mint and dill and marjoram and anise. Don't we?"

Ann Stevens lifts the glass to her mouth. "And alcohol. Don't forget alcohol."

"Even alcohol had its place." Edna suddenly feels foolish. This is *not* the conversation she came here to have. "Miss Stevens, you mentioned bedsores. Does your mother suffer from very *severe* bedsores?"

"Yes, and to be perfectly frank with you, she spends entirely too much time in bed. I hassle her, the doctor hassles her, her sister calls her from Canada and hassles her; we all hassle her about it and it does no good. So anybody going into that house to nurse her should be aware that it's a problem. She's just getting weaker and weaker. And there are people over a hundred walking around, even jogging every day, living active lives." Ann Stevens tries to smile. "Miss Nowell, if you are hired for this job, I hope you can get my mother out of her bed, get her back into life."

"Has she had any therapy?"

"Oh, yes, physical and mental. But you see, she's very set in her ways, very determined to have her way. You know the type."

"Yes, my own mother, for example."

And delightful laughter suddenly bursts from the two women; and Edna suddenly feels as though some sort of stern barrier between them has just been dispelled.

"You know, I have a feeling," says Ann Stevens. "It's just a feeling—"

"Yes?"

"A feeling that you and Deba might actually get along, that she might *like* you. You're proper and conservative, studious and soft-spoken. She likes soft-spoken women. I must admit I had reservation about hiring a colored lady. But not after meeting you. And besides, had you not told me over the phone, I would not have known it by meeting you face-to-face. So, if you're interested in the job, Miss Nowell, why, I think you can consider it yours."

Now, Edna thinks, here comes the hard part. She knows she is no longer so sure she wants the job. Something feels wrong about the whole situation. She certainly feels that she knows the temperaments of old people, but Mrs. Ursula Stevens is still too much of a mystery for her. Edna feels she needs to know more. "Well, I appreciate your confidence in me, Miss Stevens, and I certainly will *consider*—"

"Consider? You mean you came up here unsure about whether or not you want the job?"

"Not exactly. But I do feel I need to know more. I mean, just to be sure I'm the right nurse for your mother."

Now she can see that Ann Stevens has suddenly grown stiff with indignation. With her thin wet lips pressed tightly together, she's suddenly glaring at Edna. But, so far, she's speechless. Finally, Ann Stevens says, "Just what is it that you need to know, Miss Nowell?"

"Well, let's see." She opens her hand and the notepaper is still there. "I need to know the type of insurance your mother holds. I never take a private position without such information. Also who comes and goes at the house. Then there's the question of my living quarters. Your mother wasn't very clear about that."

"I see, I see." Ann Stevens reaches for the bottle of bourbon and pours herself about an inch and a half, and then she says, "Mother has Blue Cross. She was on my father's policy up till his death seven years ago and it's continued. Now what else did you want to know?"

"About my room. How is the house arranged?"

"Your room would be off the kitchen and you'd have your own bath. The laundry room is behind the kitchen. There's a washer and a dryer. Oh, yes, Mother has a cat, Lilly. Feeding and caring for Lilly would also be your job."

"May I ask who's taking care of Mrs. Stevens now?"

"A temporary nurse. How much time do you need, Miss Nowell, to make up your mind?" Ann Stevens lifts the bourbon to her mouth and drinks, this time without closing her eyes.

For the first time Edna lifts her own glass and takes the tiniest sip of the harsh liquor. Immediately she suspects it is a mistake because she sees something change in Ann Stevens' face. Edna closes her eyes for the hair of a second as the liquid slides down, burning all the way to the pit of her empty stomach. This is the first time she's ever tasted this stuff. And she starts coughing. "Excuse me," she says. If she had barnacles they would now be standing high on her back. "Tastes like something you'd put in a car."

Ann Stevens smiles. "You don't drink, do you?"

"I've been known to sip a glass of wine on occasion, usually in some restaurant with dinner."

"Your résumé says—" Ann Stevens picks it up, "ah, age thirty-three but nothing about marriage. Were you ever married? I guess what I want to know is, will you be dating, that is, men?"

Edna sighs, quickly closing and opening her eyes like an impatient child. "I wouldn't rule it out, Miss Stevens, but I can assure you that I'd *never* bring any man into your mother's house, if that's what you're concerned about. But there's another matter I wanted to ask about, a very important one. Money."

"Oh, yes, salary," says Ann Stevens. "Deba told me what your last job paid. But you didn't live with this—uh, what's her name, Wellington? Did you?"

"No, I didn't."

"In Washington, DC, that may be a perfectly normal salary, Miss Nowell, but out in Seattle, it would be a bit much, especially if you were getting free room and board."

"I see. Then perhaps you can tell me the salary you have in mind . . . ?"

"Mother and I were in the ballpark of about half of that."

Edna's eyebrows lift. "I see. Is that firm? Non-negotiable?"

"We couldn't afford any more; not with my salary and her pension and inheritance, the pittance that they are. But you know, Miss Nowell, the cost of living is so much cheaper out there, *so* much cheaper."

"Yes, I thought of that." Edna looks at her wristwatch. "My goodness, it's late!"

"Yes, it is," says Ann Stevens, glancing at her own wristwatch. "I suppose we should go down. We can have an early lunch!"

Ten minutes later at a table for two in the plush hotel restaurant, by a long trough with well-maintained ivy, Ann Stevens immediately orders the wine waiter to bring a bottle of excellent French Cabernet Sauvignon. In the background Edna heard Ravel's "Bolero," much distorted by the clicking of knives and forks and the hum of polite voices.

The waiter comes. They order.

The food comes quickly and they start eating now to the rhythm of Strauss' "Emperor's Waltz."

Ann Stevens, who is still acting remarkably sober after so much bourbon, says, "Are you still interested now that you know the salary?" She cuts into her steak.

Edna looks up from the remains of her own steak. "Yes, I think so, although I need time to consider it."

"How much time?"

"I can let you know in a week."

"A *week?*" says Ann Stevens, raising her voice. "Why so long? Are you interviewing elsewhere?"

Edna forks a smidgen of steak into her mouth and slowly chews it till her tongue is satisfied that it's ready to swallow. "No, I'm not considering any other job. In fact, I was wondering if you might not be interviewing other nurses."

She seems to almost duck from Edna's words. "We did get about a dozen responses to the ad. You're the first to be interviewed. I haven't given anyone else reason to hope. Your credentials—Howard University Hospital and the University of Maryland—were so much more impressive than the rest."

The waiter turns up again at this moment and says, "Is everything okay?" They reassure him and he goes away and comes back immediately with a colorful dessert menu but they say no.

Edna walks Ann Stevens back to the elevator doors where they stop. Edna's watch tells her it's twelve-thirty. Not a bad time of the day to get out of the city to the highway, to drive back to the District. It will be dark when she gets home. And her roommate, Tanya, a nurse from Russia, will be dying of curiosity; anxious to hear what happened; desperate to know if she'll have to start the painful process of looking for another roommate. Edna knows that Tanya dreads the thought of her, Edna, moving.

Now standing at the elevator doors, in a tired voice, Ann Stevens says, "I wasn't going to tell you this, but I might as well. There are two other candidates for the position. I don't like them." As she glances at Edna suddenly she looks exhausted. "Frankly, I like you. My mother would like you. I hope you take the job."

"Thank you, Miss Stevens, for being honest with me. And thank you for lunch." Edna is extending her right hand to Ann Stevens.

The other woman takes the hand and shakes it. "So, I'll hear from you in a week?" Meanwhile, Ann Stevens' cell phone chimes. With an apology, she quickly turns it off.

"I'll try to make it sooner, if I can," Edna says. She doesn't mean to sound so mysterious. It's just coming out this way. And she feels the awkwardness of her own smile.

They shake hands and for a moment they engage in an eye-to-eye staring contest. And if she's measuring Edna, Edna is also measuring her.

But Ann Stevens blinks first. And as far as Edna is concerned, that does it. Without changing her pleasant expression, Edna makes up her mind at that very moment.

BERNADETTE'S DOUBT

AT HIS HOLE-PUNCH MACHINE, Damon Spencer was happy and singing. He wanted to sprout like spring, dance and jump—

There I go, there I go
Thhhhhhhhhhere I go
Pretty baby. . .

trying to imitate King Pleasure singing James Moody's "I'm In The Mood For Love," and nobody could hear him for the racket of the floor full of clanging machinery.

Damon didn't care. He was feeling good.

Just before the coffee break, he turned off the punch, checked his cell phone for messages, found none, and bopped slowly over to the Pepsi machine. He knew he was pushing it. He wasn't supposed to leave his work area before the big hand was straight up. But he had an urgent plan.

And for it to work he had to be at the Pepsi machine early. He inserted money and a bottle of Pepsi plopped down the rubber chute. He got another one. Other workers were now heading for the refreshment area.

As the new girl Bernadette was about to insert her money, Damon said, "Hey, would you like a Pepsi?" And he held it straight out at her. With a smile, she took it and thanked him.

"Wanna walk outside for a few minutes?"

She looked at the time on her cell phone. "We have only a few minutes."

"We got time. Let's go."

"Okay."

Outside, on the sidewalk, in front of Universal Speakers, Inc., Michigan Avenue traffic was steady. The shadow of the red brick building stretched out to the middle of the street. Beyond was a bright splash of sunlight.

"How about dinner and a movie tonight?" said Damon.

"I can't," she said.

"I'm not gonna give up. I'm gonna keep trying till you say yes."

To his surprise, the following Friday at work, Bernadette said, "My friend Tracy and her boyfriend are having a cookout in the backyard tomorrow. Wanna go as my date?"

It was not what he had in mind but he said, "Yeah, sure."

"Tracy lives in Evanston."

Damon was definitely not anxious to go. He thought he knew what the trip to Evanston really meant. It would be pass-judgment-on-Bernadette'-new-potential-boyfriend time. After the review process they would get together for a "girl-to-girl" talk. And he would pass or fail. He felt trapped.

When they got there, Bernie's father, Dermot, and her sister, Concetta, were already there—in the living room. This was a surprise he wasn't ready for!

Damon shook hands with Dermot—who'd been watching television with Tracy's kids, both on the floor on their bellies watching the screen. Damon sat down and Dermot refocused on the TV, ignoring the new young man. Damon furtively checked his cell phone messages. No new messages!

"I'll need a ride back south with you Bernie because Daddy is leaving early," said Concetta. "Okay?"

After introducing Damon to her father and sister, Bernie marched Damon into the kitchen and introduced him to Tracy. Tracy was chopping celery.

He noticed right away that Tracy wouldn't look him straight in the eye. Instead, she gave him a half-assed sideways smile, and a hi there, and kept her hands busy on the chopping block.

Later, with a can of Bud in hand, Damon wandered outside. Marmaduke was in the backyard cooking beefsteaks on the grill. The meat was black and hard looking. Damon was self-consciously aware of the other man who was at least ten years older than he.

He stood there at Marmaduke's side watching him poke at the grilling meat, smelling the pungent smoke lift from the rack. Damon knew he should make conversation but he couldn't think of anything to say. He couldn't talk about the one thing on his mind—why Bernie brought him here.

Suddenly the wind shifted and the smoke blew straight into Damon's face. He stepped farther back. The smoke was pungent enough to choke anybody. He got behind Marmaduke, out of the smoke's path.

Then, Dermot, with the sunlight on his massive bald head, came out with a can of Bud in his right fist, a twinkle in his sly eye. "Smells good."

Marmaduke nodded and picked up his own can of beer from a stool and took a sip. "You got a free hand, put some more coals on for me, Der."

They all gathered to sit down for dinner. Attempting to be more sociable, Damon grinned at Marmaduke and said, "Hey, man, how about some music?"

And the older man said, "Sure, go ahead, the record player is in the living room."

Damon went in and put on recordings by Bags and the All-Stars, *Jamal at the Perishing*, Wardell Gray, that Central Avenue sound, and some jitterbugging waltzing by Eric Dolphy. He came back to the dinner table feeling better. The food was good.

Against the hip music in the background, Dermot and Marmaduke started talking baseball.

"You like baseball, Damon?" said Marmaduke.

"I don't follow it that much." He felt guilty.

Bernie said, "Dad, why don't you and Marmy talk about something we can all share?"

Bernie and Tracy were silently communicating by eye contact with Marmaduke and Dermot.

Dermot stood up and excused himself for skipping dessert, then waved goodbye to everybody and headed for the door.

Bernie was driving along in silence. They were on Lake Shore Drive, heading south. Bernie coughed.

Concetta was asleep in the back seat.

After another long silence, Bernie looked at Damon and said, "Okay, I may as well tell you. Tracy doesn't think we're good for each other."

He looked at her. "What's that suppose to mean?"

"It's *her* opinion. Okay? I value her opinion. Okay? She's my best friend. Okay?"

"Sure, okay." Damon looked out the window.

"It's just her opinion," she said. "But do you think she's right?"

"It don't matter what I think."

"What d'you mean?" She was angry.

Now a kind of silence surrounded them. The car roared on among the other cars on Lake Shore Drive.

A week later, Damon had calmed down. He wanted to put the incident of Tracy's opinion of the relationship behind them and go on. At the same time he reluctantly agreed to go to Bernie's mother's place that coming Sunday.

Bernie drove up to the curb in front of Damon's apartment building on Vincennes Avenue and he was standing outside waiting.

Dan was in the backyard at the grill pushing thick German sausages around with a long black fork. Blue smoke lifted from the coals beneath and the meat popped and sizzled.

Damon was sitting in an exaggeratedly relaxed manner in a plastic chair next to Tabitha, listening to her complaints about her new boss ("too stupid for words") at the government office where she worked.

Bernie moved about the yard in a restless, bored manner, tossing the ball for the spaniel, China. The dog chased it and brought it back to her then she had to twist it from her mouth and throw it again.

They heard a car stop out front and in a few minutes Concetta and a tall young man, color of tree bark, came around the house. They were both wearing shorts and sandals.

"*Surprise!*" said Tabitha.

Damon stood up and glanced at Bernadette who had stopped with the ball in her right hand and was looking at her younger sister and the young man.

Now Concetta, grinning, came over with the young man.

Damon reached down and picked up a piece of gravel and threw it out toward the back fence. Bernie came over and touched his arm. She didn't say anything.

"I wanted it to be a *surprise*. Why don't you introduce Hernando to Damon, Concetta?"

By dinnertime it was clear to Damon that Hernando was one of Bernie's old boyfriends. Seated around a big wooden table, they were eating by candlelight on the screened back porch. Damon was sitting next to Bernadette. Hernando was across from them.

Dan, at the head of the table, was focused on his plate but he was asking Hernando about his work out at Arlington. Hernando apparently worked with horses at the racetrack.

Tabitha, at the other end, was emitting a stream of chatter aimed at all of them. Midway through dinner she said, "Y'all mind if I turn on the radio or something? Don't you think we need a little music?"

After dinner, while Tabitha and Concetta were clearing away the dishes, Bernie said, "Excuse us, but Hernando and I are going for a drive. We have some things we need to talk about." While she was saying this, Damon noticed she avoided looking in his direction.

Damon's mouth opened as though he was about to speak but he didn't say anything. He saw from Hernando's face that Bernie's announcement was a total surprise.

After Bernie and Hernando left, they all moved into the house. Tabitha went to the kitchen and the rest of them to the living room. And Damon sulked. He sat on the couch and sulked.

After awhile, Dan excused himself and said he was going to bed. "Have to get up early. Going fishing."

Tabitha came in from the kitchen and said goodnight too and continued on upstairs. He could hear the dishwasher humming back there, things clanging in it.

Concetta was over in one of the armchairs. "My sister hasn't seen Hernando in almost two years."

"Well, looks like she's making up for lost time," said Damon. "Listen, Concetta. Do me a favor?"

"What?"

"Drive me home."

"You're just going to leave just like that?"

"It wouldn't be any ruder than your sister's being toward me."

She smiled. "I guess you got me there. Okay. I don't know why they're taking so long. Okay."

They went out to the street where Concetta's car was parked at the curb in front of the house.

Sitting in the car, Concetta turned to him. "Damon, don't judge her too harshly. She's not ready to settle down yet."

"I don't care."

She started the car. A pair of headlights from an approaching car behind them filled the interior with sudden light.

But instead of passing, the car drove up behind them. Damon looked back over his shoulder. He saw Bernie in the driver's seat. Hernando was climbing out of the passenger side. He climbed the steps to the dark porch.

Bernie got out too. She came up and bent down and leaned her arm on the opened car window and looked in at Damon. "Where are you going?"

"Home." He refused to look at her.

"Just like that?"

He didn't say anything. He was looking through the windshield into the darkness beyond. Concetta was looking at him too.

"You mad at me?" said Bernie.

"No, I'm not mad at you," Damon said. But he was already dreading having to see her every day from now on at work.

RUSSELL AND ME

RUSSELL AND I had been living together for about six months when I saw a small ad in *The Sacramento Bee* newspaper about a group therapy session on love relationships. The address was an office building on 3rd between N Street and O Street. There was a telephone number.

A woman named Rose Smith would direct it. The ad said she was a therapist for relationship issues. I checked her out online. Her degree was from an online university. She also had a Facebook account but it was blocked. On LinkedIn I saw her listing but there was no picture of her.

The sessions were to take place on a weekend two weeks away. It would start on Friday morning and end Sunday night. It proposed to give couples a chance to interact with other couples and thereby find ways to improve aspects of their relationships that needed work. The ad said bring your own lunch.

I showed the ad to Russell and suggested that we sign up for it. At first he was taken aback. He said you think our relationship needs work? I said all relationships need constant work. Come on Russell, it'll be fun. And after coaxing him for two or three days he finally said okay, let's do it.

So, I called the number. After one ring a woman answered, saying hello this is Rose. She sounded nice. I could tell by her voice she was a heavyset woman. I can't always tell a person's size by voice but sometimes I can. Rose told me we could pay by check when we arrive. She took our names and said you can park in the lot behind the building, just drive through the alley.

I made sandwiches of ham and cheese with tomatoes and lettuce. I packed paper plates and napkins and bottled water.

Leaving our apartment at 7:30, Friday morning, we drove there from our place on J between 17th and 18th. The streets, this early in the morning, were without the usual traffic. I loved it. Driving was easy. We parked in the lot behind the building and walked to the front. The lobby was empty. It was too early for any of the other offices in the building to be open. We took the elevator up to the third floor. The elevator door hesitated, then opened.

The conference room door was already open. As we approached, a flood of electric light poured out into the dark hallway. We entered the well-lighted large room. The woman I imagined to be Rose came toward us with a big smile. She was just as I imagined her: a big woman with blond hair and a very rosy pink face with dimples and a big smile. I told her who we were. Rose shook our hands as we exchanged greetings.

Although we were only five minutes late, two other couples, young white couples our age, about twenty-five, were already there sitting stiffly on pillows. Rose led us over and introduced us, and said, "Join the party!"

They were Lena and Scott, Rudy and Azella.

I should have taken the word "party" as a clue of what was to come, but the clue went right by me. Even before we sat down, two other couples were arriving.

Once we were all there, seven couples including Russell and me, we all got to know each other pretty quickly. We were all in our twenties and thirties.

The only other African-American couple was Cathy and Jeff. Cathy smiled almost constantly. She was cute and small, Jeff, big, tall, awkward, clearly ill at ease. I don't remember what kind of work they did.

Scott had red hair and a kindly face. He was a dentist. His wife, Lena, smiled a lot but it didn't seem sincere. She was a cute, petite blond. Both Rudy and his wife Azella were lawyers working in different firms. They were the kind of couple you easily forget soon after you meet them. I can close my eyes now and see the faces of all the others, but Rudy and Azella's faces are blank. I didn't get to know them; we never had a face-to-face conversation.

Sam was a short stocky guy with a heavy New Jersey accent. His wife, Rachel, was a natural blond, very slender, almost pretty with a southern accent. And then there was the youngest couple: Roy and Doreen. He was in real estate and Doreen was in college working on a BA. She was nervous with a perpetual frown.

Rose told us to spread out around the room, so we all got up and moved about till we formed a circle around her as she stood in the center of the room. We were all sitting on big fluffy, colorful pillows on the floor.

Rose said, "Let's get started. I want everybody to relax and have a good time. The more relaxed you are, the more receptive to improving your life you will be. Talk among yourselves and socialize a bit. I'll be right back."

Rose waddled across the room and went on out into the hallway. For a moment there was silence then laughter. I think Lena laughed first then Phyllis giggled. She was a high school teacher. So was her husband, Tom. Cathy, leaving Jeff on the pillows, came over.

She said, "You guys live in the city?"

"Yes," I said.

And so we all made small talk till Rose returned.

"Okay," Rose said, "Let's get started. I want to start by asking each of you to talk a little bit about your relationship, tell each other what you want that you are not getting. It can be anything. Anything! Just look at your spouse or companion and say what you wish he or she did differently. Let's start with you, Lena. What do you wish Scott did differently?"

"Well, it's not so much what I wish he did differently," she said, "I wish he would go down on me more often."

"Okay," said Rose. "That's a good start. Let's stay with that thought. Scott?"

"I like to go down, I mean I like oral sex but—"

"You like it done to you," said Lena.

"Do we have a selfish issue here?" said Rose.

And one by one, couples around the room talked openly about their sexual activities, or the lack of such activities. I was watching Russell on the sly to see his reaction. When it came our turn to talk, Rose asked me directly how about you, Darla.

I didn't feel secure enough to talk as openly as other women had; besides, Russell and I hadn't known each other very long. Some of these people had been together for many years. Sheepishly, I said we don't have any problems.

But the truth was I wanted Russell to be rougher with me, to spank me, but I didn't have the nerve to ask him. I wanted him to take me across his lap and spank me. Not real hard but hard enough. But I didn't have the nerve to ask him to do it. I felt he should already know that was what I wanted. But I knew that feeling was silly. How could he have known? I also was hoping he would turn out to be open-minded. My fantasy had long been to have two men make love to me at the same time. I was afraid to say this to him or anybody.

"Everybody has areas they can improve in," Rose said. "That's why you are here, to improve."

"I didn't know this was going to be just about sex," Doreen said.

"Sex is a big part of any love relationship," said Rose.

"But—" said Doreen.

Rose cut her off, "If a relationship has problems it usually stems from some issue in that area." She was now addressing the whole group.

Somebody coughed.

Then directly to Russell, Rose said, "What about you, Russell? What do you want Darla to do differently or to improve on?"

I grew tense, waiting for his answer.

He was hesitating. "Well," he said, "It's hard to say, because she's so perfect." He was grinning like a Cheshire cat, and I had the feeling there was something on his mind, but he was not going to say what it was and that left me vaguely troubled.

Rose continued with this line of probing and when the talk wandered away from sex to things like sharing household responsibilities, she brought it back to sex. This was where she wanted to keep the focus. This went on all morning. We couples took turns airing our emotions right up till lunchtime.

We'd all brought our lunches so we all relaxed and ate and actually talked, couple to couple, more easily during lunch than we had before. We shared lunch with each other too. That was the fun part. We were relaxing more, and talking more openly, not about sex, but about day-to-day matters, such as where one might find good tomatoes in Sacramento, or which dry cleaners in midtown were the best. At one point, Azella recommended her favorite restaurant. Roy said real estate was picking up and that it was a good time to buy a house because it was a buyer's market. That was the sort of talk we engaged in.

After lunch, more of the same, more talk about sex; but now that we were more relaxed after sharing food and engaging in ordinary conversation, the sex talk seemed easier to manage. Even Doreen seemed more at ease with it.

Saturday? The same thing: talk, lunch, more talk.

Then Sunday, everything changed.

In the morning Rose said, "I want each of you to select a mate from among the other couples, to talk with, to even touch. This is a test of jealousy. If any of you are hiding jealous tendencies this will bring those tendencies to the surface. Jealousy is a destructive emotion. It needs to be dealt with before a relationship can be fully healthy."

I looked around the room at faces. At first, most of us were puzzled. What did Rose mean by touching? Where was this session going? I was surprised by this turn of events. I kept looking around, trying to gauge reactions. Rachel and Doreen both had lifted eyebrows. That said a lot. But they were also grinning. The men all seemed okay with it, including Russell. They were smiling. Don't get me wrong. I was okay with it too. It was just that I hadn't expected Rose to request such a thing.

Rose said, "Select someone you are attracted to. Just look around the room and make your choice. If you can't make a decision I will select someone for you."

She was standing in the middle of the circle, turning about, looking from face-to-face; waiting for the first person to start. So far, no one had moved.

"Come on," Rose said, "let's get started."

For a while couples talked among themselves, trying quietly to make decisions about who they wanted to sit with, who they wanted to talk to, who they wanted to touch.

Cathy, Jeff's wife, was chosen by Tom, the high school teacher, and Phyllis' husband.

I chose Jeff. He was tall with strong facial features. Unlike Russell, who was light skinned and average size, Jeff was tall and muscular, and his skin was a beautiful blue black.

Scott chose Doreen, the college student and Roy's wife.

Russell chose Lena. She seemed pleased that Russell selected her. Her secret smile suggested this. She constantly blinked in a fake innocent manner. I didn't care for her. She was too cutesy.

And so the selections continued until everybody was sitting with somebody other than their mate.

Then Rose said, "I want everybody to undress. Come on. Don't hesitate. Take off your clothes. This is an essential part of becoming completely open and honest with yourself and each other. When you are undressed, you are in your natural state. That is where truth and honesty begins."

The men were first. They were watching each other. Rudy was the first man to fully undress. I could see why. He was well hung and obviously proud of it. When Jeff was finally undressed, I was impressed by the beauty of his body.

I looked across the room at Russell and Lena. Russell was down to his underwear and Lena was slowly unbuttoning her blouse. She still had that little fixed smile.

Other women were beginning to peal off clothing. Phyllis was the first woman to stand before her pillow fully naked. Her stomach was flat, her breasts small and well shaped. She was beautiful.

"Okay, don't start touching yet," said Rose, "Talk for a time and get to know each other."

Every once in a while I looked over at Russell and Lena. I noticed that Russell was doing the same thing. Occasionally, he shot a glance my way. But he and Lena were not talking. Lena's hand was resting lightly on his thigh. It was very close to Mr. Know-It-All. And Rose hadn't yet given word to touch. Goodness! Lena was eager to get her hands on my man! I tried to read Russell's expression but couldn't. He was keeping a poker face.

Meanwhile, Jeff was telling me about the Honda he had just bought. He was very excited about it.

Rose said okay, "I would like for you all to just gently touch each other: on the arms, legs, anywhere. Just touch, gently."

We obeyed our teacher. I was getting turned on as Jeff stroked my arms and thighs. He took my feet in his big hands and massaged them gently. He was breathing deeply and heavily. I could tell his lust was rising.

Across the room Lena was lying flat on her back across the pillow. Russell was stroking her stomach, then he ran his hands down her thighs. I was curious but I felt no jealousy. He kept doing this very slowly. Her eyes were closed.

I closed my eyes and let my mind follow the comfort of Jeff's hands. Nearby, I heard a guttural sound then a cry. "Oh, my God!" It was a woman's voice. I saw Tom behind Cathy. They were both on their knees. He was grunting and humping away. And she was crying out "Oh, my God! Yes! Yes!"

Rose said, "It's all right, follow your desire. See where it takes you." She was standing a few feet behind Tom watching with assumed detachment.

Then she touched Tom on the back and said, "Stop right there! Come with me, I want to talk with you about your emotions."

I thought what a hell of time to stop a man—just before he is about to finish. But Rose was definitely in charge. Even of Tom's release.

Tom stood up with his erection standing tall, and Rose took his hand and led him out into a small side room.

Four or five other couples were now making love. The sounds they were making were such wonderful animal sounds. I thought, how beautiful the human animal! This is the human animal at its most natural!

Across the room, Russell was on top of Lena. Her legs were spread and locked around him. What did I feel at that moment? What did I think? I do know I did not feel anger or jealousy. I guess I was surprised that Russell would make love to another woman in front of me, and in front of all these people. But since other people were doing it first, it probably made it easier. When in Rome! I remember thinking that people are just like sheep. They follow the leading sheep.

Meanwhile, Jeff was still stroking my body. I could tell he wasn't about to do any more than that. Had he wanted to, I would not have objected.

I began to think this was what Rose intended all along. The slow build up to this. The fancy talk was just a prelude. But what was she doing with Tom?

Soon it was obvious when we all could hear Tom releasing himself with a cry like a bull's guttural cry at the moment of castration.

And across the room Russell made a similar sound—one more restrained but an unmistakable cry of urgent release. And Lena was saying, "Give it all to me! Give it all to me!"

I took Jeff's hand and placed it you know where, hoping he would get the idea. I wanted it now. Why not? Russell had already redefined our relationship. We'd never talked about possible sex with other people. But maybe now we didn't have to.

But Jeff removed his hand. He was shyly looking around the room and occasionally grinning at me. I then noticed that he was busy watching other couples while stroking me absentmindedly. Meanwhile, his wife, Cathy, was lying on the pillow where Tom left her, with her arms locked around her knees. Her eyes were closed in deep concentration or deep disappointment.

At this point, Rose and Tom came back into the room together. She was smiling and he was looking a little embarrassed or guilty. I couldn't tell which.

"Okay, guys," Rose said, "It's time to talk about what we felt. So get dressed and let's start talking."

Everybody got dressed.

Rose questioned each couple about their feelings during the swapping. Then she came to Scott.

"Scott, how did you feel about Russell being with your wife?"

Scott didn't say anything.

Rose said, "Did you feel any jealousy? Did you feel threatened?"

"No, not at all," said Scott.

Rose said, "Russell is a good-looking man. You weren't worried about Lena becoming seriously attracted to him?"

"Not at all," he said. "I might have been, I guess, if he'd been white."

"Wow!" said Russell.

Roy said, "Scott, that sounds like racism."

Scott turned red. "It's not racism. I'm not racist! I just know my wife. I know she's not interested in a serious relationship with a black guy."

Everybody looked at Lena. With eyes downcast, she was smiling. She avoided returning the gaze by looking down at her own hands folded on her lap.

Then Rose said, "How about you Russell? How did you feel about Darla being with another man?"

"It was okay. They didn't do anything anyway."

Everybody laughed.

"You had to be watching to know that, right?" Rose said. "Were you glad they didn't do anything?"

"I don't know, Rose. I have to think about that one. Besides, I only glanced over there a couple of times."

Rudy said, "That's all you had time to do. Right?"

Everybody laughed again.

"And you, Darla. How about you? What did you feel about Russell and Lena being together?"

"Actually," I said, "I liked it. I know Russell loves me. I love him. I've long felt that sex has nothing to do with love. Love is in a realm by itself. And sex is just sex. Because he did it to another woman doesn't mean he lost his love for me."

Rose said, "You feel the same way, Russell?"

He hesitated. "I have to think about it, Rose."

That answer worried me. Looking at his troubled face, I immediately had the feeling that our having participated in these sessions would eventually lead to the demise of our relationship. Ironic, because I had set out with the notion that they would help to bring us closer together.

Finally, at the end of the day, we all said our goodbyes. The sessions were behind us. Even as we left the room, walking out into the hallway, Rose was trying to get commitments for another session, in the near future. Nobody was ready to make another commitment. But some said, "Maybe."

When we got home, Russell slammed the door angrily and walked straight to the refrigerator and got a beer. He leaned against the counter and snapped it open and took a long drink. I watched him.

"Are you okay?" I said.

He looked at me a long time. His eyes were burning with contempt. Then he said, "I'm okay." He took another long drink of beer and again said, "I'm okay."

VICTORIA

IT WAS A COLD MONDAY MORNING, in November, with nothing above Chicago but a thick grayness that passed for a sky. The view from Victoria Fouche's large living room bay window, looking out onto South Parkway, showed an occasional car going by north or south; but mostly what Victoria saw were the women walking by going to the bus stop, half a block north of her white stone house.

She stretched and contracted her fingers, trying to free herself of the stiffness that, lately, lasted most of the day. Arthritis! She had three vacant rooms in the basement she felt she needed to rent, and the ad in the *Chicago Defender,* Saturday, so far, hadn't brought hordes rushing to her door. People passing by on the street, unless they were looking for such a sign, didn't notice her *For Rent* sign in the upper left corner of her bay window.

Also, for three days now, Victoria's beloved dog, Baby, had not come home. Victoria tried to remember exactly the last moment she saw Baby. As nearly as she could remember, she last saw Baby Friday afternoon around three. She was going down the front steps.

Baby was an old, overweight, black mixed breed—mostly Lab—who could barely walk. It was unlike Baby to wander off like this. She was old in dog years, sixteen, and it had been at least six or seven years since she'd gone off on an adventure. Victoria feared the worst. Normally, on a morning like this, Baby would be resting on the porch right at the edge, watching the people and the cars going by. The mornings, and the rest of the last three days, hadn't been right without Baby.

Victoria felt all she had left was Baby, her house, and her hats. She sold the hats—they *were* for sale—and she rented out every crevice of her house she could get away with.

This morning, two years after the end of the Second World War, in her normal way, she sat in her parlor window surrounded by an array of bright and fancy hats—hats made for her by a talented hat maker, Mrs. Sarah Mae Jackson, in Atlanta, Georgia. Mrs. Jackson's cut was fifty percent. Had it not been for the hats, and Victoria's age, she might have been taken for a 1890s New Orleans prostitute, at the window, soliciting customers by tapping on the window with a quarter.

Actually, in her younger days, she *had* been a New Orleans Creole prostitute, who, with a quarter, tapped on the window to attract male passersby. She never talked about it to anybody nowadays; and although she remembered the times with a sense of loss—it may have been her lost youth she was lamenting—she, at the same time, knew in her bosom that they were mean, and often brutal, dishonest, and desperate times.

Now, in the bay window, with a cup of coffee sitting on the window ledge, Victoria watched for neighborhood women, not men; and when she saw a likely candidate, using the edge of a quarter (or, when she didn't have a quarter handy, her wedding ring) to tap on the window to attract the female passersby. And she knew most of the women, either on sight or by name. Some of them took the bus to the north side to do house cleaning. One was a manicurist at the Metropolitan Barbershop. Others worked in factories. They knew her too—knew her as the hat lady with the stone house on South Parkway across from the Ritz Hotel and Lounge, where jazz musicians played late into the night, giving the neighborhood a warm and happy,—even cozy—feeling. It reminded Victoria of New Orleans.

But Victoria, this morning, was also waiting for Chaucer. He'd promised last Thursday that he would stop by this morning to finish the plumbing work on the sink in the basement apartment so she could rent it out.

None of the rooms in the house, with the exception of Victoria's own bedroom, were bigger than a large closet, and everybody, with the exception of those in the basement, had to come through Victoria's living room to enter or leave. Victoria herself both liked and disliked this arrangement. On the one hand she could keep her eye on everybody—make sure nothing unacceptable was going on—and on the other, she was annoyed by the constant intrusion, the foot traffic, kids running in and out, leaving the front door open.

But in a way, she'd come to think of some of these people as family. Regina Ashe, with her two kids, Luke and Willa Mae, moved in only a year and a half ago, but already Victoria thought of Regina as a friend.

On her way out to work, Regina, who was passing for white on the job, had told Victoria that Luke was staying home sick today, and to make sure he didn't try to go outside and play. He was supposed to stay upstairs in bed.

Victoria thought about Regina passing and smiled. Funny how a colored person can tell but the white folks can't. She remembered going into Carson's and seeing Regina behind the jewelry counter. She smiled and winked at her and kept walking.

Now Victoria sat there waiting and watching, feeling unusually excited, despite her depression over Baby. She didn't know why but she just had a feeling she was going to get lucky this morning and sell a hat. She was feeling this way when she spotted one of her oldest neighbors, Mrs. Ruby Louise Young. Mrs. Young had to be in her sixties, yet she got on that bus, come rain or shine, and rode up north to clean house once a week for the same white family she'd been with for the last fifteen years.

The moment she saw Mrs. Young, all bundled in her shabby gray coat, Victoria tapped three rapid times on the glass, this time with her wedding ring. Mrs. Young was stepping along briskly, in her nurse-type low heels, walking faster and looking livelier than lots of folks twenty years younger than she. Victoria fingered for her to come in.

Victoria watched Mrs. Young climb the steps, holding onto the black iron railing, till she gained the porch.

When Victoria opened the door for Mrs. Young, Regina's boy, Luke slipped by Victoria and went out with a bag of garbage. She noticed him and didn't notice him because she was so focused on Mrs. Young. "Come on in, Ruby." said Victoria.

"Victoria, I'm late for work, honey. What is it?"

"It'll take just a minute. Just one minute. I just got this new shipment in Friday." She closed the door and took Mrs. Young by her coat sleeve and literally pulled her through the living room over to the parlor window, where the hats were spread out on the parlor bench.

Victoria picked up a silly looking yellow hat that looked like an upside-down bird's nest with a black veil attached to it. Victoria was saying, " . . . And the minute I saw it, I just knew it was you. It was just made for you, Ruby, girl."

She was holding it out in front of the flustered Mrs. Young. "Here," Victoria said, "Try it on. Wear it to work! Go on! Keep it! Just see if you like it! I know it is perfect for you. Go on, put it on."

Reluctantly, Mrs. Young took the hat in one hand and pulled her wool cap off with the other.

Victoria pulled her over to the wall mirror in the foyer. "Here," she said, "let me turn on the light here, so you can see." And she hit the button and pushed Mrs. Young closer to the mirror and under the ceiling light. "Isn't it a darling? I think you just look *darling* in that hat."

Mrs. Young looked critically in the mirror, at herself, turning her head from side to side, saying, "Victoria, now you know I ain't got no time to be trying on no hat this morning. I'll come back when—"

"Sure, sure," snapped Victoria, "just take it with you. I'm sure you'll love it."

"Victoria, now you know I can't wear no hat like this to work." Mrs. Young screwed up her face, looking at her old friend. "It's pretty but sho ain't gon keep my ears warm." And she carefully lifted the hat off and handed it back to Victoria.

But Victoria would not take it. Instead, she said, "Let me give you a bag. I'll put it in a bag for you. Don't you like it?"

"It's—"

"You'll like it. You just have to give yourself a chance, Ruby, girl. You have to wear it. Take it home and keep it for a few days."

"I can't take it to work, Victoria. Here, you take it back, and let me get out of here. I've already missed my bus."

"Then you'll pick it up on your way home?"

Mrs. Young was headed for the door. "Maybe. Let me think about it, Victoria." She reached for the doorknob. "I'm not sure I like it very—"

Victoria blurted out, "By the way, Ruby, you haven't by any chance seen my dog Baby down your way, have you?"

Mrs. Young shook her head. "I've got to go."

"It's darling on you, I'm telling you."

But Mrs. Young was out the door now and going down the steps.

Victoria was sick and frustrated as she closed the door, and returned to the parlor bench. The hat was just right for Ruby Young. She just needed to give herself a chance with it. Not just any woman could wear a hat that looked like an upside-down bird's nest. Victoria smiled faintly as she refocused on the street, touching her hair, making sure all the strands were in place. It was a habit she'd picked up years before when she was turning tricks in New Orleans, before her marriage to James, a porter on the railroad. She just had a feeling about it. James was probably dead by now. With his drinking and gambling, he wasn't cut out to last long.

She turned and looked over at the clock on the wall in the foyer, alongside the mirror she had forced Mrs. Young to inspect the hat in. It was eight-fifteen and Chaucer had said he'd be here between seven-thirty and eight. Always operating on CP-time. That was Chaucer. A wonder he'd done so well with his little plumbing business all these years. But then again people always needed plumbers, so they were pretty much at his mercy, which meant he could call the shots.

She got up and went back to the kitchen to get another cup of coffee. Polly, in her big cage, said, "Polly want a cracker, Polly want a cracker." Sometime when Baby was out of the house, Victoria let Polly out so she could wander around through the house just to exercise. And as Victoria poured coffee into her cup, she heard Luke's voice out in the backyard shouting, "It's Baby! Miss Fouche! It's your dog, Baby! Better come, quick!"

She climbed down the steps, holding onto the railing, and walked around the house as quickly as her old legs could carry her.1

In the backyard she saw Luke down on his knees, looking under the house.

"What is it, Luke?" She could hardly catch her breath.

"It's Baby! She's under there! She's not moving! I called her but she wouldn't come out."

"Oh, my God," said Victoria with her hand over her mouth. "Crawl under there, Luke, and pull her out."

Luke flopped to his belly and started crawling under the house.

"Be careful," Victoria said, "if she's sick, she might bite you."

Luke crawled under the house; and a moment later he backed out, pulling the stiff body of Baby by one of her back legs.

"Oh, my God," said Victoria. "She's dead. Baby is dead. Oh, my God. Oh, Luke, what am I going to do? Oh, my God!"

Luke said, "We'll have to have a funeral."

"Oh, my God; yes, we'll have to have a funeral."

THE EXCHANGE

"There are some secrets which do not permit themselves to be told."

—EDGAR ALLEN POE
"The Man of the Crowd"

WHEN I DECIDED to exchange teaching posts with another professor on the other end of the country in which I was born and in which I remain a citizen, I had the hardest example of my own inability to reduce disorder to an acceptable level. The initial idea of exchanging was his. This was in the early 1980s.

The other professor, who shall remain nameless, taught a rather strange version of the same subject I teach at my university on normal occasions. He described in detail his approach. He was enthusiastic but fearful that my university might not approve of his method. I quickly reassured him of the department's flexibility.

In his trickle of letters, my potential exchangee presented himself as a "laid back" person who had learned to accept the calamities of life. Well, I said to my wife, this exchange should be pleasant. I had heard from my colleagues that exchanges could turn out to be nightmares. This would be my first. Judging from his letters, I could not have hoped for a more understanding person with whom to trade.

I'd said no dogs or cats in the house and he assured me there would be none. I knew from my own series of dogs and cats in my previous homes that animals could cause wreckage—especially to furniture and carpets. I was simply trying to head off a problem.

It took six months' worth of correspondence to set up the transfer. I negotiated with our course committee and won its endorsement on what my substitute would teach. I told him everything I could think of about our house: its advantages and shortcomings. I drew up a long list of telephone numbers and addresses of local merchants I thought the best or most dependable along with the names and numbers of repair services. I told him exactly what to do in emergencies, gave him our doctor's name and address, and told our doctor about my exchangee, his wife, and their son. My wife arranged for the boy to be enrolled in the neighborhood high school. He was fifteen. Let's see. What else? God, I can't remember everything but I do remember my wife and I thought they deserved the best care we could give.

All during the six months before the exchange, I wrote to him two or three times a week—about the house, the school, insurance, the mail service, garbage pickup, the yard, lawn, helpful neighbors. In the whole time I got, in return, maybe one third as many letters from him. Well, I thought, he's busier than I plus no doubt more efficient and better organized and therefore in no need of having to write so often.

As I said, he lived on one coast and I on the other. My end was warmer than his. This fact brought us to consider the practicality of also exchanging cars. His was better suited for mountains (of which there were plenty in his area) and mine was a fair-weather one. The question was resolved quickly: we would leave our cars at home where they functioned best. The minute the decision to swap cars was made I phoned my car insurance guy and made the necessary adjustment. Then I quickly sent word that all was well on my end where the car was concerned, assuring him that he would be covered while driving. Three weeks later he responded saying he hadn't gotten around yet to seeing his guy. I waited. Finally, after two more weeks he sent a hasty note saying he had made the insurance arrangements. His car, he assured me, although two years older than mine, was in excellent condition.

My wife and I continued to work hard to get the house in the best possible shape. We replaced the worn carpet in the hall, repaired some of the siding on the windward side of the house. On the kitchen floor where the tile was cracked we replaced with new squares, had our neighbor the plumber install a new drainpipe under the kitchen sink because the old one leaked. We also depersonalized the house by taking away our most personal objects—such as family pictures—and storing them in the shed out back. In this way, they might claim the space better.

When there was only a week to go before the actual move was to take place, he wrote with the distressing news that his department still had not approved what I had requested to teach. Five months earlier, I had been led to believe otherwise. Thinking all was settled concerning the four courses, I had spent many hours preparing my materials, and now I had no time to junk those plans and start over. I telephoned him—in distress—but there was no response. In a few hours I tried again, and by then my anger was somewhat under control. When his wife got him to the phone he stammered an apology and told me that, although the titles of the courses were now different that I should not hesitate to use the same materials I had already worked up. Nobody, he said, would know the difference. Thanks a lot, I thought. Well, they wouldn't quite fit but I figured I could bend them a bit.

Then the time came.

We left the keys with a neighbor and took a taxi to the bus station then the bus to the airport. Once my wife and I were buckled into our seats on the airplane we agreed that there was nothing further we could do to make the exchangee and his family comfortable in our house. We'd left brochures for the furnace, the TV, the stove, the fridge, and the record player, along with a welcome note on the table. If there were problems each family was only a telephone call away. I took my wife's advice now and pushed my thoughts toward the coming adventure. We would enjoy the other coast and the mountains. I suddenly felt carefree and ordered a scotch on the rocks. My wife requested a Coca-Cola, as usual.

We knew where to look for the keys: under a loose plank on the porch. A plant in a flowerpot would be sitting on the particular plank. We also had the name of the neighbor to the left who was friendly with them but I did not want to have to go asking questions or favors right away.

Our plane landed and we claimed our bags and after the hassle of getting out of the airport, got to the town by taxi. At one point during the hour's ride I hugged my wife and kissed her cheek. She squeezed my hand and kissed her wedding ring.

The keys were indeed under the plank. The house had been described to me in an early letter. It looked far better than I had had any right to expect. It was a ranch style house.

But the front door didn't work too well. You had to wiggle it from side to side till you disengaged the lock. I think, after I was exhausted, my wife got the damned door open after ten or fifteen minutes of wiggling the key.

With the door opened, we began taking our luggage in from the driveway, where the taxi driver had dumped it. When this was done, I look the car keys and went out to the driveway to take a look. Up close, the car looked muddy and rusted out along the fenders and the lower body—especially around the bottom of the doorframe. I got down and checked the tires. They were worn unevenly and badly.

I got in. It was a delight to find that the seat covers were of cloth rather than that horrible plastic stuff. I moved the seat closer to the wheel; tilted it a bit. While sitting there, I became aware that the entire dashboard was filthy with food grease and dust and something else I have no name for. Then I saw the cracks in the plastic around the radio and the ashtray. I opened the glove compartment. It was stuffed with a jungle of things: a deck of cards, broken sunglasses, cassette tapes, a greasy rag, and a flashlight with a corroded battery spilling out of its case. I closed the compartment. Then I put the key in and turned it just to listen to the motor. I had to turn the key ten times before the engine kicked in. When it did, the thing groaned as though in physical pain.

Once I was back in the house, I called out to my wife. And she called back that she was in the kitchen. I found the kitchen by taking the direction from which her voice had come. I felt frustrated by my experience with the car and wanted to tell her what I had learned. But when I got to the kitchen, I found her sitting slumped in a chair at the table, looking very dejected. What was wrong? She told me to look at everything. Everything?

I looked around. I began to see what she was seeing. Beyond being in a kitchen that appeared to be normal, I found myself standing in an abnormally dirty kitchen. There were dirty dishes in the sink, dishes that clearly had been there for weeks. The counter was filthy with smudges of jelly and butter. Ants were crawling into and out of an opened loaf of Wonder Bread. With every step I took, I was walking on crumbs and grime. My wife told me to take a look in the refrigerator. I didn't know if I wanted to. But I did. I opened the door and looked in. On first sight it seemed that every inch of space was crammed with stuff. Among the many, many things were a half-used carton of milk with an expired date, a topless plastic tub of butter with toast crumbs stuck here and there where a knife had stabbed, a moldy pack of bacon, an array of left-overs wrapped in aluminum paper. Behind me, I heard my wife tell me to take a look at the vegetable bin. I reached down and pulled it open. I saw two rotten heads of lettuce and three or four shrunken lemons with a stack of other things beneath, which, at one time in the past, had been either green or yellow but were now all the same color of brown. I guess I shook my head in disbelief. I heard my wife begin to laugh at my bewilderment or out of frustration, I don't know which.

I closed the fridge door and turned back to my wife and reminded her that we were on an adventure. I said these are minor matters. The house itself seemed sturdy enough. No danger of it falling in on us in the night while we slept.

Besides, my exchangee and his family probably thought they were doing us a favor by leaving the car and house in the condition they were in. Since there was no welcome note anywhere in sight, perhaps this and the lived-in look of the rest of the kitchen was meant to be a kind of sincere, warm handshake. I always tried to put the best face on things.

Next, we explored the bedroom. There were family pictures on the dresser. The room itself was much smaller than I had been led to believe. I tested the mattress by pressing my hand on it to see how much resistance it could give. I was delighted to find hardness necessary for my bad back. Meanwhile, my wife had opened the closet door and made a sound closely related to a scream. I turned to see her standing there with her hand over her mouth. Had she stumbled upon a corpse? Surely she was overreacting to something. There couldn't be a dead body hanging in there! I went to see what was wrong. The closet was full of books! I couldn't believe it. From floor to ceiling: books! Not an inch of floor space left. Entry was impossible. (At home we had cleared out all three closets in anticipation of the exchange.) It wasn't even possible to force a shoe into that closet, let alone garments.

I dashed through the house to find the study where there was supposed to be another closet. There was. It was much smaller, but empty of clothes. Yet, a disassembled bicycle took up most of the floor space.

We found the boy's room and opened the closet there. A huge greasy boat motor had been placed on the floor on an opened newspaper. I swore. My wife told me to calm down. She was right. The space above the motor, she said, was free. There was no reason why we couldn't hang our clothes there. We just had to be careful not to drop anything or to hang anything too long. Or move the motor? Well, this whole trip was an adventure, and...

We fetched hamburgers and fries at a nearby fast-food place and came back to the house. We ate and went to bed. All night I tossed and kept my wife and myself awake. By morning I fell asleep telling myself that so far we'd not encountered any serious problems. And it was true!

Over the next three or four days, weather-wise, we felt we were at the beginning of fall. We could indulge our passion for hiking and do some weekend camping before the cold weather came. We planned to discover those much-written-about mountains of the area! There was a fireplace in the living room. There, in the freezing nights of winter, we could make love or read to each other. It was going to be a very, very good adventure!

Then I met the people at school.

First, the secretaries! I figured out pretty quickly that they had a "slot" for me. I was the exchange guy. This meant that I was temporary. In academia, when you are temporary, you are not necessarily treated well. If you are lucky you are treated with respect if not care. There was trouble finding an office for me. Something they should have figured out before my arrival! They forgot to give me a mailbox. When they apologized, I smiled and assured them that there was no problem. After all, I was on a fun adventure!

Next, the professors! I met three or four in the mailroom. One was extremely friendly and suggested we have lunch together one of these days. Perhaps in the next century? Another said hi and welcome.

There was no formal reception for me (although, I later learned, on the other coast, there was one for my exchangee).

Then classes started and I met the students. Aside from a girl who was obviously having emotional problems, they were—as a group—more serious-minded and hardworking than I could have hoped for. Going to class became a stimulating challenge. Some of them dreamed of careers; a few expressed a passion for philosophy or art or physics. It was refreshing.

Meanwhile, my wife and I adjusted to the house and to the car—despite small daily car and house problems. The car was slow to start and it leaked oil. I bought bug spray to try to get rid of the ants on the kitchen counter. I refused to let such problems get me down. These were simply the pests of daily life. I put the annoyances to the back of my mind. My wife, on the other hand, was growing more and more irritated by these things.

We hiked; we camped. We drove along the coast. We stopped in cozy little ocean-side restaurants where we ate fried oysters or squid. The mussels were good too.

We never wrote or called my exchangee to complain about any of the problems we encountered. They, on the other hand, contacted us constantly about issues they were having with our house. For a while they thought the stove had a faulty oven but it turned out his wife didn't know how to turn it on.

There were other complaints. Students complained about his method of teaching. He said the Chair was cool toward him. Some driver had dinted the finder of my car. But the insurance company covered the cost of fixing it. His wife had a cold. Every time we heard from him, whether by phone or letter, he had a complaint.

Before we knew it, spring was here: shrubbery and trees in the front and backyard began to show signs of new growth. The last snow fell in the middle of April. We began to hike more and to camp on some weekends. One time we saw a huge bear, walking upright through the trees. We stood still, holding our breath till he passed. We explored the coastal area, going farther up than we had in the fall. Now, my second semester was easier than the first and I liked the new students. Although my exchangee's car had cost us a lot of money in repairs, we told ourselves things could have been a lot worse.

The time to leave drew near. We spent a week at the end cleaning the house—hopefully, not as a cynical statement. We were just in the habit of cleaning up after ourselves. My wife called a professional carpet cleaner who came out and did a fine job. We put new washers in all the faucets; replaced a broken glass and one cup. We left the refrigerator empty and clean as a whistle. There were no dirty dishes in the sink—of course—and the counter was clean. The tiled floor was clean enough to eat on. When we arrived the bathroom seat cover had been loose. Now we bought a new one. We probably overdid it a bit.

Then we called a taxi. It was a fine day in the middle of the month as we were driven to the station and from there on to the airport. At one point I almost leaped into the air and clicked my heels but the weight of the luggage kept me grounded.

On arriving home we found the door closed but not locked. It was mid-day and they had left the day before. I was furious! My wife gave me the look that said, Calm down; do you want a heart attack? She grew up in the country where people rarely locked doors, and I, in the city, where only fools did not. One of the upstairs windows—I had noticed the minute we stepped out of the cab—was open and therefore also unlocked.

We went in. The house smelled bad—like dirty socks. With the door ajar, I began to bring in the bags. Meanwhile, my wife was already exploring the house. She came back to the hall holding her face. Her eyes were closed. She said the whole house was filthy. Well, I thought, she was probably exaggerating.

I had to go to the bathroom. When I finished I noticed that the tub was dirty with grease and hair; the face-bowl contained a similar coating of the same sort of human waste. There were, on the counter, fingernail polish stains and a scattering of face powder. The mirror was cracked in the corner. We hadn't left it this way.

Okay, okay, so, you say, I'm making a mountain out of a molehill. Perhaps I am, but I believe in simple common civility and respect for others. One oversight can be overlooked but when a multitude of little oversights line up in a long line of them, then they, collectively, amount to a problem.

On the way back to the front hall, I glanced into the bedroom and the study. The bedroom stank and the study had been rearranged for some reason. The carpet beneath my feet was filthy with what looked like dog hair and God-knows-what else. Had they had a dog in here? We had explicitly told them no animals in the house!

I found my wife in the kitchen looking into the refrigerator. I went and looked over her shoulder. Every inch was stuffed with things they'd left. Among them, I noticed right away, a half-used carton of milk with an expired date, a topless plastic tub of butter with toast crumbs stuck here and there where a knife had stabbed, a moldy half finished pack of bacon. I didn't want to see any more. I backed away and stepped on a dead mouse. We had never before had mice!

I was speechless. My wife turned and wept on my chest. I held her close. I comforted her by telling her we would call in a house cleaning service. Then I proposed, in a soothing voice, that we go out to dinner then check into a motel and pretend we were just beginning to get to know each other. We would make love with the passion of those gripped by wonderment. Then watch the late movie—and it would be about a couple learning the mystery of love and how to trust it, and also about how they finally come to accept the problems they know are always coming. It would be a perfect family story!

THE DRIVER

THE SUN WAS GOING DOWN at JFK in Queens. We would travel about fifteen miles through heavy traffic to get to Manhattan.

"Just take us to the city. I'll tell us where to stop," I said to the taxi driver. Up ahead, through the windshield, I could see the comforting, persistent lights of the great city, New York, and its skyline.

In his rearview mirror, the driver kept giving us quizzical looks. And I kept looking at his audacious name: Gunman. Is he for real? Is he a man simply doing his job? Or does he represent a plot?

And Helga, beside me, was tired from our flight. So was I. But we were happy. We were headed for a new life together.

I watched the back of the driver's head. He gave a quick boorish laugh and called over his shoulder something—due to the roar of expressway traffic—that was unclear. I called out, "What'd you say, pal?"

"I only was trying to remind you folks that I haven't the slightest idea where I should take you. How about Brooklyn?"

Silently, I pondered the possibility of Brooklyn. What I knew about Brooklyn was what I had read in stories and newspaper articles. Nothing was especially bad or good about Brooklyn.

"The only reason I suggested Brooklyn is there is a lot of superstitious people in other parts of the city. I live in Brooklyn myself; you'd never know it, though, because I don't have a Brooklyn accent—did you notice?"

I nodded, though I was sure he had a Brooklyn accent.

"Well," he said, "you folks are obviously from out of town so you didn't notice. I even grew up in Brooklyn, and I don't talk like your ordinary taxicab driver; if you know what I mean."

Helga, in a cheerful voice, broke his monologue, announcing, "Didn't you use the word superstition?"

"Yeah, lady, that's what I said; but I'll explain to you what I mean by that, if you give me a moment." He now raised his voice: "Can you hear me back there?"

"Loud and clear," I said.

"Like, the gentleman called me pal. I know you didn't mean nothing by doing that, but it just proves a point; the same thing I was talking about, the way I talk. I mean I never call a person who is not my friend a pal. You know what I mean? In Brooklyn we don't do that."

I felt his passionate desire to turn around to witness my reaction but he was a safe driver so he was stuck looking forward.

"Calling people pal," he said, "that's the way cab drivers talk, you know. Anyway, the young lady asked me about superstition in this city. It's rampant! Now, I ain't—I mean I *am not*—no expert on the real nature of these kinds of things, and I don't know anything about you people. I mean, whether or not you two are married or just friends or what have you, but I know this, that—except for Brooklyn—a mixed couple, and as I say, I don't know if you are a mixed couple, I mean if you two are—you know what I mean, married or going together—for all I know, you are just friends or just business associates."

"Right," I said.

"And I really don't care," he said. "But in case youse in some way romantically involved—" For the quickest and most tense moment of his speech he suddenly and automatically lifted his thick hands from the steering wheel to form the beautiful phrase "romantically involved." He did so by throwing his hands up, forming a circle, as though holding something round and invisible. "If youse guys are a couple I would suggest Brooklyn because there is less hard feelings there against, well, you know what I mean. In Brooklyn, you will never find people going around using bedbugs, for example, as a curse for sore eyes. But in Manhattan—*Oh Christ!*—there're folks there who do this kind of thing: they actually mix bedbugs, all crushed up, you know, with salt and the human milk of a pregnant woman, if they can find one; and not only for sore eyes but the poorer people, in the ghetto, or the hood, as they call it, they're even dumber than just the average guy, they even take it internally; they claim it cures—get this!—urban hysteria!"

"Urban hysteria?" Helga said.

I thought, Oh merciful gods, spare us this sideshow! But, to hear better, Helga was leaning forward. He had peaked her interest.

"It's witchcraft," he said. "Witchcraft is what it is."

"Are you saying this is generally true of everybody who lives in Manhattan?" said Helga.

He defensively snapped, "Do you know what literal means, young lady?" In his rearview mirror he was watching for her reaction.

"I know what literal means."

"Yeah, you do, huh. Well, that's the way I mean it. I wouldn't tell you anything that isn't true, the literal truth." He hunched his shoulders in a show of innocence.

Helga said, "How come we never heard anything about this on the news?"

"Because they don't want you to know. Think what it would do to the tourist industry! Ask yourself: what can I get out of lying about this. I'm just trying to be a decent fellow and tell you why you should go to Brooklyn rather than Manhattan."

I started laughing.

"You can laugh all you want," he said. "I can tell you things you wouldn't believe about The Bronx and about Queens and Staten Island too."

"Such as?" I said to humor him.

"In the other boroughs you find superstitious practices but to a lesser degree, because, well, those people they've had a little more education but Manhattan is the worst of all."

I could feel Helga's excitement and frustration and confusion. She obviously wanted to argue with the driver but didn't know how to start. His voice was so coolly antiseptic, so sure.

"My son-in-law," he said, "he's a lawyer, told me just the other day, believe it or not, that a Manhattan lady came to him to file for a divorce from her husband. Want to hear the reason she wanted a divorce?"

"Why not?" I said.

"This husband of hers, the poor guy, he dropped a black ace of spades—*accidentally!*—while just playing a normal game of cards"—he pronounced the word *cads*—"in their living room. You know, just sitting around with the fellas playing cards!" He laughed, waiting for our reaction. "That's why she wanted a divorce. Ain't that something?"

We laughed too.

"And before you call me a liar, I'll tell you this, my son-in-law is, first, a good Catholic, a Harvard man, a responsible gentleman who maintains his ethics, and a decent husband to my daughter. They're even buying a home in Brooklyn Heights. And if you knew anything about the city here at all you would know what *that* means."

"Mister Gunman," Helga said, laughing, "You must be putting us on."

This of course steamed him up again. "Look!" he snapped ambitiously, "Do you know anybody, in your hometown, wherever you come from—"

"Chicago. We come from Chicago," she said.

"Well, do you know anybody in Chicago who hangs garlic around in their home? I mean to keep evil spirits away?"

"Not personally," Helga said. "But I've heard of that one."

"Well, they do that in Manhattan. Everybody! Not just a few people! Everybody!"

It was all so absurd I was laughing again.

"Have you ever heard of people who go around rubbing the bald-headed heads of helpless old men just to try to improve their own memory? They all do that in Manhattan. I'm not kidding you."

I was watching his face. He was keeping a straight face. What a comedian!

"Or how about this theory that water is fattening? You know anybody who stopped drinking water because it's fattening? No? Well, there is a trend now in Manhattan of people who are doing just that to lose weight."

"People die without water," Helga said.

"Right!" he said. "And they're dropping dead too. Believe me! Some of them won't drink anything that even contains water." He shook his head in disgust. "And there are thousands and thousands of voodoo rites in Manhattan."

"Voodoo?" Helga said.

"Voodoo! And I don't mean concealed in some basement. Right out in the open. Other people for certain reasons put people under a spell. They're actually held like that as victims."

"But why?" Helga said.

"It's all very secretive. Nobody knows why."

"They use everything from rotten apple roots to certain kinds of perfumes to get certain effects; it cause people to go insane or walk around zombie-like. They get restless and can't sit down. They just keep going till they drop dead. A lot of them are young people like you two. They've been hexed. And I'm not trying to scare you. It's just that if you go to Manhattan you got to know what you are doing."

I decided to play along with him. "Well, you've scared me, all right. We were planning to go to Manhattan but now, I'm not so sure it's the right thing to do."

"Manhattan uptown is the worse—nothing personal to you, sir, but the colored people are the worst of all."

"How so?" I said.

"It's like a religion to them," he said. "But it's not just them. I don't want to give you that impression. It's all of New York City. I say, except for Brooklyn. It's really funny sometimes. You can be driving around in Manhattan and see people strutting and just ah strolling along and everybody, I mean everybody is carrying an umbrella—"

Helga cut in: "But why?"

"Well, you see, they have this belief, it's like part of Manhattan culture, you know. They believe that if you carry an umbrella that that will forestall rain. Seriously!"

"How do you know that is why they carry umbrellas?"

"What else is a umbrella for but rain?" You could tell he believed his logic was impeccable.

I cut in: "But you are still taking us to Manhattan, right?"

"You see, it's a long drive in," he said. "And right now you still got a chance to choose. Like they say on television, when they're talking politics, you have an alternative—" He chuckled, his shoulders rocking. "That's a nice big word, huh?" He stopped laughing, then said: "I don't mean to dwell on this subject. If there's anything I hate, it's somebody who dwells on a subject. But while you're making up your minds, let me ask you a question. You sir, or, the lady: have either one of you heard of the art of capnomancy?"

I said, "The art of what?"

"It's an evil art that is practiced in Manhattan. Some people call it pollution. Seriously!"

Helga cut in: "But how about the Village?"

He cut her off: "The Village is no different. Of course you may find some strange people there, you know, they're all weirdoes down there. Really weird people! And as I say, some of them might call it pollution but the true name of it is capnomancy. It's an art, like I say. It's done with smoke. And it's very deadly. So, if you decide on Manhattan anyway, just remember that. You can't say I didn't warn you. Because you 're gonna come up against it."

"But if it's smoke," Helga said, "certainly it would drift to Brooklyn too."

"Nope! Never happens! We don't have that sort of thing in Brooklyn." His tone was self-righteous.

I said, "Then what *do* you have in Brooklyn?"

"We have good people, that's what we have in Brooklyn."

I looked out the window. We were shooting straight ahead toward the city. The sky was growing darker.

I said, "I can tell you something you may not know that I've heard about Brooklyn."

"Like what?"

"Like the fact that they have body snatchers there; but don't go around talking about this to anybody you don't know because you could easily get into trouble. Brooklyn is a hot spot but it's happening all over. People are being snatched off the streets under the cover of night and taken to certain places, usually hospitals, where very rich or important people, who have heart trouble, are in critical condition, are about to die. They call these captured people—who are always poor and defenseless—*donors*. They're especially interested in pregnant women because their hearts are in better shape."

"No!" said the driver. He chuckled, obviously not believing me.

Helga was listening intently.

I continued. "You see, the only way the operation can succeed is if they catch a person who is healthy, walking around with good blood circulation. They have to act quickly. And they use very sharp instruments. They have everything in the operation room already in place. Then *shuph!* Cut out the donor's ticker and get it into the other person's chest pronto."

"Holy Christ, in Heaven! What are you talking about?" he said. He was truly alarmed.

As an afterthought, I thought it only fair to add: "Of course, they use antiseptics and all kinds of—"

He cut me off: "Just hold on a second, will you. Answer me this. What has this got to do with Manhattan?"

"Nothing. In fact, Manhattan is the only place where they are not snatching people off the street."

"Yeah," he said. "They shoot them instead."

"Despite your kind warnings," I said, "we want you to drop us off at Washington Square Park in Lower Manhattan. We'll find our way from there."

"Look!" he said, obviously offended. "Where you go is your own business. But don't say I didn't warn you!"

Through the windshield I could see the black mouth of the Queens-Midtown Tunnel up ahead, specked with yellow lights. As we sped under the East River, I reached for Helga's hand, which was already resting on my knee, and squeezed it.

SKETCH

MORNING, on the terrace. I can hear Jean Baptiste Quenin crooning "Veilleur de toutes les nuits." Radio in the kitchen. Middle of February. New Grumbacher French Portable easel out here on the terrace. A sketchpad against my lap. A particular pen. A particular brush. Things changed.

Things continue to change. Here, we are somewhere else, knotted, unknotted, and the wallpaper, the sky, everything is different. If this is doppelganger-time, you are not my uncle, not my brother, not my Other, but me. I can't capture you in lines. We live in the spasm of each other's sagging lives. While shopping at the old market today I saw you look suspiciously at me (in a mirror) the same way you looked suspiciously at the onions, the red fish, the aged cheese. How are we sleeping these days? Orthodox or paradox? I'm the ox but I'm also the bull.

My wife? She's in there, in the cool house, sitting up in bed reading a magazine, no, reading a novel. We have a particular morning ritual. We donate time to thoughts like clouds, they linger over our heads, mackerel-sky-stuff, then I'm up and the coffee is going, and she's up too. But this morning, she's hanging out in bed, coffee at bedside. Marie-Paule Belle singing "Les Petits Paletlins." Is that really our kitchen radio or the neighbor's?

Running out of things to sketch? View from café-bar at corner of rue Alphonse Karr and rue la Liberte. Quick action of people walking. Juxtaposition. Traffic jam. Noise into the clashing of lines. The rue de la Liberte traffic is hectic with honking and fumes, shouting hot, shouting cold. Four figures of the left hand. Flower spikes!

The view from the mall with its potted tropical shrubbery at Palais de Quency against the gray of the old apartment buildings. Concentrate on this. Where are all my Arab friends this morning? Insults floating over their heads—no grass grows under foot—like scripture in a Negro church. *Une negresse morte*, or should I say dead soldiers? But my Arab friends don't drink red wine, and empty bottles are as taboo as, uh, *sheygget* (disgusting!) to Behane, my friend from North Africa, born to a Jewish mother, which is all that counts, so they count him in high places. A firebrand. Son of sorrow. To Behane. I'm as clear as Running Water, so he never calls me *shokher*, no sir.

But the question arises: What else is there to draw here? I've done the faces—spirited, noble, valorous, comely, harmonious, bright, lily-like, hospitable, fair, helmeted, feminine, animated, veiled, pleasant, blooming, wise and unwise—and though I know there are still endless uncharted faces, all different, damsel and gazelle, I'm sagging like a palm tree with face-boredom.

So go home. What's home? Whose home?

At the end of February. A bar across the street from Hall du Voyage. The crowd is younger here. Motorbikes crowding the curb. British music, French kids, jukebox screams. Yet, moderation, moderation. The Russian with his coffee at the back table. Tatiana in apron. Sidonia in the doorway. Tara coming in with a shoebox under arm. My sketchpad on table. My hand waiting for a jewel, a sea, a prosperous moment, the tip-off for the right motif. A thick forest of ideas floating just out of reach. Outside, a double-parked delivery truck. That's good enough for the moment, but move fast. Girl with white mane blocks view. (So stick her in!)

The lycee crowd, this. View of street construction crew and trip hammer, drill-noise creating gems of terror, rosemary-throbbings. But any of this could be anywhere, in the City of Light or the Eternal City. Nice is nice. I nickname it Salty, Reborn, Without Fault, The Happy Peaceful Place, Patrician Nymph of Ageless Lust, Opal. Café across from Hotel Vendome on Pastorelli? Orange plastic chairs, white metal tables. This is the right stuff, the honored model, no, ideal model, the archetypal—simple things. Metal tables. Chairs.

Sit here as in a dream house, dazed but alive as Mars. Sketch the Arab street sweeper washing and sweeping the sidewalk with fire hydrant water, cleaning the street of its unending string of dog turds and piss.

Keep the hand moving. Care not to knock over the coffee. Two francs, not three. An old woman in a third-floor window as she opens her shutters with a bang. Her eyes connect with mine; she draws back as though slapped. Rebellion-face, a face belonging to Bitterness, to the Ill-Tempered Kingdom. Seventy different meanings for such a face, Mary, Mary, quite contrary. Touch it with a laurel, cast it in a battle, under a lime tree or keep it with the barren, the diseased. Find the right motif to move with the hand, as now the voice of Catherine Ferry singing "Bonjour,

Bonjour," in the spirit of the Roman goddess of spring or the Serpent of Light.

Even this late in February, this cozy, translucent, ceramic-white sunlight, multicolored sunlight pours down in the nickname of Joy, on my sketchpad. And page after page, I am filling it. Fulfilling it, like a promised oath. A name, a bond, a lilac in a meadow. Before leaving for Old Town, I do this: My Wife Sunbathing, her bra beside her on the towel.

Sitting with coffee. Artist with Coffee and Sketchpad.

Across from the Palais du Justice where the fisherman parked his pushcart. Early, old shoppers trudging into rue du Marche. Three young girls skittering by in *les jambierres* and shiny boots. Ambulances from Saint-Roch Hospital. Delivery boy unloading bottled water.

Along Jean Medicin. Panoramic. Like a staircase of tinsel sweethearts, complex crisscrossing, violent black-and-white, red-and-white forces—sound, light, supplanted, protected by its own wild goat-spirit, its vine-like network reaching out from some absolute Wrathful but Gracious Sanity.

Along the Promenade. A medley of TV antennas over on the roofs of the big hotels, roosting pigeons. Winter sky, winter light, February strife, unsurpassed. Skyline, bathers, strollers, supplanted strollers, supplanted bathers, supplanted delivery boys. Thirst. A burst of rain shoots down from the splendid sky with its hedgerow-shaped clouds out over the sea.

Run across the wide, wide boulevard. Brightness and simplicity follow me all the days of my uncluttered life.

Pivot, enter a small street. I wear a mask of comfort, pass doors I will never knock on, draped windows through which other lives peer in the same wonderment I have known since the beginning of Human Time. Clothes strung on short lines drying between buildings not more than ten feet apart. The Palais parking lot and the big clock in the beige bell tower. I've done that before, done it from three different angles. Rushing walkers under umbrellas and snug in raincoats. How come I didn't know? Two women talking Dali.

Brazzerie le Liberte. A seat at the bar. Overhearing a conversation, in French, of course. He wanted her to do this unmentionable act with another woman and himself. She got sick of the whole affair. Nothing to sketch in such a Post-Modernist moment. It's a verbal corridor leading to an architectural disaster, partitions of pain and staircases of desire, gifts, and habitation, the archer's arm stretched. The gap.

Sunday morning. Walking along rue Patorelli. At Gubernatis, stop. A cloudy day. Strange, powerful forces at work. Keep moving. Something is bound to give. You're onto something, something like you've never captured before. I can taste it, hear it. It's flourishing, animating me. I know for the first time I was never a Tower Dweller, always an earth-level observer of the Mighty Moment, the Silent Splash. Cross Square Dominique Durandy. A river crosser, this ancient resolution. Even today the mood as Crosser remains that of a wolf or a raven. There is resolution in crossing. Firmly I cross Square Dominique Durandy!

Cross and enter a crowd. Crowd gathered around philatelists huddled over their precious, beautiful stamps. In each tiny stamp I am somewhere different, on a carpet flying over India, in a California gold rush, on a Mediterranean island, a dairy farm, a homestead, with a prince, gazing into the eye of a conqueror.

These stamps Teutonic and Anglo-Saxon gaze back, occasional disquisitions of brilliant design—in fern green, mosaics, in gold, in stairway blues, in nineteenth century Bordeaux reds. Wonderment stamped, stilled, held down with ink. Clustered narrowly, spinning in the spacious eye. And seagulls coming overhead from the slap of the sea, circling, nosy, checking us out.

I'm looking slowly, looking. And when there's this much already accomplished, when you see its Power even in miniature, it's hard to raise the rooftop from inspiration, to let it soar, to give Nature undivided attention or to take it. So you move on. Wading, as one who moves homeward, a full sketchpad under arm, the known plot of What Comes Next already thick with afterthought.

A STORY OF VENICE

I COULDN'T BELIEVE I was actually waiting for her to call. The next morning I didn't even go out for my morning coffee ritual. After showering and washing my hair, I stood at the hall window looking down at the service boats going by on the canal and alternately at the people on the fondamenta on the other side. The water was unusually high on the walls. At a low place in front of an apartment entrance directly across the way the fondamenta had collected about three inches of water nine to ten feet wide. When I got bored with watching the redness of tomatoes and the yellowness of squash on the boats going by just below my window I focused on the people puzzling over the problem of the flooded area in front of the apartment entrance. You could almost see their thoughts. They would come merrily along—from both directions—and suddenly stop upon seeing the water. The approaches to the problem varied. About half tried to wade or tip or hop or skip through; the others took the time to retrace their steps either over the bridge by the post office or going all the way back down to Hotel Navona and crossing at the little stone bridge there. There were exceptions of course. A boy hoisted his girlfriend onto his back and waded through the mess in his tennis shoes just to show, I guess, how tough he was. Two boys climbed the wall of the building, holding onto electrical tubing, which ran along above the doorway.

The water was high like this because it had rained in the night and the tide probably had come in but more probably the flooding—which no doubt was a problem in spots all over the city—was due to those damned channels they dug years ago from the sea into the lagoon to let the great ships in. Because of those profit-motivated trenches the whole of Venice was slowly, slowly sinking into the mud, I had read.

In one sense I was waiting for her to call because she had, without knowing it, given me new hope, and in another, she had stirred some emotion in me I had not felt in a long while. I wasn't yet ready to identify this emotion but it was interesting to watch it from the distance I placed between it and myself. Meanwhile, being in the apartment like this gave me a slight feeling of uneasiness akin to claustrophobia. By noon on the first day I was as restless as a fifteen-ounce Yorkshire terrier.

I didn't go out for lunch. I settled for scrambled eggs and a hard roll. I ate at the kitchen table although I had a large dining room. As I sat in the kitchen I could hear the expressive fellows downstairs in the restaurant below my window talking politics and philosophizing about life in general and about life in Italy in particular. I'd eaten lunch in that restaurant two or three times and could picture the guys crowded at the bar drinking to delay lunch as long as possible. They did it every day and it was fun listening to their urgency and seriousness. The wife of the owner washed tablecloths and napkins all day and she strung them on the ropes that ran parallel to their kitchen window and mine. As I ate I could hear her pulling the lines and taking in the dry stuff. No doubt she'd hung up the things she'd just taken from the washer.

I waited and the phone still didn't ring. I went over my notes, and coming across the manuscript of the rough bibliography of Faber I had in progress, I remembered that I had not yet made a photocopy for Angel. I made a mental note to do so. I also made a mental note to remind myself to remember the mental note. By mid-afternoon I was exhausted from waiting and went to bed. I dreamed the phone was ringing. I got up and answered it. It was my ex-wife saying she had seen her lawyer and was seeking to increase the amount of the child support. I turned over and moved into another dream. Mrs. Faber brought a caged bird to my door and handed it to me without so much as hello. I had no idea how I knew who she was but I did. Around six I got up and dressed.

I went over to Lidia Faber's campo with the intention of eating in one of the restaurants there. The lights were on in her flat. I went on. I stopped and examined the first posted menu on an easel set on the sidewalk out beyond the tables with their freshly starched and ironed white tablecloths. As I stood there I became aware of a small group of old men and women chattering frantically just inside the shadows of Corte del Fontego. They were gathered around a small shrine of the Virgin perched in one of those little wall indentations you see all over. I wandered over to get a closer look. Over their heads I could see the thing. I had the feeling I had seen it before and that it had glowed in the dark or some such crazy thing. Anyway it was unusual to see this many people gathered at once around such an ordinary shrine. And at this hour? Normally old people will cross themselves as they pass such a thing without even stopping. This Madonna was pretty and bright. She was made of marble and was a relief. I swear she had Picasso's eyes and there was, cross my heart, something also Grecian about her!

When I had had enough of listening to their sighing and watching the Madonna's beauty, I went on beyond the restaurant I considered earlier and looked at the menu of the next one farther on in the campo near the church. The church bells were ringing.

I went into the restaurant and the waiter showed me to a small table in the front by the window. Something in his manner told me he was a person of pride. He liked me. I liked him for it. From my little table, I could see the campo and the shops across the way. The shopkeepers were letting up the glass covers and pulling back the gratings from the doors. The lights came on in a sprinkle. Suddenly, people came out of side-calles and began to move along the line of shops. They moved quickly and gestured to each other with excitement. It was as though something really wonderful was about to happen. What I didn't know at the time was: it was already happening.

Immediately after dinner, I rushed back but the phone remained silent. I turned on the TV for the first time. Frank Sinatra in a dubbed movie. I watched for maybe a half hour before I couldn't stand any more. I made coffee and poured brandy in it and went to the study which was just a little room across the way. I sat in the easy chair and picked up from the lamp table one of the various mystery novels strewn about, left no doubt by earlier tenants. It was one by Mary Roberts Rinehart. From the first paragraph I discovered what a wonderful prose stylist she was: but even with this I couldn't concentrate for long.

The next morning the postman woke me with his buzzing and I leaped out of bed and jumped into my jogging suit, which was the easiest thing to get into pronto, and buzzed him in. Actually, I buzzed him in as I climbed into my jogging suit. Sometimes he simply left the mail in the box inside but for some unknown reason at other times he waited for me to come down so that he could hand me the things directly. Maybe he simply wanted to say *buon giorno* and *a domani* or *arrivederci*. He handed me a large manila envelope. I saw that it was from my department. I said farewell to the postman and went back up and made imported instant coffee—which tasted terrible compared to Italian. I sat at the kitchen table and opened the manila envelope.

The first thing that struck me was a Venezia postmark and an Italian postage stamp. The return address was Lidia Scarpa Faber's! Above the address there was simply this: Faber. The letter had been mailed fourteen days before. I tore it open and tried to calm myself in the same instant. I read: "Dear Professor Foster: I am writing to express my regrets that we did not have a chance to meet while you were visiting Venice earlier in the summer." She went on to say that the mix-up was understandable. Her maid was not careful enough in giving me proper directions. Venice, she said, was difficult enough to get around in but Sophia's English was not so good, which made matters difficult. In any case, if I ever decide to return to Venice, I should inform her ahead of time and she would personally pick me up from my hotel and take me to dinner just to safeguard against any mishap. Meanwhile, she said, she was writing to me about another matter. "As you may know, I have been working with my husband's literary executor on various legal problems concerning his literary properties, both published and unpublished." She said Professors John Kinzer and Ruth Gwertzman had agreed to help as advisors. "Both recommended you to me, you may remember; and they again recommended you as possibly someone who might be interested in also serving in an advisory capacity on literary matters." She wanted to know if the idea sounded like something I might be interested in considering? She hoped so. She wrote, finally: "Meanwhile, I look forward to hearing from you at your convenience." She closed with good wishes and hoped that I was enjoying late July. She remembered it to be her favorite time of year in New York. "With best regards, Lidia Faber."

Well. Need I tell you that I read the whole thing over again and that I felt shocked, confused, pleased—actually stunned. Here I was still in Venice and Mrs. Faber didn't even know it! All I had to do was pick up the phone and Lidia and I could become close friends for life; I could learn all I needed to know, start my biography, spend hours before her with the tape turning, explore the unpublished manuscripts. I leaped up and knocked over my coffee, which spilled onto the letter, turning it brown. I swore. Then grabbed the dish cloth and dabbed at the sheet but it only made matters worse: the blue ink smeared against the burnt umbra and more than half the meaning was lost.

I knew I had to calm down before making a decision about what to do next. When I'm too excited to think clearly, the best thing for me to do is walk. I took a shower and got dressed and burst out the door with no particular plan. I didn't have my camera or the guidebook. I walked quickly over through Giardino Papadopoli Park and along Fondamenta S. Simeone till I reached the station bridge. I took the steps two at a time for no particular reason. I hurried left, along the Old Spanish route, that is, into Lista di Spagna, the way I had walked with Angel. I continued past the restaurant where she and I ate and crossed the bridge over Canale di Cannaregio then impulsively whipped left, heading away from the heavy flow of human traffic. I walked a few feet before I saw in English and Hebrew the sign over the entrance to The Ghetto. I entered and within another few feet, I was in a little old campo where a group of tourists stood looking up at the building. I heard New York accents. I rushed by them. I gained a large campo and stopped. To my right was a little museum. On impulse, I went over and poked my head in the doorway. It was dark inside but I could make out on the walls blowups of Hebrew writings. It was just what I needed: something I couldn't understand, something remote and serious and awesome to the point where the body could almost shudder before its depth and age. I stepped inside.

It was cool and dark. I saw blowups of tombs snapped at the Jewish cemetery on the Lido. The word was that if you went along the lagoon from Santa Elizabeta to the monastery of San Nicolo al Lido you'd come to the cemetery. That struck me as a very interesting idea. The thing about it that was so immediately captivating was its remoteness from my plans: it was simply something that a large number of people might be interested in knowing and that in itself gave me the distraction I needed.

I climbed the steps and bought a ticket and explored the little museum, and then a girl came into the recessed room and announced that she was about to conduct a tour of the three synagogues. The oldest one was right there upstairs in the museum building itself. Along with three or four other drifters, I followed her up into the elaborate room. She told us to sit down. I took a seat on one of the narrow benches where worshippers once sat. Before me was a locked desk-like contraption, obviously a receptacle for a holy book. As the girl talked rapidly in Italian about the room, I looked around, not trying too hard to follow her words. It was obviously a room not originally meant to be a place of worship. I looked up at the gallery where women were obliged to sit in the ancient times and wondered at that custom and what they could hear up there.

Meanwhile, the tour guide finished her little lecture and asked us to follow her to the Levantina Scola which was just down the way. It and the Spanish-influenced one, Scola Spagnola, were still in use, she said as we walked with her down the steep stairway. She used her huge key to open the giant wooden door with its metal strips. The vestibule was a dungeon. We followed her upstairs and sat in the cool darkness on the slender benches. This one she said was built in the late 1530s. Longhena worked on the exterior. Brustolon was thought to be responsible for those intricate wood carvings which graced the rotunda where the rabbi held forth. Slowly I became aware of a growing impatience in myself as I listened to her. It was like an itch I couldn't scratch because I couldn't locate it.

On the way to Scola Spagnola I attempted to break away but the guide turned sharply and gave me a wonderful cherub-smile which snagged my escape-attempt. I sheepishly fell back in with the others and when we reached Scola Spagnola I made it my business to stand close to her; as she unlocked the door I asked when this one was built, just to show my interest. Around 1535 or so. Once we were upstairs she pointed out that around 1635 or so Longhena probably directed the work on the interior. She talked about the manner of worship. You could tell she wasn't happy about the women being stuck upstairs. Today, she said, the men and women are still separated but the women can sit down here now, back there, she pointed to the last rows, behind the men. Her smile was bittersweet. She waited for questions. There were none.

That restless feeling, or rather my itch, was no better even as we followed her down and waited in the vestibule for her to lock the huge gate to the upstairs. Now, she stood at the door to the campo, as we filed by her out into the hard clear day. I thanked her and she thanked me back.

I raced toward the iron bridge which was, I guessed, the way out, walking swiftly across the large campo surrounded by tall Seventeenth-century buildings. A dog was lapping water from the side of one of the old wells at the center. A twelve-year-old girl in black stockings was waiting for the dog to finish. Although I hadn't smoked a cigarette in ten, maybe eleven years, I now had a burning desire for one.

At a tobacco shop in Rio Terra S. Leonardo I stopped, intending to buy a pack of one brand or another but my sight fell upon a pipe with the face of a monk carved on the front of its bowl. Without thinking about the price I bought it as though I knew what I was doing, bought a pouch of tobacco, too. The clerk was friendly and in English told me I couldn't go wrong with this brand and the pipe had been carved by his own father.

Once I headed toward Ponte delle Guglie I wondered what the hell I would do with a pipe. A couple of teenage kids sitting on the steps of the bridge seemed to be laughing at me as I climbed toward them. I decided not to drop the pipe into the canal because they were watching me. On the other side, in Saliz S. Geremia, I threw the tobacco in a trashcan but held onto the pipe as though my life depended on contact with it. As I entered the S. Geremia Campo area I stuck the pipe in my mouth and put on my dark glasses. I felt like General MacArthur. But I probably looked like a fool.

I decided not to call Mrs. Faber. The calm thing to do was to send her a note telling her I was still here. I wrote it seven times before I got the right tone, the right turn to my letters. At the post office the clerk wanted to know why I was wasting a stamp on such a thing. He said I could walk to Campo Santa Margherita in less than five minutes but that it could easily take my letter a week to get there. I said I wanted to mail it anyway. He snickered and in Italian told the story to the clerk manning the window next to his. They both looked at me and laughed together. I took the damned stamp, licked the spot where I wanted it stuck, stuck it on, and waved goodbye to the merrymakers. Outside, I dropped it in the box and felt that the matter was out of my hands. I'd given her my phone number and now I had only to wait. As I headed for the nearest coffee shop, I wondered how long that might be.

Sitting at one of the outdoor tables was Beckmann. A small glass of wine was on the table in front of mine and he was sketching the canal in his sketchbook. He smiled broadly when he saw me and invited me to join him. I did. The waiter came and I ordered brandy. He brought it. It wasn't very good. From the moment I sat down, Beckmann—without stopping his furious sketching—began telling me how delighted he was to have read Faber's collection, *The Bridge and the Church*, which he'd found in paperback. Of the five stories, he especially liked the title one, which, of course, deals with a black milk deliveryman's affair with a white housewife. Beckmann was amused by the outcome of the story: the woman turns to Christ after an abortion. I failed to catch the humor but despite my own bewilderment, I chuckled with him—feeling a little strange and foolish all the while. I quickly recovered my composure and asked him what he thought of my own favorite story, "The New Sax," from that collection. It's the one about the player Gershwin Jones who discovers his roots in Africa. Beckmann hadn't read it but he had read, "Teresa Leaves Home," and "In December the Faith Died."

He asked how my work was coming along and if I was still enjoying Venice. I babbled something about so many distractions and seductions . . . He shook his head knowingly. I told him those Faber stories were all right but that he should read one of the novels, the novels were better, much better. Which one should he start with? I offered to lend him a copy of one. He seemed touched but begged me not to go out of my way. He could just as well pick up whatever I recommended in the English language bookshop in San Barnaba. I decided not to insist and dropped the matter; finished my drink, shook his hand, and told him I'd see him around. While going through these final motions, I realized there was in Beckmann a stuffiness I was both attracted to and repelled by.

As I climbed the steps to my apartment I heard the phone ringing but before I could get the door unlocked it stopped. I told myself it was Angel. Who else could it be? I got a lot of wrong number calls, calls for previous tenants, and once a person conducting a survey called but I played the dumb American and hung up—politely of course. It was a quarter to eleven—just the time Angel would call. I could see her at her desk—if indeed she worked at a desk—at the hotel with the telephone to her ear. Three days had passed since our last meeting. She was the kind of person who would think that the proper amount of time to wait before ringing.

I took off my street shoes and put on my house shoes and turned on the radio to the classical music station. The radio was in the kitchen. I opened the kitchen window. I could hear the guys downstairs getting ready—rather, they were already far into readiness. They were clicking glasses and singing. The woman across the way was hanging out the wash. With the window opened I couldn't hear the music so I turned off the radio. The guys made better music anyway. I made myself a cup of coffee.

I needed a good book to read: that was the thing missing in my life. I had never been without a book. I explained the lapse, telling myself that the first two months here had been given to adjustment, recovering from jet lag, culture shock. I didn't fully buy my own rationalization. Why hadn't I been reading something? The minute I faced the question I knew the answer. I had, long before coming here, sold myself on not having time—ah! time was the culprit!—to read for pleasure or even enlightenment: there was only time to read for work, for tenure. Blast tenure! Damn tenure! Must everything be for tenure? Must my whole life focus on tenure? Is there no pleasure left in this world? How ironic it was that I found myself in a great city with some leisure and was unable to relax, unable to even take the time to read a simple book for simple enjoyment! The sad fact was, the only book I could bring myself to read was one I had already read—not for pleasure; certainly not recently!—as a stone in my stairway of research.

As I began sipping my coffee, I heard a buzzing in my ear and wondered if, like Colonel Cantwell, I might be on my last leg, war-scarred, falling apart, in need of drugs, a young innocent woman of royal background to inspire me to renewal. The buzzing got louder. Then it clicked. It was a mosquito! Occasionally, I had been bothered by them in the night but this was the first little bastard zanzara to come trying to get my blood in the broad daylight!

I lost track of the names of the days as I waited for the telephone to ring again. If only I could have waited with the ease of an old dog sleeping on a warm rug by the fire! I do remember that it was midmorning and the church bells were dinging madly and profusely when the phone finally rang. Rather than saying pronto I said hello as usual because I wanted to start out with the understanding that I was going to speak English and not Italian. The voice said, "Mister Foster, this is Lidia Faber."

Just as I was about to leave to meet Mrs. Faber for lunch at "a great little restaurant" (her words) she knew about in Campo San Barnaba just off Calle dei Traghetto, the phone rang again. (Mrs. Faber no doubt: calling to give me a bit of further advice on getting there. She didn't need to worry so: I wasn't going to screw up again. I'd learned to play the game in this city for walkers: it was a chessboard you could walk across and with skill you could win; which is to say you could find your way even without counting bridges.) But the caller was not Mrs. Faber. Angel said, "Forgive me, Murphy, for the long time I waited. I call now. My little boy Rolando has had a sickness and I was not able to leave him." She went on to say that she wanted to take me to lunch this very moment—or when it was convenient. I felt myself smile as she described a "wonderful little trattoria" in Campo San Toma where she knew I'd love the pasta and they even served tripe there. I forgave her her assumption!

The hesitation and disappointment were obvious in her voice when I responded with a request to postpone till tomorrow. I gave her no excuse, except, I think, I muttered something about being overwhelmed. I wrote down the name of the trattoria and agreed to meet her there at one. As I locked my door and descended the stairs, I thought: what rotten luck! what great luck!

I was early. I went in and stood at the bar and drank a glass of the *vino bianco secco di casa*. It was crisp and dry. I looked at myself in the bar mirror. I needed a haircut. It was a thing I'd do myself rather than trying to find the right barber. I felt my knee throb a bit.

I drained my glass. As though a stage director had worked out the timing, a woman I took to be Mrs. Faber came rushing in. She was smiling nervously as she came toward me with an extended hand, ready to be held and shaken. With her was a man with white hair and wearing an expensive blue-gray suit. The woman introduced herself as we shook, then introduced the man. He was Signor Gino Camerino. He and I stood awkwardly while Mrs. Faber exchanged greetings with the waitress, who, I gathered, was also the owner.

The waitress showed us to a table in a small dining room in the back. A couple of women in cotton suits and a boy and a girl were already eating at two tables pushed together and at a single one a very obese gentleman sat with his napkin tucked in his collar. Daylight came in through a muted window in the ceiling. The fat man was chewing with the sleepy precision of a cow on a warm day in an English meadow. The minute we were seated, I learned that Signor Camerino was the same Camerino who had translated Faber's books into Italian. Mrs. Faber insisted on apologizing for having brought him along without prior word.

I waved away her apology as he made a joke, saying something about having twisted her arm.

Mrs. Faber explained to me that this was a family restaurant. By that she meant that customers simply ate what the family cooked for itself. There were no menus. I quickly told her that in that case I'd have exactly what she herself was going to have. Camerino laughed and, in accent more Tuscan than Venetian, told her he too was going to rely on her expertise. Meanwhile, the waitress approached and stood with a fixed smile as she clasped her hands together against her apron. She looked as though she was admiring an infant trying to take its first step. In rapid Italian she and Mrs. Faber had an exchange and I assumed all was fixed.

The waitress went away. Then Mrs. Faber leaned toward me and asked if I knew Italian. I waved my hand like sea motion and she got the point. In that case, she said, she would translate. She ordered the house wine, mineral water, and a three-course meal consisting of sausage antipasto, the spaghetti—which was the best in Venice—and a platter of grilled cefalo. She said we could count on having more than we could eat because the servings were enormous. As she talked I was thinking what a handsome woman she still was in her pale green suit and with her gray-green eyes and they seemed never far from a show of excitement, maybe even wonderment. I liked her face very much.

The waitress brought the wine and the water and the antipasto, and then went away. Mrs. Faber quickly reached for the wine pitcher and poured some into each of our wine glasses, put the thing down, and turned again to me. I felt a fine sweat break out like oil on water in my armpits. I took my fork and stabbed at a piece of sausage and guided it to my mouth. I watched my own hand shake. I glanced at Mrs. Faber. She was watching it too. She smiled.

"So you've fallen in love with Venice. You can imagine how surprised I was to get your letter from Santa Croce!" She laughed and looked at Gino. Judging from the way he grinned I gathered he knew the whole story—everything. My stomach sort of turned over like a whipped dog.

I assured her I not only loved Venice but I was getting a lot of work done on my projects. The last of course was a lie. But it came out before I had a chance to cover myself in a way closer to the truth.

She asked me to tell her again about my project. The way she put it told me she didn't need to hear me recite it but maybe simply wanted to see how I would do it. I was being tested and I resented it a bit. I took up my wine glass and sipped the wine. Then I told her calmly and briefly all the things I'd already told her in the letters. She kept nodding as I talked. I watched Signor Camerino when I wasn't watching her. That way, they both knew my words were shared.

When I finished, there was a long, rather tense silence, then she lowered her head to a forty-five degree angle and lifted her eyes so that she was looking at me through her lashes. She gave me a suspicious smile which I could have put a wedding ring on and lived with forever. She spoke. "Your book sounds very ambitious. I suppose you already know that it would be impossible to write it without access to the collections at Yale and Buffalo. Oh, I suppose a person would need to look at some of the things I have, too." This last bit was obviously ironic and she knew it and she knew I knew it. She gave me that smile again and I almost proposed to it. But she was obviously waiting for another kind of response from me.

I tried to think of the tactful thing to say but all I managed was a shrug which was a lame attempt to conceal my desperation. I then showed her my palms and held the shrug just to show my helplessness. I was over a barrel and I wasn't going to deny it. All the while I was giving her my best smile or the one I imagined to be my best. I hoped it didn't say, "Have mercy." She held a good hand and she was a brilliant player. I had the feeling she would not only see through mine but straight through me as well. The last thing I was about to say was that Faber did not belong to her now but to the world.

She suddenly looked very serious, even a bit worried. Meanwhile, the waitress brought the spaghetti and took away the antipasto dish. Mrs. Faber reminded me—unnecessarily—of the contents of her recent letter to me. The "advisory capacity" she had alluded to had to do with the idea of a Ronald Faber Society, she said. Many old friends of her and her husband had urged her since his death to start a society. She had put off the idea, thinking it too self-indulgent, too egotistical but everyone—Remick-Wynegar, Truscott, Brook, Sanchez, Kinzer, Gwertzman—had convinced her that it was the humanitarian thing to do, that Faber himself would have approved. She stopped and asked me at this point if I wanted to hear about it.

I did indeed! I folded my arms. Signor Camerino began to eat and Mrs. Faber shot a glance at him. He put down his fork. She turned back to me. "The idea, one of the first ideas," she said, "is to form a board of directors or advisors. This body would be made up of scholars and writers and perhaps some other people in the arts. The important thing is that it must be international.

Gino here has already agreed to serve. My husband's works, as you know, have been translated into all the major languages in the world so it might be possible to enlist the service of various translators or scholars who've dealt with his works, say, in France, England, Poland, Russia, even China, wherever—! Its main function would be to oversee the Society and to screen potential new members, to organize conferences, select lecturers, raise money. For a couple of years now I've been in touch with various friends who have already put together a potential list of members. The consensus seems to be, at this point, that we should charge fifty dollars a year for membership. The benefits would include rights to attend the annual conferences, to lecture at them, to nominate potential members and so on." She stopped and gave me half of that previous smile, then without releasing it, said, "We've already applied to Delaware for an Incorporation permit."

As she talked my excitement was growing. I blurted out, "What about a newsletter?"

"Yes, a newsletter, too. But here's how we plan to do it. It will run as a regular feature of a quarterly—which Kinzer has already agreed to edit, at least for the first two or three years. I tell you, man," she said with rising excitement of her own, "a lot of people are already hard at work on this dream!" She hit the table with her small white fist.

I noticed how Bronx her accent really was. "And this is where you might come in. I mean, the quarterly. John suggested you for the list of associate editors. Would you—?"

"Of course!"

"He also told me you have contacts and might be able to tap them to raise money to get the magazine started. We need all kinds of help. Can you—?"

"Well—" (I tried to keep the worry out of my voice.) "I could ask, uh, uh, a few people. Money is a touchy subject."

"I know, but if we—" (the "we" did not escape me!) "—approach only those *sure* friends of Ronald Faber then we're not running the risk of embarrassing. . ." She broke off, grabbed her chin, turned it with her delicate fingers, said, "Hhhhhhhh." I watched her focus on her previously unseen spaghetti. Then she seemed to *see* the spaghetti. "Our food is getting cold." She looked at me apologetically. "Forgive me for going on so—"

"No problem," I told her. "I'm absolutely delighted by the idea of the Society. I'll help in any way I can." Meanwhile, I was beginning to feel that I was perhaps the most isolated person on Earth: how could such a society have been in the works for—what? a couple of years?— and I hadn't heard of it? Why hadn't Ruth or John told me? Don't get paranoid, I told myself, after all, you were recommended. I picked up my fork and aimed it at the spaghetti.

Within a few minutes I was nearly choking on my spaghetti because it began to dawn on me that what I had just given approval to was a plan which might by its very nature spell the death of my own efforts. As Signor Camerino began speaking to Mrs. Faber in Italian about problems he was having with a publisher they both knew in Milan, I chewed spaghetti and tried to plan my next move. Mrs. Faber had clearly dangled the prize in front of my nose when she said anybody planning to write about her deceased husband's life needed her cooperation. But this Faber Society might easily turn out to be the opposite of a delightful idea. Was I mistaken in now suspecting she was deliberately making a connection between access to the Faber papers she possessed and serving the Society? Plus there was another more variable potential problem: the emergence of such an organization might crowd—not help—my cause. My chance of being the first to come out with the definitive critical-biography could be reduced if not completely eroded. I rolled the same network of spaghetti on my fork eight times—and dropped it eight times—before I got it into a tight little bundle, neat enough to fork up onto my tongue. Funny things: I knew this was good spaghetti but it tasted like a shredded rope no longer of use to a gondolier. Don't ask me how I know what such a thing would taste like.

I was silent through the coffee.

Outside, Signor Camerino asked me if I was walking toward the train station. He had to take a train to Milan to see a publisher. We walked with Mrs. Faber as far as Campo Santa Margherita then stopped there with her in front of her door. She took my hand and shook it. Her wicked smile this time wasn't quite so attractive. I thanked her and told her to call me if there was anything I could do to help in any way. Before I turned her hand loose I said, "I also hope you'll let me take a look at the documents you have. I'm not asking for anything personal—" She cut in and, still smiling, told me that she would think about it.

Signor Camerino led the way along a shortcut through narrow streets behind the government buildings. He told me to call him Gino. As we approached the Santa Croce area he said that the Faber-business could get very sensitive, even sticky. How? Well, there was a young woman here in Venice who claimed to have had a more than, how do you say, friendly relation with Faber. The point of course was once the Society got going one wanted to avoid such people as this woman who could only cause confusion. She was an obvious liar. All great men's names were plagued by such people who wanted some part of him. We stopped on the bridge over Rio Delle Burchielle because I was going to turn and he was about to go on. Autograph hounds were only the most harmless of these types. The worst of course were those who loved their heroes madly, sometimes to the point of killing them. This woman who professed a claim on Faber was the dangerous type. Were there others? He laughed. No doubt there were! Perhaps around the world. But he knew only of this one. Did Mrs. Faber know about the woman? Yes, but never mention her to Lidia. Lidia had had two nervous breakdowns and could not bear much unnecessary bother. The reason he brought up the matter of the crazy woman at all was due to my obvious interest in helping with the Society. He smiled, took my hand, shook it, and said he would be late for his train if he didn't run.

For a moment I watched him running down the steps and across the fondamenta, then I, more bewildered than ever, began the short walk home along Rio di Garraro. I wished I'd asked the woman's name. Oh, well. Maybe he wasn't referring to the person I feared he was. For the moment I wanted only to escape my own confusion. I determined to go home and sink myself into a tub of hot water and re-read some of the poems in *Tunnel in the Body.*

I carried out my intentions: I got into the tub and began to read the poem "Neighborhood Thunder," but read it through twice before I realized my thoughts were elsewhere: on another Faber work. I was thinking of Ruth, the character, in *Ruth with Eggs*. I had believed that Mrs. Faber was the model for this Ruth but now, after meeting her, I wasn't so sure. I still believed Faber based the protagonist, George the painter, on himself. It wasn't unusual for writers to do this. You can think of as many examples as I can. If they don't change themselves into painters it's musicians or some other type of artist. Nobody's fooled. Of course from the point of view of pure scholarship, I never confuse the real model with the character—yet one can't help tinkering with such thoughts.

In *Ruth with Eggs,* George loves his Ruth passionately. He paints her dozens of times in different poses holding a basket of eggs or placing eggs into the basket or taking them out. George has a whole exhibition of this series and gets good reviews by the top New York art critics. The reader is supposed to think of her as a sort of fertility goddess with a Bronx accent. If you know the Bronx accent you know how funny the image is. I myself like this and think that Faber intended it humorously. Other critics—even John Kinzer and Ruth Gwertzman—have doubts. George's best friend, Mark, a fellow painter, is envious of George's success with the show but eventually has an even more successful one. Meanwhile, Ruth's family—after ten years—is beginning to recover from the shock and sadness they felt at her marriage to a poor struggling painter who, worse than that, was black. The first time George is invited to have dinner with Ruth's parents and her brother and sister in the Bronx is a sensitively rendered moment. It is also heartbreaking for what it says about the relation of the individual to the family and about marriage and in-laws. But the novel moves on away from New York to Paris and finally ends in Venice. It succeeds in being as much about George's relation to Mike as his relation to Ruth. Even after the setting is Paris and Venice, Mike still turns up vying as always with George. They clearly need each other as some sort of stimulus. But to get back to

Ruth. How could my beloved Ruth be in any way related to that woman I had just had lunch with?

I pulled back. I tried again to focus on "Neighborhood Thunder" and at that moment the phone rang. Dripping wet, I dashed out to the hall and answered it. The caller was Angel. She was profusely apologetic for calling in mid-afternoon when perhaps I was taking a nap. She rushed on to say that tomorrow would be impossible and apologized again for that, then rushed on again to say she would like very much for me to come to dinner tonight if possible. I wanted to be sure I understood. At her house? That was correct. She apologized for the short notice. If tonight was no good, perhaps next week, early. I assured her that tonight was just fine. How could I resist? I didn't feel a bit hungry and couldn't imagine ever being so again but more than food was involved. She gave me her address and instructions on getting there. She said seven then she bade me farewell.

I set out early, headed for Angel's place in Santo Stefano, because I wanted to walk slowly, partly because my right knee was hurting from where I had pulled a muscle six months before while playing tennis with The Chair, and partly because I liked the noise and busyness of the people on the streets. I went the busiest way, down Minotto and over, avoided—for some reason—Santa Margherita, through San Barnaba and on across the Grand Canal on the big bridge there into Campo San Vidal where a hundred and six cats live and on around the big church. As you turn the corner there you can see the huge campo which is Santo Stefano. Some people call it Campo Morosini. On the way there I passed the guy on the street barking neckties, scarves, guanti, foulards. I kept one eye aimed at any possible new posters announcing art shows. It was still August and the streets were crowded with tourists. I stopped and wrote down the information from one poster which promised an international show of paintings by the wonderful polish painter Duda Gracz, the brilliant Hans Christopher Rylander, of Denmark, and the Belgian sculptor, Jose Vermeersch. It was like somebody had put those artists together just because they knew I loved their work so. De Cirico's drawings were also showing somewhere. I didn't write down the information. When I reached Campo San Vidal I saw a well-dressed young woman squatting in the clearing petting the mob of cats. They kept pushing each other aside trying to get under her hand.

Angel opened the door and she was dazzling and behind her were the soft lights of her home. Behind her I also saw a long hallway with old Venetian prints on the walls. I heard voices off in the direction where the living room should be. Angel pecked a kiss on my cheek—and I one on hers. As I followed her along the hallway she asked the routine questions one asks on such occasions. I'm no expert but the prints seemed excellent. Views of Ponte Rialto, Ponte di Lido, San Marco, Bridge of Sighs, a grand view of the Guidecca. I'd learned a few things already by prowling through the old print shops of which there were hundreds in Venice.

I made a mental note not to call her Angel, to call her Angela. I followed her past an open door to a room filled with books and warm light. I felt at home in a strange place. When we reached a giant plant in a pot on the floor by the hall window we turned right into the living room and came face-to -ace with two people: a man with a kindly face and straight, slicked-down hair and a woman who was pretty with bright eyes. Her hair was almost red. The man was holding what I took to be a glass of scotch and the woman had obviously just put down her glass of champagne on the coffee table where Angel had left hers. It all made sense. Introductions were made. We shook. He was Lamberto. She, Maria Antonizzi. Mozart was also in the room with us.

While Angel fetched me a drink the boys came and Lamberto introduced them as his rascals. Although he did it in Italian I understood. They were cute kids. Then they politely excused themselves and dashed off to another part of the house where I'm sure the TV set was still on.

Angel brought me a glass of wine she said came from the grapes they grow at Tramin. Lamberto told me you couldn't do better than that for grapes. It was good. Meanwhile, something was happening to me. I was feeling a thing turning around inside like a winter bear changing its sleeping position. Each time I glanced at Maria it happened. I kept my eyes away from her face.

As Angel made small talk, trying to get a conversation going in English *and* Italian, I stole a glance at the room. It was beautiful. I imagined ancient Venetian ladies in long silk dresses in this room—in the fourteenth century. I looked quickly at everything and everybody except Maria. Lamberto was helping his wife now: using the few English words he knew when he could stick one or two into an Italian sentence. So far Maria had said nothing beyond hello.

I couldn't resist any longer. I looked at her. She was a paper doll cut out of a sheet of pink construction paper. She gave me a look that said there are things to come, adventures to survive—or the look said, Keep your distance. I looked away and looked again. She was all human, all real, flesh and force. Her eyes were large and blazing with emotion. I didn't know what to make of her. My bear got up and turned again.

It was a long, elaborate dinner. Lamberto kept pouring the Tramin wine into the glasses. At one point Angel excused herself to answer the phone. It was her mother, Ennia. Her father, Benedetto wasn't feeling well. Her brother Alfonso was planning to go to London so he could study English and therefore get a better job. At another point Maria was sort of forced by Lamberto to talk about herself—as if he didn't already know her! She laughed at him and herself too. What was work like these days? Nobody at the Biblioteca Nationale Marciana worked except the lowly ones. Had she heard anything from Giuseppe? No, and she didn't want to. She tossed her short hair from her eyes and wrapped spaghetti around her fork.

It was Lamberto, who much later, first mentioned the name Ronald Faber. He was fishing. Angel had to restate in English what he had asked me because—due to the thickness of his tongue from the wine—I had missed it. He wanted to know if I knew this man, Ronald Faber. No, but I liked his work.

Meanwhile, I knew Maria was watching me. Then Lamberto said something that caused deep silence—at least for two minutes. He said: "Signor Ronald Faber, he is to plague my life!" He said it like this in English. I looked at his face. Whatever forces lived inside this man were now beating upward for exit. He was eating ice cream but it might have tasted like fire on his tongue.

I looked at Angel. She lifted her eyebrows and made her mouth into a fistula.

Maria avoided my eyes.

I focused on the bubbles around the edge of my ice cream. One popped.

We lingered over coffee for an hour and finally Lamberto and Angel said goodnight to Maria and me at the door.

I walked with Maria to her apartment building in Campo San Luca. Just as I was about to say *buona notte*, Maria asked me if I'd like to come up for a "spot" of amaro from Sicily.

I accepted. It was Averna, and quite good!

We kissed. I tasted the amaro on her tongue.

From her bedroom you could see the Grand Canal and one side of Palazzo Grimani which was now a government building.

We finished the amaro and undressed. After this point, I don't remember more than three or four words passing between us. Her tiny body was all movement. Her yellow eyes were full of light. The lights in them moved constantly.

We made love very quickly the first time.

Then we sat on her bed and I gazed out the window at the tops of buildings across the canal while she talked. She told me she lived here on a ruined altar. I didn't allow my gaze to linger long on her bare small breasts. I quickly got drunk on her smell: it was thunder in a wet tree stump. I tried not to look farther down her stomach—although I had already penetrated her as deeply as I ever would.

We made love again, this time with the lights on, the windows opened. We could hear the vaporettos and other boats going by on the Grand Canal and we heard the tourists lost in the streets below, trying in the dim lights to read their infernal maps. I, meanwhile, lost all control in the high luster of her spirit, in the slippery curve of her body's intelligence. I feared, even in the leap of passion, I might fall in love and I couldn't think of anything less untimely or more stupid.

We rested, then made love yet another way and with renewed energy. The sounds of lapping water, the lone cry of the gondolier, the speed of a police boat, you name it, the sounds came into the rhythm of our tunings and sighings. Her little bird calls punctuated my gruff groans.

When I slept I had tiny dreams of weird things: being on the one hand some exotic bird, on the other, a common seagull out sleeping on a black canal.

Our sweat dried and we woke and started a new sweat. Silk rustled against the damp cotton of the sheets. As she came, I thought I heard her calling out for fresh garden flowers. She was not speaking Italian.

Deep in the night, I was lost with no firm ground to stand on. I turned into a quivering jellyfish. I was sure I was halfway through some strange, unwanted journey to a place of ruined stones, echoes of whimperings, the debris of cavalries.

And that wasn't the end of it. By noon the next day, she and I were waking and smiling at each other. I can't imagine what my face looked like after such a rough and elusive and exotic and beautiful night but I *felt* like I was smiling back at her smile. She kissed my nose.

She made coffee and we drank it and ate cheese and crackers then talked plainly the rest of the afternoon. She was not ready for a serious relationship. A casual affair would be all right. She told me stories of her marriage and her affair with Andre Lobetti, the guy recently busted for possession of cocaine by her former husband, Giuseppe. It was all too much and she didn't need the headache of any of it again soon. She liked her job at the Biblioteca. She wanted to keep things simple at the moment. See her friend Angel. Fuck a man once in a while. That was it. I told her I understood. I told her about Anna and Pattie. She asked if I loved anybody right now. I laughed and told her I loved my mother and father. And she laughed too. She wanted to know about them. They lived in Brooklyn, I told her. Coretta and Randolph were the happiest couple she'd ever want to see: their happiness was enough to make you sick. She told me she figured me to be an only child and probably a little spoiled. Then the talk got rifled back to us. She said, as you Americans say, let's just hang loose. We'd see each other when or if we felt like it. I told her that suited me just fine.

I may have had no passion for falling in love but I had a passion for my work and since I liked teaching I was committed to holding on to it. I didn't tell her any of this although it was fully on my mind. I confess to you now of having had unethical intentions. But at least my efforts would benefit the world of knowledge and culture. No? I intended to attempt to get a look at the Ronald Faber things Maria was keeping for Angel. I had no idea just where they were kept or how I'd manage it without detection.

I had not trapped Maria into an affair. It happened just as I say. I was innocent of any secret mission yet it was inevitable that I should come around to such a commitment. I couldn't very well ask Maria to show me the things and I didn't at the time think it wise to ask Angel. That would have been like asking to see the interior of her mouth.

One day while Maria was taking a bath I went gingerly through her belongings—the dresser drawers, the trunk at the foot of her bed, her roll-top desk—and looked under the bed. Her smell was everywhere. I could hear her singing as I searched her bedroom. I had little hope of finding the papers in this room. No doubt they were locked away somewhere, perhaps in the living room where there was a locked, grand desk she inherited from her great-grandmother who claimed to have been a princess because of the nobility of the Russian side of her family. I didn't have time to search the living room and I knew it. Already I heard the water being drained from the tub and I was sure she was by now standing on the fluffy rug drying under her delicate arms. With only a few minutes left, I opened the closet, intending to give it a quick once-over. The light from the window dimly showed its contents. There were shelves above the clothes-pole. On the top shelf was a large cardboard boot box. I don't know why but I had a hunch it did not contain boots. I lifted it down and took the lid off. My hands were shaking. Right on top was that copy of *The Education of Elena Miller* and beneath it were various copies of Ronald Faber's other books—autographed no doubt. I didn't bother to check. Beneath the books were about sixty typed manuscript pages. I leafed through them quickly. My heart was making its beating reverberate in my ears. The manuscript appeared to be a novella. Beneath the pages was a scattering of postmarked envelopes. The return address varied but the name above them was consistent: Ronald Faber.

Just at that moment I heard—rather, thought I heard—Maria coming. I quickly replaced the lid and pushed the box back in its high place, backed out of the closet and eased the door shut. I expected to turn around and see her there in the bedroom doorway watching me with astonishment.

I turned.

She wasn't there. I tiptoed back to the bed and climbed under the covers and closed my eyes. I had a throbbing headache and my hands were still shaking. A chill ran through my entire body.

Nothing now would stand in my way! It was just a matter of time!

*

I had only to wait for the right moment. Meanwhile, August went fast. I saw a lot of Maria. I often met her at the Biblioteca and we would have lunch together at one restaurant or another in the San Marco area. One Sunday we took a waterbus out to the end of the Lido. We'd packed a lunch. We rented bikes and rode on out to the very tip and had a picnic. It was fun. Another time we went by boat to Burano and walked around and looked at the leaning campanile. On Torcello we explored the old Cathedral Santa Maria dell'Assunta with its Veneto-Byzantine Ravenna-type basilicas. Parts of it were being restored and therefore were closed off. We peeked through the planks at the wonders. The menu of the Cipriani restaurant was promising but the prices were expensive so we moved on. A fisherman gave us a ride for a few thousand lire over to Murano. The spirit of the Altinos was still here everywhere. The people had been making glass since the thirteenth century. We went into a couple of the factories to see the brilliant colors with the light coming through them. We found a trattoria late where the prices were sane and the grilled fish excellent. One Friday morning when she didn't have to work we went over to San Erasmo and took the long walk out the country road away from town. It winds along the coast with vegetable farms on both sides all the way. It was a cool morning for August but the mosquitoes were already bad. The irrigated ditches were neat but the Lagoon out there smelled horrible. On the way back I took pictures of the ducks on the sand bars. Laguna Veneta by noon was getting no breeze at all from the Adriatic. Back in Venice we had a drink at Florian's, inside, not outside with the tourists. I liked being with Maria despite her tenseness and the sudden—alarming—high pitch of her nervous laughter. Her eyes still amazed me. I'd grown accustomed to her quick movements. I was nowhere near to giving her up. I saw her usually not more than two or three times a week.

While I waited for the right moment, I felt myself become more emotionally involved with Maria than I had intended. She knew a lot and shared with me what she knew. She liked old prints and so did I and we spent hours in print shops. She showed me Tintoretto and sunsets and the correct way to eat spaghetti and how to avoid being taken for a tourist and how to avoid tourists and the best churches and the museums I couldn't have found on my own and together we went to two or three concerts and one opera. As a librarian she had specialized in art history and for hours she sat telling me amazing things about Venice I never dreamed of knowing. She had theories too. Being in Venice, she once said, was like always being on stage. Or you could see it another way. It was like being in a crowded gallery where everybody's shoulder to shoulder, feeling slightly annoyed but being polite and tolerant. I almost thought she might introduce me next to the Contessa Alte-mura. Once Maria pointed out an old woman whom she called Gina Lollobrigida, the Cat Lady. Maria said Gina the Cat Lady walked all over Venice throwing sardines to the cats. They followed her across every strada and down every fondamenta and under every sottoportico in all the six districts. Everybody knew Gina Lollobrigida, the Cat Lady. She apparently had cat friends in every riva and knew where hundreds of litters were, even in the most remote rughettas and calles and along all the wide rio terras and ramos. We watched her once in the piazza feeding about two hundred cats out of her shopping bag.

So, this was the way I was waiting and it wasn't a bad way to wait yet most of my time was spent alone, working. I developed a new outline for my critical biography. I remember the morning when I got it into the shape I liked best. I stood by the window reading it aloud. It was an exciting moment to see the whole thing fall together. I could see the title page: *Ronald Faber: A Life and The Work*. By Yours Truly. And beneath this, a few words from James Joyce's *A Portrait of the Artist as a Young Man*: "To live, to err, to fall, to triumph, to recreate life out of life . . . " Just perfect! Dedication? I thought something simple: "To my father and mother who always encouraged me to". . . to what? Well, I'd work on it. I had time. The foreword would consist of my thanks to the people and the institutions who had given me assistance. Also perhaps a word or two about the development of my interest in Faber, our common Brooklyn backgrounds, et cetera. Part One, ho boy! The South and Brooklyn: 1915-1922. Chapters in Part One would be: a) The Discovery of Being Different, b) First Love and Art, c) Becoming a Young Man and a Young Writer. Part Two: Years of Ambitious Struggle: 1922-1943. Chapters would be: d) A College-Dropout Finishes His First Novel, e) A Writer in Uniform: Writing for Stars and Stripes, f) On the G.I. Bill and *The Alarm Clock*. Part Three: *We Shall Arrive* and Money 1944-1948. Chapters would be: g) First Marriage to Diane Armas and the work on *No Entry,* h) Divorce and the Love of Lidia, i) *The Day Before*: A War Novel set in France. Part Four: Friendships and the Literary Life at Home and Abroad: Chapters would be: j) *Inclusive Terms* and Exclusive Relations, k) Wynegar, Smith, and Remick, l) Truscott, Brook, Sanchez. Part Five, which was as far as I had gotten, was called Ascending and Descending: 1960-1972. Chapters would be: m) Collecting the Scatterings of the Past, n) Finding the Tunnel in the Spirit, o) Home Among the Children of the Lagoon. There would be at least one more section with three chapters. What went into it—and to a large extent what would go into the first five—depended on the success of my stay here in Venice. Of course I'd end my grand opus with Sources and Notes, Debts and Credits, and an Index.

Not bad, huh?

I could tell Maria suspected nothing. I'm not even sure she knew the depth of my interest in Faber. We never—rather, hardly ever—talked about his work. I think she had read only one or two of his novels although she remembered him and the lecture he gave at Universita di Venezia Ca'Foscari.

As I say, August went fast. Angel came for the bibliography which I hadn't duplicated. Together we went downstairs to the Copy Center, which was right next door, taking my original. One day I knew for sure I'd see it in the boot-box. She was in a hurry so she turned down my offer to have lunch together. Meanwhile, I got in the mail a printed letter from Mrs. Faber outlining the next steps for the Faber Society. She had herself listed as President. Gladys Utecht was Business Manager. A letter from Ruth Gwertzman came from Puerto Rico. She was on the beach, having fun. A student I had given an incomplete/failure sent an essay. It was horrible. I gave him a D. At times I felt homesick.

It was quite a chance to take but I had no choice. I took to carrying my large briefcase all the time. Maria wanted to know why. She laughed when I told her I was working on an idea and never knew when I might need to whip out my notes for reference. The truth of course was I was waiting for the chance to stuff the case and—well, beyond that I wasn't quite sure what I might do. I vaguely planned to cart the stuff off to the photocopy shop, I guess, and happily return the originals before Maria noticed their absence. It was a dangerous and mad thing to do and the plan kept me on edge for two weeks before my chance came.

It was a Saturday in the middle of the afternoon. She left me lying in bed and got up to take a bath. As she left she said she was glad August was over. The minute she was gone I leaped up, grabbed my briefcase, dashed to the closet, and snatched down the boot-box. Leaving the books, I took the typed manuscript pages and the letters. I stuffed the whole pile in my trusty case, quickly zipped it shut; returned the box; quietly closed the closet door. I could hear her running water into the tub. I thought of going in and kissing her neck or lower just to show her some affection. I really felt affectionate at that moment. But I didn't go because I was still shaking and if she noticed she might have gotten suspicious. I got back into bed. I could make up an excuse to leave but no duplicating shop would open till four-thirty or so. Of course I was dying to read the letters and the manuscript. It took all of my willpower to stay there looking across the room at my case on the chair with my clothes. I held out for less than five minutes. I got up and looked out at the Grand Canal. I leaned out and looked straight down. A little fast-stepping woman was moving right along with an ugly little dog whose mouth was muzzled. A dog without an owner or a muzzle suddenly came out of a calle and tore into the muzzled poodle. The lady screamed as she pulled at the leash. The law in Venice said that all dogs must be muzzled. The woman finally lifted her dog from the bloody teeth of his attacker and held him against her bosom. On the other side of the canal I noticed a woman in a window watching too. I remembered something somebody once said about Venice being a series of reflections: I thought of the woman across the way as a kind of mirror of myself just as the two dogs below mirrored each other. Everything here was double, I suddenly realized: even Angel was in some twisted way Mrs. Faber's double. No, fancy thinkers would have her as another sort of symbol. She'd be an intellectual's fountain of youth, some hazy version of the world's unconscious. Yet nothing was what it seemed to be. The lion wasn't really a lion. The money-lender wasn't really a money-lender. All that glittered really was gold. There were no real dragons in sight. By now Maria was singing an American song. She had a pretty good voice. It was three. An hour and a half to go.

Maria finished her bath and made tea and we sat in the kitchen and drank it and ate tea biscuits. She was telling me about some sort of work she was doing on film at the Biblioteca. I had a very hard time concentrating on what she was saying. I burned my tongue. She had been given a special assignment to organize a film display or to catalogue films set in or made about Venice or something like that. Apparently I checked my watch three times in the half hour we sat there. She finally asked me what was up. I told her I had some typing to do at home but that I wanted to come back, say, at seven and take her out to dinner. Her face clouded. She thanked me but said no, she had another date, with another friend. She also said she thought perhaps we were starting to see too much of each other. She said she was beginning to feel an attachment to me that she had not wanted. I gave her a helpless smile. I could see she wasn't impressed.

At five she walked me to the door. I of course was carrying my case. She said, "You know, I never see what you carry in the cartella." I grinned and told her it was a secret plan. I told her I worked for the CIA. She didn't think it was funny. I was stepping through the doorway when she said, "Murphy, it would be good to suspend the relationship for a while. Do you not agree?" You can imagine my panic. I told her it was a crazy idea. She said, "At least until next weekend. This is okay, no?" I couldn't speak. I babbled something or other. She pushed me out the door, playfully of course. "Call me tomorrow. Let's talk about it on the telephone."

There I was in the hallway and she had closed the door. For a moment I knew I was going to burst back in there and give her the manuscript and letters and confess everything. God, what a mess!

I didn't really have a plan but I knew I needed to act quickly. I took a Number Two to the Piazzale Roma stop; went over the bridge and through the park at a trot; bumped people, excused myself; bumped more people, excused myself again. The Copy Center in my block was closed. I went upstairs and poured myself a glass of scotch and stood at the window drinking it—too fast. At five-thirty I took the briefcase and went back down. I could see somebody through the plate glass window in there moving around. I rapped sharply on the glass and jabbed a finger at my watch. She shook her head patiently then slowly came over and unlocked the door. A group of French tourists following their guide went by. A police boat shot up the canal. They rarely came over this way. For a moment I almost ran. Then I saw myself getting a bullet in the back. The photocopy woman opened the door and I almost fell into her arms.

I told her in Italian I wanted one copy of each page. She said she couldn't do so many pages right away, I had to leave them. I told her it was an emergency, that I would pay double—triple. She gave me a quizzical look. Then she went into the office at the side. When she came back a young man in a suit and tie was with her. He smiled at me. He wanted to know what I wanted. I told him I needed the pages copied right away, that it was a matter of great urgency that I have them. He smiled sympathetically and reached for the stack of pages and almost instinctively I withdrew them, holding them firmly to my body. I'm sure he thought I was a madman. I think about it now. How could he have thought otherwise? In English he said he needed to see how many pages I wanted duplicated. Reluctantly, I gave him the pages. The letters were still in the briefcase. I intended to take them from their envelopes and to have them too duplicated. In my confusion and haste I had forgotten. He looked through the pages then asked if I was a writer. I blurted out that I was and even added that I needed to send these things off right away—that I had already missed my publication deadline. He seemed to understand as he once again gave me his sympathetic look. The woman, meanwhile, stood by the photocopy machine looking as though she was about to take flight from an approaching beast. The young man wanted to know if I might leave the pages at least for an hour. I insisted on waiting for them. He said he understood and handed them to the woman. He told her in rapid Italian to go to work on the pages. With tight lips and fluttering eyes she turned on the machine and began feeding the pages—starting with the last one—into the machine. I stood there dazed, watching the light each time a page was duplicated. The young man pointed to a chair by the window, inviting me to have a seat, then he went back into the office from which he had come.

I sat for perhaps five minutes before I was on my feet again. I paced a bit, I guess. I knew the woman was watching me from the sides of her eyes. There was no way to assure her I wasn't going to suddenly strangle her. The door opened and a man came in. I looked, as did the woman, at him. His face brightened as though he recognized me and he came toward me with an extended hand. I backed away a few steps, unable to place him, not trusting his motives. He called me Murphy and I reluctantly shook hands with him. Then his face clicked. He was Lamberto! I hadn't seen him since the night I had dinner at his home. I felt embarrassed and apologized. I shot a glance at the woman who had stopped feeding the machine because, wouldn't you know, she'd jammed one of the pages and was now digging the damned thing out of the machine. With my luck going the way it was, the machine would break down in five minutes.

Lamberto said he was walking by and saw me through the glass and just came in to say hello. I thanked him nervously—for what, I don't know. I was a character in an opera of conflicting themes. This was deep travail, or a hellish melodrama. If I was the author of my own hell I had no authorial confidence at this moment. Lamberto asked if I was making copies of my own great works of scholarship. I saw him looking at the pages. I spoke to him from some sort of abyss; I must have babbled something to his satisfaction because he was now grinning at me and shaking my hand again. He turned to leave, then turned back. He said that, at another time, he wanted to speak with me confidentially about a matter I might find interesting—and perhaps even profitable. He winked and rushed out.

The woman had the machine going again and I was back at the edge of my own personal hubbub. It suddenly occurred to me that I had in my briefcase letters another man had written to the wife of the man who had just left; although those letters were written before her marriage to this man, still somehow it suddenly seemed to me that I had thoughtlessly gotten myself almost in the middle of a sordid situation.

We were way the hell in the next century when the woman finished duplicating the pages. She wanted a hundred lire per page, which was the regular price. No extra charge for fast service. I then remembered the letters again. I slapped my own forehead so she'd see my state of mind. I begged her, as I took them out, to please make one copy of each page. I took them out of the envelopes for her. She sighed and set to work. I stood literally breathing down her neck till she turned and gave me a sharp glare. It drove me back to the chair.

I thought she'd never finish but when she did I finalized my business with her and bounded out of there.

I tripped running up the stairs to my apartment and hit my chin on the marble step.

In my study I placed the copies in my desk drawer and used the bathroom quickly then took up the briefcase and hit the street again.

When I got back to Maria's I pounded on the door rather than ringing the doorbell as I normally did. I didn't expect her to be there. When she opened the door I could see she was dressed to go out. She looked so alarmed it gave me a sudden sense of how crazy I probably looked.

I pushed my way in without being invited. I told her I had to talk with her right this moment, that I couldn't be put off. She shifted gears: took the posture of appeasing me; in a friendly gesture she took my hand and pulled me toward her living room. She asked me to sit down. In a voice louder than I meant to use I told her I didn't wish to sit. I blurted out: "Maria, I love you—I love you. I want to marry you. Will you marry me?" I hadn't intended on saying that; in fact I had had no plan at all except to get inside the apartment. I was there now and didn't know what to do or say. She gave me a conciliatory look then turned around and went to the couch where she sat lady-like and crossed her legs.

She finally asked me if I had forgotten the things she and I talked about at the beginning of our affair. She reminded me that I had agreed to "hang loose." She went on to say that she feared something like this would happen and she was sorry that I was showing so little self-control. That did it. I exploded. I began shouting at her, calling her insensitive, cold-blooded. I don't know what all. I paced back and forth in front of her, stopping to point my finger at her when in my verbal attack I used the second-person pronoun. I could see meanwhile that she didn't know or hadn't decided how to take my performance.

Suddenly I broke off in mid-sentence and ran from the room, into her bedroom, slamming the door behind me—but not locking it. I could have locked it because the three-inch long key was always in the keyhole on the inside. I quickly unzipped the briefcase, snatched open the closet, grabbed the boot-box, lifted the books out, dumped the manuscript pages in with the letters—which I had forgotten to return to the envelopes. In my haste I wouldn't have known which ones went where. I placed the books back as I had originally found them, on top; returned the box to the top shelf. All of this was done in, oh, less than ten seconds. Meanwhile, I heard timid knocking at the bedroom door. I closed the closet door and threw open my briefcase in the usual chair as I tiptoed quickly and quietly across the room and stood looking down at the darkening water of the Grand Canal. Behind me I heard her open the door and come in.

"Murphy," she said, "you are upset. We cannot talk with you this way. Besides, I must leave to meet my girlfriend. We are going to the opera."

Without turning, I said, "An opera a day keeps the doctor away."

CLARENCE MAJOR is a prizewinning short story writer, novelist, poet, and painter. As a finalist for the National Book Award he won a Bronze Medal for his book *Configurations: New and Selected Poems 1958-1998.* Major was a finalist for the Los Angeles Book Critics Prize and The Prix Maurice Coindreau in France. He is the recipient of The Western States Book Award, The National Council on The Arts Award, a New York Cultural Foundation Award, The Stephen Henderson Poetry Award for Outstanding Achievement (African-American Literature and Culture Society of The American Literature Association), the Sister Circle Book Award, two Pushcart prizes, the International Literary Hall of Fame Award (Chicago State University), and the 2015 Lifetime Achievement Award in the Fine Arts, presented by the Congressional Black Caucus Foundation, among other awards. He is distinguished professor emeritus at the University of California at Davis.

CPSIA information can be obtained at www.ICGtesting.com
Printed in the USA
LVOW08*1408150816

500044LV00005BA/5/P